Eric Dinnocenzo

The
Tenant
Lawyer

iUniverse, Inc.
Bloomington

iUniverse books may be ordered through booksellers or by contacting:

iUniverse
1663 Liberty Drive
Bloomington, IN 47403
www.iuniverse.com
1-800-Authors (1-800-288-4677)

Because of the dynamic nature of the Internet, any web addresses or links contained in this book may have changed since publication and may no longer be valid. The views expressed in this work are solely those of the author and do not necessarily reflect the views of the publisher, and the publisher hereby disclaims any responsibility for them.

Any people depicted in stock imagery provided by Thinkstock are models, and such images are being used for illustrative purposes only.

Certain stock imagery © Thinkstock.

ISBN: 978-1-4620-0477-5 (sc)
ISBN: 978-1-4620-0478-2 (ebook)

Printed in the United States of America

iUniverse rev. date: 11/11/2011

"I will turn your raw deal into a rare meal, with steak and moneybank sauce."

— Ray Stone

PART ONE

1

Thursday was eviction day at the Worcester Housing Court. Typically there were about a hundred cases on the calendar, and the lobby was jammed full of people. The lucky ones got seats on the four old wooden benches that lined the dull gray walls, while the rest stood around looking as if they'd been waiting for hours at a bus station to go to some unexciting destination. Some were alone, some talked to their lawyers, some talked to friends or family members, and some talked to other tenants who were also being evicted. All waited for their cases to be called.

This Thursday was no different, I observed, as I entered the housing court lobby and merged with the vast, throbbing crowd. A small lump formed in my throat and my heart raced. I was always nervous on the days I went to court. In the four years that I'd been practicing law, it was something that had never gone away.

As usual there was a loud buzz from the conversations in the lobby, like the sound of heavy machinery at a construction site. The noise made it difficult to talk to clients so that I sometimes had to almost shout in order to be heard. I took a look around the lobby. I always had trouble discerning who was a landlord and who was a tenant—something that still amazed me. Two years earlier, when I first went to the housing court, I had expected a more striking class and racial divide between the two groups. But that was not the case. There was, however, one notable exception—there were always some people there who looked very poor, who looked as if they were down and out. And they were always tenants.

At the housing court you never saw a landlord or a tenant dressed in a suit, or even a shirt and tie. For that matter, the lawyers didn't dress particularly well either. It wasn't uncommon for them to wear sport coats and slacks. Their suits, when they wore them, often looked dated and out-of-style, not to mention wrinkled and worn. On this particular morning, I felt a little overdressed in my Burberry suit, a remnant of my previous life as an associate at a large Boston law firm.

Maneuvering through the dense crowd, I passed by a few lawyers I had been up against in the past who were speaking with their clients. I traded friendly nods with the ones who made eye contact with me. They represented only landlords, since tenants couldn't afford to pay their fees. As the resident legal services lawyer, I represented only tenants and did so free of charge, which meant that I was pretty much the only show in town for them.

Roughly ninety-five percent of the tenants at the housing court were from the slums of Worcester or lived in public or government-subsidized housing. Rarely did you see working-class tenants there. In most cases when they received eviction notices, they either paid the back rent and the case was discontinued, or they vacated their apartments before the trial date and moved in with friends or family. But the poor usually didn't have those options, so they showed up in housing court to fight their evictions.

I finally made it to the far end of the lobby where a set of glass doors led to the clerk's office. The first thing I wanted to do was file pleadings for some of my other cases, cognizant of the fact that if I got held up in conversation with one of my clients I might forget to do so.

A young girl, who looked to be between five and seven years old, suddenly darted in front of me, and I came to an abrupt stop to avoid a collision, my briefcase knocking against the side of my leg. Looking up at me with a startled expression, the girl ran back to her mother and wrapped her arms around one of her legs, then looked up at me with wide eyes, as if assessing whether or not I was dangerous. I smiled at her and, in response, she loosened her grip on her mother's leg and her expression softened. Meanwhile, her mother continued her conversation without even noticing what had happened. They were obviously tenants. Landlords didn't bring their children to court with them.

In addition to being nervous, I felt wired and tense, the result of a lousy night's sleep and two large cups of coffee I had consumed that morning to try to make up for it. My girlfriend, Sara, and I had gotten into an argument the night before—one that felt as if there was no way out of it, as though we were on opposite ends of a carousel going around and around a center that neither of us could reach, and I ended up lying awake in bed for a couple hours until I finally nodded off. I was usually able to fall asleep after our arguments, but this time I had trouble doing so. Truth be told, I couldn't even remember exactly how the argument had started, except that it had been over something small and inconsequential. That was how many of our more serious arguments started. We'd bicker about minor things, and then it would snowball until both of us were hurling all kinds of accusations and past resentments at one another. Those past resentments—which neither of us could seem to fully put behind us—always remained just underneath the surface and would bubble up and explode from time to time.

Our relationship had been changing for the worse for some time. And that night, lying in bed, trying to fall asleep, I felt sadder about it than any time I could remember. I felt we were about to head over a cliff, and while I could see the cliff up ahead, I was powerless to stop us from going over it.

"Baker versus Gonzalez!" a female voice shouted, its sheer volume causing my head to swivel in its direction. Standing in front of the clerk's office holding a manila case file in her hands was Carol, one of the housing court mediators.

Another tenant is going to get pressured into a bad settlement, I thought.

The court employed four mediators in total who were charged with facilitating settlement agreements between landlords and tenants. Before the parties went in front of the judge, they first met with a mediator to see if they could resolve the case. Without the assistance of the mediators, the judge would be faced with the impossible burden of hearing hundreds of eviction trials each year. And as all of the lawyers who practiced at the Worcester Housing Court knew, Judge McCarthy wanted to hear as few cases as possible.

Carol had a well-deserved reputation for stripping unrepresented tenants of their rights in mediation. Once she got them behind closed doors, she'd side with their landlords and put the screws to them, despite the fact that she was supposed to be impartial. "When can you move out?" was often the first thing she'd say to them, in a way that sounded much more like a command than a question. Because she was a court employee, many tenants saw her as an authority figure and gave in to her. On the occasions when she was met with resistance, she was known to employ dirty tactics, like misrepresenting the law in order to make tenants think that they were going to lose at trial if they didn't accept what she was putting on the table. More than once she and I had clashed during mediation when I thought she had pushed too hard against me and my client in favor of the landlord. The result was that neither of us were big fans of the other. It didn't take me long after starting work at legal services to learn that, in the world inhabited by the poor, justice is often in the hands of low-level bureaucrats.

As I walked past Carol and into the clerk's office, I smiled and said good morning to her in a pleasant tone. I generally had to be nice to her, as she was a court employee and one who reportedly got along well with Judge McCarthy. She returned my greeting with what appeared to be a forced smile.

Glancing to the side as I went through the door, I caught a glimpse of one of my clients, Maria Roman, and quickly moved ahead, hoping she didn't see me. I needed to file the pleadings before doing anything else, and I knew that if she got hold of me she wouldn't let go, as she was one of my most demanding clients. Working at the front desk of the clerk's office was Penny, a middle-aged woman with short hair and silver wire-framed glasses who had always been friendly to me.

"How are you doing today, Mark?"

"Okay." I handed her my pleadings. "I think I had too much coffee, though. I feel a little tense."

"Oh."

I realized that my response might have come off as a little odd. "So how are you?" I asked, hoping to rehabilitate our conversation.

"Oh, just the same as every Thursday morning. You know how it is here, always a zoo. Do you have a lot of cases today?"

I stuck up two fingers. "Two."

"That's less than usual. Well, good luck."

"Thanks."

As I turned around to head back into the lobby, Penny said, "Oh Mark, one other thing."

I spun around on my heels. "Yes?"

"There's a woman outside who needs some help. I told her that you'd talk to her, if that's all right."

"Certainly," I replied. "Who is she?"

"She's Hispanic, thin, probably in her late-thirties. Oh geez, I forget what she's wearing. You know, I just saw John go out into the lobby. He'll know who she is."

John was the court officer. He was a heavyset guy with a goatee and light brown hair that was thinning at the top. Although we were both in our early thirties, he looked a good deal older than me. I looked young for my age and still got carded half the time when I went to bars and liquor stores. I was six-one and one hundred eighty pounds; due to jogging three or four times a week, I had pretty much the same build as in my college years. When I located John, he directed me to a thin woman dressed in jeans, sneakers, and a puffy black winter jacket. Just as I began to approach her, I noticed Maria Roman lock onto me with a piercing and intense gaze, and she began to walk in my direction. Reflexively, I raised my index finger in the air to signal that I needed a minute, and to my relief, she backed off.

The woman John had pointed out was somewhat attractive with full lips and almond-shaped eyes, but she had the tired look of someone who had lived a hard life. Her hands were clasped together in front of her holding onto a piece of paper that I could tell from its small print was an eviction complaint. I introduced myself to her as a legal services lawyer and told her that one of the court employees had said that she needed help.

"Yeah, I need a lawyer. I'm being evicted."

I pointed to the paper in her hands. "Can I see the complaint?"

She handed it to me, a little surprised that I knew what it was, and I quickly read it over. "So you live at George Washington and you're being evicted for the drug arrest of a household member?" I asked. George Washington was the largest and most dangerous public housing complex in Worcester. It seemed as if I was always hearing or reading about someone getting shot there or a massive drug raid taking place.

"Yeah."

"Who's the household member?"

"My son. But he don't live with me and he ain't done nothing wrong. You see—"

"Just one second." I took another look at the complaint. "You're not getting evicted today. Your trial date is one week from today."

"I know that. It's on that paper."

"I'm just mentioning it because you just told me that you're being evicted."

"I *am* being evicted."

"I know, but not today, not right now,"

She gave me a look as though I were from another planet. "Listen, you're the lawyer. I'm the tenant. I told you I was being evicted." Her tone was like that of a scolding mother. Most lawyers probably would have found it offensive, but it actually kind of amused me.

"Okay, okay," I replied. I looked at the complaint to get her first name. "It's Anna, right?"

"Yeah."

"All right, let's take this one step at a time. What was it you were about to say to me before?"

"My son don't live with me and he was at the wrong place at the wrong time. It was his friend who was dealing the drugs, and my son didn't have nothing to do with it, but since he was there in the car, the cops arrested him."

"Is he on your lease?"

"Yeah."

That wasn't good for her case.

"How long have you lived at Washington?"

"Fifteen years. My rent is only one hundred fifty dollars and I can't afford to lose that apartment."

I took out my wallet and handed her one of my business cards. "I'm busy with cases right now, but you can come to my office tomorrow, say at two, and we'll go over everything. Can you come then?"

"Yeah." She nodded eagerly.

"Make sure to bring all of your eviction papers. You should have received a notice before this eviction complaint called a notice to quit."

She put a finger to her lips and scrunched up her eyes. "I think I got that at home."

"Bring it with you. Also, could you bring your son with you?"

"Why does he need to come?"

"Because he's the reason you're being evicted. His version of what happened is important."

"I'll try, but I don't always know where he's at."

Just then someone bumped into me, and I turned to see a middle-aged man walk past. It irked me that he didn't say excuse me. I hated the close quarters of the housing court lobby on Thursday mornings.

"Also, if you have any other documents, like your lease, for instance, bring them with you, too."

"Okay. I know I got my lease."

I handed the complaint back to her.

"Don't you want it?" she asked.

"No, you keep it. But make sure to bring it with you tomorrow."

I had a couple of reasons for not taking the complaint. First, if she chose not to show up to our appointment, I didn't want to be in possession of what might be her only copy. Second, keeping it might give her the idea that I was going to take her case, a perception that I didn't want to encourage. Drug eviction cases from public housing were extremely difficult to win for tenants such as Anna, and I had become selective about which ones I accepted. The "One-Strike" law passed by Congress during the Gingrich revolution permitted the eviction of public housing tenants if any household member or guest engaged in illegal drug activity, even if it occurred outside of the apartment. Unfortunately for Anna, her son was listed on her lease, and he had been arrested for illegal drug activity. That meant the housing authority had a strong case against her.

The "One-Strike" law was considered by tenant advocates to be extremely draconian and unfair. A lot of innocent people had been harmed by it, forced to suffer the consequences of crimes committed by family members and significant others. Legal services challenged the law all the way up to the Supreme Court in a case entitled, *Department of Housing and Urban Development v. Rucker,* where it lost in a unanimous decision. For Anna and other tenants like her the stakes were high and the odds of prevailing were slim. It didn't matter that Anna might not have had any control over her son or knowledge of his illegal drug activity. All it took was a drug arrest of a household member or guest, and as a result, the entire household could be put out on the street. In the case that went before the Supreme Court, a 63-year-old grandmother who had lived in public housing for thirty years was evicted because her grandson was caught smoking marijuana in the parking lot.

Making matters worse for innocent tenants like Anna, the housing authority only had to prove that the drug activity occurred under the civil standard of a "preponderance of the evidence." In layman's terms that means "more likely than not," a far easier standard to satisfy than "beyond a reasonable doubt" which applies in criminal cases. Accordingly, the simple fact that the police had arrested Anna's son meant that the deck was already heavily stacked against her.

Although I took most of the eviction cases that came my way, I had over time tightened my standards for drug cases and now only took a slim percentage of them. After losing a few battles in court, I came to realize that it made little sense to put time and effort into a case that would have little chance of success—time that I could spend helping other tenants with better cases. Besides, there was often more to these cases than clients initially related to me, which made me even more wary about taking them on. More than once I had listened to a mother fervently profess her son's innocence at our first meeting only to discover, once the case was underway, that the housing authority had convincing evidence of his extracurricular activities. To make matters worse, the guys who got arrested for the drug activity usually weren't of much help. They rarely showed up at my office to prepare for trial, and when they testified in court they frequently made poor witnesses. Furthermore, if they had prior criminal records, as they often did, they were vulnerable to impeachment on cross-examination.

So far Anna's case looked like one I would reject. I figured I would probably help her fill out an Answer and Demand for Discovery, which would set up her defense to the case with the court and postpone her trial date for two weeks. Then I would give her some advice on how to represent herself in mediation and trial, and that would be it.

When Anna and I said goodbye to one another in the lobby, she smiled, giving off a warm vibe, and all of a sudden I felt rather sorry for her. She hadn't done anything wrong but was about to lose her affordable housing anyway.

My clients were mainly single women with children who lived in the projects, for the most part Puerto Rican and Dominican. Through representing them I learned about the lifestyles of the men who were their sons and boyfriends and the fathers of their children. Many of the guys lived fast-paced lives, partying for days on end, driving around in unregistered vehicles, and fathering children with different women. Domestic violence was not uncommon. One case from about two years ago, shortly after I started working at legal services, always stuck with me. I was defending a Latino couple in their early-twenties who were accused of fighting with each other late at night and causing a lot of noise and disturbance at their apartment building. They both denied the allegations and maintained that the complaints were manufactured by neighbors who disliked them due to a disagreement over a parking spot. On one occasion, I met alone with the girl, who confided in me tearfully that the boyfriend would beat her when he got drunk at night. I was shocked by what she told me, but nodded with understanding, and then advised her to report him to the police and seek domestic violence counseling.

Right after she left my office, it dawned on me that I had made a mistake from a professional standpoint. I had given her advice that was harmful to another one of my clients—her boyfriend—creating a clear conflict of interest. Even if I hadn't done that, I still had a conflict between one client, the girl, who had basically admitted that the allegations in the case were true, and another client, the guy, who had previously denied them to me. I quickly came to the conclusion that I had no choice but to withdraw from the case.

Some days later, I stood in front of Judge McCarthy and asked for permission to withdraw, fully aware that without representation the girl would probably get evicted and end up homeless. After the judge granted my request, I started to walk out of the courtroom and noticed the girl looking at me with utter helplessness in her eyes. I absorbed her look for a few seconds, then turned away and kept walking. Her look haunted me for days afterward.

Many of my female clients didn't know where their boyfriends were at any given time. They were like phantoms who flashed in and out of their lives. One day I was doing an intake of a girl of about twenty who was being evicted from public housing because her boyfriend allegedly lived with her as an unauthorized occupant. She denied the allegation, but when I asked her where he lived, she responded that she didn't know.

"How do you get in touch with him when you want to see him or talk to him?" I asked.

"He calls me when he wants to see me."

"But how do you get in touch with him? Does he have a phone?"

"He uses people's phones."

"So you can't really get in touch with him?"

"No."

This state of affairs amazed me. In contrast, Sara generally always knew where I was and what I was doing. Some guys I knew were resistant to being in that type of relationship, believing that it infringed on their freedom. But I figured that if two people were in a relationship, they should each know what the other person was up to. Anyway, I had no distractions or social activities that made me yearn for freedom away from Sara. I really liked being with her and never tired of it. However, truth be told, sometimes she could be too possessive and too fervent in keeping tabs on me, which I didn't care for at all, and on occasion we got into arguments about it. "Where were you?" "What were you doing there?" "Why didn't you let me know?" These were questions that I sometimes got from her that I didn't think were justified or deserved.

The previous summer I suggested that we attend couples' therapy to try to mend our relationship. Our therapist, Eileen, a thin, elegant woman in her late fifties, told us after our second session that we had communication problems. We talked right past one another, not listening to what the other person was saying. We were also quick to interpret each other's words in more negative terms than they were intended, a major reason why our fights often escalated. About me, she said that I was a "fixer" rather than a "listener," meaning that when Sara came to me with problems, I didn't provide her with compassion and understanding but instead would focus on how to fix the situation. That was something that came as a revelation to me. At the same time, I thought that Eileen had a more negative view of our relationship than was warranted. Despite our problems, there was a tangible energy between us that a lot of other couples didn't have. I could see it in Sara's eyes sometimes when we engaged in a little back-and-forth teasing; they'd open wide as if a current of electricity were running through her. We had lively conversations and joked around and laughed a lot. We were never bored with one another.

Eileen tried to help us. She gave us communication exercises to perform at home that required us to sit across from one another holding hands while we each took turns talking about our feelings for five uninterrupted minutes. Admittedly, I ruined the exercises. It simply ate at me to have to sit there quietly and listen to Sara say things about our relationship that I felt were inaccurate or blown out of proportion, and so at times I would interrupt her in order to set the record straight. Afterwards I felt bad for doing that, but then the next time we did the exercises I'd do it again. It really upset Sara.

The rest of the therapy wasn't very successful. Eileen kept trying to open us up to each other's perspective, but after years of arguments and grudges, we were too entrenched in our own separate camps to reach a middle ground. After six months we gave up on therapy altogether.

2

Over my two years at legal services I had grown so accustomed to handling eviction cases that they had become routine. The landlord would file a non-payment of rent action, and I would assert sanitary code or security deposit violations, or both, as defenses. At court, the parties would usually reach a settlement requiring the tenant to move out within a few months that included a waiver of the back rent. If the landlord brought a case based on tenant misconduct, I would assert a general denial of the allegations. The case often settled with a probationary agreement allowing the tenant to stay in the apartment, but authorizing a quick eviction if the misconduct continued. Every once in a while a case would go to trial.

Over time I came to see myself as someone who was simply performing damage control, rather than working to improve housing conditions in Worcester. From a professional standpoint, I felt that I wasn't fully developing my legal skills. In eviction cases there were generally no complex issues and discovery was limited with no depositions. Trials were conducted without a jury, were brief in duration, and the lawyers did not deliver opening or closing statements. Sure, I got to conduct more trials than my peers at large law firms, but they were constricted trials. Altogether, I felt I was more or less running in place and not moving forward in my career.

The next thing I did, after talking to Anna, was go over to Maria Roman. Although I had told her to dress nicely for court, she was wearing skin-tight jeans that were fairly provocative. Oh well, I thought, nothing I can do about it now.

"So what's going to happen now?" she asked me.

"We go to mediation. Either the case will settle or we'll have to go to trial."

Like Anna, Maria was being evicted from George Washington, but her case was based on different grounds—that her boyfriend, Jose, resided with her as an unauthorized occupant. At my request, Jose had accompanied her to court in the event the case went to trial so that he could testify that he lived at another address, which was the story that he and Maria had all along insisted was the truth. The problem, however, was that he had no proof that he lived elsewhere.

Public housing authorities routinely moved to evict tenants who they believed had unauthorized occupants living in their apartments. There were three policy-based reasons for this. First, a tenant with an unauthorized occupant could be bilking the program, because public housing rents were calculated based on household income. For instance, if Jose lived with Maria and he earned a good salary, enabling them to afford a market-rate apartment, she would be depriving low-income people who really needed public housing. Second, before they were given public housing, applicants were subjected to a screening process that included a criminal record check. Obviously, an unauthorized occupant evades this requirement. The final reason was plain old social engineering. The government wanted to prevent female public housing tenants from sleeping with their boyfriends and having out-of-wedlock births which would entitle them to more public benefits.

Many tenants I represented in the past failed to understand that they could be evicted for having their boyfriends live with them in public housing. They thought that whatever went on inside the four walls of their apartment was their own business.

"What would be a good result," I advised Maria, "is if you could get an agreement where you won't have Jose stay overnight anymore for the next six months or so—it's called a probationary agreement—and if you comply with the agreement during that time period, your case will be dismissed. Jose could start visiting you overnight in accordance with the terms of your lease, which means up to twenty-one nights a year—"

"Twenty-one nights a year?" Jose said incredulously.

"Twenty-one? That's ridiculous," Maria chimed in.

"Unfortunately, that's the rule in public housing," I responded. "It's in your lease." I had previously explained this to her in detail in a meeting at my office.

"That's unfair," Maria snapped. "Other people don't have that rule."

"I agree, it is unfair," I said, "but you give up certain rights when you live in public housing. It's the way it is."

I sensed that some of Maria's anger was directed at me, as if I was somehow responsible for the twenty-one night rule or was trying to sell her down the river with a probationary agreement. That anger showed up in more than a few clients, since I was the one person who stood between them and the legal machinations of the housing court. When I informed them of the law, so that they would understand what they were up against, they didn't see me as an advocate who was on their side. They didn't see that I was simply providing them with information, but instead considered me to be advancing the landlord's position. It could be very frustrating. I wondered if this occurred because I failed to communicate the information in a sufficiently understanding and sympathetic manner, but it was hard to tell. It was hard to objectively analyze myself and make that determination.

"Keep in mind," I continued, "if the housing authority claims in the future that you violated the probationary agreement, it can bring you back into court really quickly with only four days notice. So there's that risk. But, on the other hand, you'd get to leave court today staying in your apartment, which isn't a bad way to leave housing court."

Maria folded her arms across her chest. "He don't live with me. How can I get evicted just because they're saying this? You're telling me it's in my lease, but you're not telling me how they can get away with sayin' that."

I lowered my briefcase to the ground. Having already gone over this with Maria, I felt a little frustrated that I would now have to do so again. My time this morning was precious since the motion session would begin soon, and I was acutely aware that I needed to speak to my other client. "Because it's all a question of fact to be determined by the judge. If he believes Jose lives with you, you'll get evicted. If he doesn't, you won't."

"Even if he did live with me, which he don't, what we do shouldn't mean nothing to nobody."

"Maria, we've been over this," I said wearily. "I've seen people in your shoes get evicted. The law allows it. I don't know what else to tell you. I'm trying to recommend solutions because I don't want you to get evicted. If we stand here and bemoan the state of the law, we're not going to get anywhere."

Maria tapped her foot on the ground and looked around the lobby with a really pissed off expression. I could almost see the wheels turning in her mind trying to think of other ways to defend her case. She turned to me and said, "They can't prove that Jose lives with me. Don't they have to prove that?"

"They have witnesses, specifically your two neighbors whom they've subpoenaed—"

"Yeah, Crystal and Amara. They're both liars. That's what they are," she snapped at me.

"Maria, I'm not your enemy." I put my hands up in the air, almost like I was the victim of a stick-up. "I'm just telling you what the law is and what we're up against. I have to do that. It's my job. The law says he can't live with you." I pointed at Jose. "The judge will hear evidence and determine the facts, meaning determine if Jose lives with you or not. If the judge believes you and Jose, you win. If he believes the housing authority and its witnesses, then you lose. Now, aside from your neighbors, there's also an officer from the security department at Washington who's going to testify that he regularly saw Jose's car at your place overnight. On your side, we have your testimony and Jose's testimony that he doesn't live with you. But a big problem, and I've told both of you this before, is that we don't have real proof that he has another address. No phone bills or credit card bills. No cable bills." I shrugged to accentuate my point.

"I live with my brother, man," Jose said. "I don't have any of the bills there in my name. You know, I don't have a cell phone, I don't have a lease. And sometimes I leave my car for Maria to use. They know that over there. The manager just doesn't like Maria and so she's trying to get rid of her any way she can."

I nodded understandingly. "Okay, but I'm not the one you have to convince. The judge is the one."

I was pretty sure that Jose lived with Maria. The lack of proof of another address was an indicator, along with the way they both reacted to the mention of the twenty-one night limit. They had a right to be upset by that restriction, since it didn't allow them to live on the same terms as the rest of the population, but the nature of their reaction told me they were living together. Where would Jose or most other guys in his shoes choose to stay—with his girlfriend or with his brother? I kept my opinion to myself, though, knowing that if I ever communicated it to them, they'd flip out and my ability to represent them would go right down the toilet.

"I'm still advising you to do the probationary agreement," I said, "assuming one's on the table. I mean, we probably shouldn't even be having this discussion because one hasn't been offered yet. But just think about it, okay?"

Maria said, "Crystal doesn't get along with me because she's going out with this guy, Luis, who used to be my man before that."

"I know—"

"That's why she's making stuff up. She thinks that if he's around Washington and I'm around Washington, that he'll want me or something." Maria gave a dismissive wave of her hand. "She can have him. I don't like him. He's trash. The other one, Amara, is Crystal's friend, and she goes along with anything Crystal says. Trust me, she don't have a brain of her own. She's like a robot."

"All right," I said. "Let's see what the housing authority says."

Maria turned away, and as she did so, I noticed that her facial muscles suddenly relaxed and she wore a vulnerable expression that I had never seen before. Even though she had just put up quite a fight with me, it appeared that she was losing her resolve and her spirit was weakening. Jose put his hand on her shoulder in a comforting way. I realized right then that I shouldn't have gotten into a discussion about a probationary agreement since one wasn't even yet on the table. If one didn't end up being an option, then I had just stirred up the waters for no reason. A more seasoned attorney, I thought, would've taken things one step at a time.

3

My other client, Kendra Clark, a black woman in her mid-twenties, had been waiting patiently on one of the benches in the lobby while cradling her one-year-old boy in her arms. The boy was wearing a blue winter jacket and a red hat with tassels coming down at the ears, and he looked up curiously at me with big brown eyes. Kendra's five-year-old daughter was standing next to her, twirling one of her braids with her finger, as was her ten-year-old son who looked at me with suspicious eyes and a sullen expression; you could tell almost immediately that he had been exposed to things that a kid his age shouldn't see.

A few weeks earlier, I had been in housing court with Kendra when her landlord had first taken her to court for non-payment of rent. Her boyfriend, who was also the father of her children, had been the one working and paying the bills, while she stayed at home with the children. One day he suddenly and unexpectedly left and never came back. Because she was only qualified for low-wage jobs and couldn't afford to both work and pay childcare at the same time, Kendra went on welfare, but the benefit it provided was not nearly enough to cover the rent, and she fell behind.

When I was last in court with her, I worked to forge a settlement agreement that allowed her to stay in the apartment on the condition that she paid the rent going forward plus an additional one hundred dollars a month towards the arrearage. She had owed three month's rent, but I managed to cut that figure in half due to bad building conditions, which included a mild roach infestation and leaky ceilings. That day at court I watched Kendra sign the agreement with a slow, careful scrawl, knowing that ultimately she wouldn't be able to make the payments, and it wouldn't be long before we'd be back in court again. But there were no other options for her. If she took a move-out date, she'd still have to pay the monthly rent going forward and also raise enough money to put a deposit down on a new apartment. Besides, she wanted to stay in her apartment to ensure that her ten-year-old could remain in the same school system.

Kendra never said anything good or bad about the boyfriend to me and instead just stoically endured her situation. Sometimes it felt like I was angrier at him than she was. It was my belief that she didn't express any emotion about what he had done because she was a proud and private person. She looked at his leaving her as a simple fact of life that she had to deal with as best she could. But there was a persistent sadness that she always seemed to carry, that was draped around her like a cloak, and I wondered if there would come a time when she would finally break under the weight of it.

"What's going to happen?" she asked.

"The landlord wants possession of the apartment, so we're going to have to go before the judge. Is there any way you can pay the money you owe? If you can at least make some type of promise in front of the judge, you have a shot at not being evicted."

"I get my next welfare check in about a week."

Suddenly I felt a little hopeful. "Good. How much will that be?"

"Three hundred."

My spirits sank. The payment she missed was eight hundred dollars. Anything else besides that?"

"No."

Kendra's one-year-old began to cry. "That's okay," she said to him softly. By tilting her head and rolling her eyes off to the side, she indicated that she wanted me to take a few steps away from her other two kids so we could talk out of their earshot. "I can't get evicted. I just can't," she said with desperation in her voice. A vulnerable look that I had never seen before flooded into her eyes.

"Okay, Kendra, but I …"

"Mark, I can't—" She sniffled and looked away for a moment. Her eyes welled up with tears. "I can't be evicted. I just can't."

"Let's just take it one step at a time," I said gently.

Right then out of the corner of my eye, I saw John, the court officer, walk into the lobby with a bunch of files in his hands. Shit, I thought, the motion session is going to start. John came to a stop and shouted above the clamor: "Listen up, everybody! Motions! If you hear your name on the list, please enter the courtroom."

"Time to go into the courtroom," I told Kendra.

We joined in at the back of the crowd and shuffled into the courtroom as John read aloud from a list of names. My throat was parched, my heart raced, and I felt like I was perspiring a little. I pictured myself speaking to the judge in front of a courtroom full of people and worried that my voice would shake. I extracted my bottle of spring water from my briefcase and took a sip. Don't be nervous, I told myself. Don't be nervous. You've done this a bunch of times in the past and you've always done well.

From a physical standpoint, the courtroom of the Worcester Housing Court wasn't much to behold. It was a far cry from those magisterial courtrooms that you see in the movies with high-vaulted ceilings and large galleries with rows of stately wooden benches for spectators. The courtroom was approximately 30-feet by 30-feet with only three rows of old wooden benches for seating, and they were covered with nicks and scratch marks. Immediately to the right upon entering the courtroom was the jury box, a cramped space with swivel chairs that looked like they belonged in an office.

Although the courtroom itself wasn't terribly impressive, the presence of the man who presided over it, Judge McCarthy, was larger than life. He was in his sixties and had a stocky build, thinning white hair that was combed-over, and a pudgy face with light blue eyes. Initially appointed to his judgeship by Governor Michael Dukakis about twenty years earlier, he was widely considered to be both the most colorful and cantankerous jurist in Worcester County. No one was spared from his tongue. There were many mornings when his dry remarks had everyone in the courtroom laughing. One morning the housing authority lawyer, Kevin Merola, who for years had appeared in front of him on a weekly basis, introduced himself to the court by name as lawyers customarily do: "Kevin Merola for the plaintiff."

In response Judge McCarthy huffed, "I know who you are!"

Legend had it that Judge McCarthy had initially ascended to the bench with the gusto of a revolutionary toppling an established and corrupt government. There had never been a housing court in Worcester County before his appointment. Housing cases were piled onto the district court docket where the judges lacked an in-depth knowledge of housing law and the particular challenges facing low-income tenants. When Judge McCarthy took the bench, the state sanitary code was strictly enforced and the slumlords were kept in line for the first time in the county's history. After hitting a few landlords with sizeable judgments for failing to maintain their buildings in a safe and habitable condition, he became known as a "tenant judge," and landlords became fearful of having their cases tried in his courtroom. Over the past ten years, however, the pendulum swung back the other way with Judge McCarthy more or less migrating to the center. He less frequently penalized landlords for breaching their obligations, while at the same time he became stricter with tenants.

I believed the cause of this transformation was that he had simply burned out. I thought I could see it in the way he slowly lumbered up to the bench, his shoulders hunched over a little and his head angled slightly downward. For years, he had seen thousands of landlords and tenants come through his courtroom with the same issues: non-payment of rent, tenant misconduct, and sanitary code violations. It was like an assembly line of legal claims, all of them pretty similar in nature, and it had probably worn on him over time. And over the years he had signed off on the evictions of thousands of people.

The work of a housing court judge was often not intellectually challenging. The vast majority of tenants were unrepresented and thus did not raise and argue points of law. On the comparatively rare occasions when interesting legal issues did appear and lawyers were present on both sides, the judge had such a large number of cases to deal with that he often had neither the time nor the resources to really engage with the issue. It was difficult to spend half an hour, or even fifteen minutes, presiding over an oral argument when fifty other cases were waiting to be heard in a single morning.

After only two years as a legal services attorney, I was beginning to feel a little burned out myself. Most of the tenants who sought my help were a number of months behind in rent due to some calamity like a serious illness or job loss, or just a terrible life decision. One tenant was famous in my office for paying her cable bill instead of her rent, even though it was explained to her that having cable TV would mean very little if she had no home to watch it in.

Since they had little or no income, these people's tenancies couldn't be salvaged. There was little I could do for them, except to try to puff and negotiate for more time, since I had almost no bargaining power on my side. It was a dispiriting role to play, making me feel kind of like a doctor who only tends to dying patients and, unable to cure them, on his best day makes the end of their lives only slightly more bearable.

Judge McCarthy often gave me a hard time when I appeared before him, something I attributed to my being a young lawyer, since he didn't act that way to more seasoned lawyers. It started with my first trial in front of him. I was cross-examining a landlord and asked for permission to approach the witness, which he granted. When I requested permission to make a second approach, he said tiresomely, "Mr. Langley, you don't have to ask permission every time you approach a witness."

"Yes, Your Honor," I replied. "Sorry."

When it came time for me to approach the witness again, I did so without requesting permission. Judge McCarthy snapped, "Mr. Langley, what are you doing?"

I looked up at him with a startled expression. "Approaching the witness, Your Honor."

"You ask permission before you approach a witness in my courtroom!"

"Oh, I'm sorry, Your Honor," I stammered. "May I approach the witness?"

"Well, what's the point now?" he bellowed. "You already did it!"

Worcester. At certain moments like this one, waiting for Kendra's motion to be called, or while driving my car to and from work, it would dawn on me that I was working in my hometown. Worcester was a place I had longed to escape during my adolescence and had, in fact, managed to successfully stay away from after going away to college—up until the last two years, that is. In my view, Worcester was a place where you were born and raised, not a place where you remained as an adult, especially when Boston was only fifty miles to the east. The sour taste that Worcester left in my mouth, I knew, was largely the result of getting picked on as a kid in school and feeling like a social outcast. I had always reassured myself back then that one day I'd leave Worcester and prove that I was meant for bigger and better things. Returning to Worcester, even just to work there, was a persistent reminder that I had failed in that endeavor.

My parents had lived in Worcester all of their lives, as had their parents, and it was hard to picture them living anywhere else. In fact, they hardly traveled outside of the area except for a week's vacation in Florida in the winter and a week in Cape Cod in the summer. Even visiting me in Boston was a big trip for them, and I could only recall them bringing me there a handful of times when I was a kid. They had come of age in Worcester when it was a solid middle-class city with manufacturing jobs and a vibrant downtown. But as had occurred in many mid-sized New England cities, the manufacturers had closed down or moved away in the 1960's and 1970's, and for years Worcester had been on the decline. In conversation I would sometimes make jokes at its expense, like that the downtown was so desolate after six o'clock that you could see tumbleweeds rolling down Main Street. I once heard a comedian at a comedy club in Cambridge, riffing in a derogatory way about his hometown of Buffalo, say, "Buffalo is pretty much like Worcester, but with a football team." To my mind, that pretty much said it all about Worcester.

I was well aware that my return to Worcester was of my own doing. After law school I worked as an associate at a prestigious Boston law firm and subsequently got fired. The only job I was able to get was as a legal services lawyer in Worcester, where I made only a fraction of my former salary. At the law firm I practiced in the Labor and Employment department, and because I had an interest in litigation, I was staffed mainly on employment discrimination cases in which the firm represented management. In my heart I wanted to represent the plaintiffs, but I figured that I could suck it up for a few years, make some money and get good experience, then leave the firm and switch to the other side.

One case I worked on was brought by an attractive single mother of about forty who worked in sales at a Fortune 500 company. She alleged that her manager, a portly and extremely arrogant guy in his fifties, had subjected her to unwelcome sexual advances and comments. At her deposition she testified that he had cornered her next to the coffee machine late one evening and groped her ass. Another time he told her that if she made a certain sale, he would give her a bonus, that bonus being what he called a "naked workout" in a hotel room. She said that he would regularly leer at her body and a few times had stared directly at her ass and said, "Man, I'd like a piece of that."

It was during the manager's deposition that I realized that I couldn't do what I was doing any longer. At a break he and I were both in the bathroom washing our hands at the sink and, while looking down, he said, "You have to K.O. this bitch." My resolve as an advocate for his company broke at that moment, like a shelf that collapses under too much weight.

A couple of months later, the partner I was working under told me that I would be responsible for briefing and arguing a summary judgment motion in the case in federal court, which was a lot of responsibility for someone only two years out of law school. I told myself that I'd be able to do it, that I could do it in a clinical way and get it over with. I was ambitious, and I wanted to take on that responsibility and add it as a notch on my belt. Even if I had been determined not to work on the case, there would have been no way to get out of it with my career at the firm still intact. I couldn't tell my superiors that I had a moral conflict. It just wouldn't fly. They would have scoffed at me and said that a lawyer is an advocate for a client, not a moral compass. I also couldn't make up the excuse that I had too much other work to do, because they would've told me to work nights and weekends. Quite simply, any attempt to get out of arguing the motion would have been interpreted as a sign of weakness or an effort to avoid work. I might as well have just written my resignation letter as made an excuse to avoid involvement in the case.

When the day for oral argument arrived, I went through the doors of the courtroom and saw the woman there, which surprised me because usually just the lawyers were in attendance. She was standing demurely with her hands clasped in front of her, wearing a dark blue business suit and white shirt. Her dark brown hair was tied back and she wore pearl earrings. She looked at me and then quickly turned away, which made me feel wicked and impure, as if I were in league with all of these men conspiring against her. Her eyes had unwillingly betrayed vulnerability, but after she looked away from me they had a determined focus.

I intentionally lost the motion. I didn't make solid arguments, and I let the woman's attorney get the better of me. Everyone in the courtroom knew that I was taking a dive; the judge looked at me curiously a couple of times when I spoke, as if he couldn't figure out exactly what I was saying and why I was saying it. And, at one point, the woman's attorney turned towards me after making an argument, as if expecting me to respond, and when I didn't he just steamrolled ahead. The partner I worked underneath was seated next to me, and I could feel his eyes burning through me, but I didn't dare look at him. When I returned to the firm he gave me a good dressing down behind the closed door of his office, then met with the other partners. I was gone by the end of the week.

My job search was fruitless for the next few months. Boston is a small legal community and word of what had happened traveled fast. No law firm wanted to hire a lawyer who scuttled his client's case because of his own moral qualms about it; hell, doing so was a breach of legal ethics. Plus my firm was not exactly willing to give me a good reference.

I received unemployment insurance and Sara paid the lion's share of the rent, since I had virtually no savings. She wasn't at all upset about what had happened. She thought I had done the right thing and was proud of me. She told me, "I don't know how you represented that guy in the first place." She had a very carefree, romantic attitude towards life, so whether or not we would be able to survive financially wasn't something that she particularly dwelled on. But the situation certainly worried me, since her earnings at the real estate agency were inconsistent and not very substantial. On top of that, maybe due to machismo, but more likely due to always being a self-sufficient person, I didn't like being supported by her. Eventually I landed the job at legal services in Worcester, far enough removed from Boston so that the people there were unaware of what had happened to me at the firm. I never asked, but I assumed they never called my old firm for a reference.

So I knew that there was only one person responsible for my ending up working in Worcester, and that was me. I missed being able to get up in the morning and walk through the Boston Common to my office. And I was certainly no fan of driving one hundred miles round trip each day to Worcester. Though money wasn't very important to me, I missed not having to worry about it, which was the case when I worked at the firm. Rent, student loan payments, gas, car insurance—they all added up, so that I had very little spending money. I often wondered where I would go for the next step of my career, or really, for that matter, if there would be a next step.

Judge McCarthy heard about ten motions before Kendra's case was called. Most involved tenants who violated agreements to pay off rental arrearages that had been entered into weeks earlier in mediation. There was one tenant who claimed not to have had heat for the past two days, and Judge McCarthy sternly ordered the landlord to restore it. Another case involved a noble-looking Greek landlord of about sixty with a thick white moustache who brought a temporary restraining order against his tenant, a hefty Latina who wore her hair in a tight bun and donned large gold circle earrings, because she had refused to allow him into the apartment to perform repair work in the bathroom. That was something you didn't see every day in housing court—a landlord asking the court to force a tenant to allow him to make repairs. Usually it was the other way around, the tenant asking the judge to order the landlord to make repairs after many ignored requests. According to the landlord, on two prior occasions he had given the tenant advance notice before going there with workers, and each time she had refused to allow him access. He had lost money paying the workers to show up at the building, he said, and couldn't keep dealing with this.

When it was the tenant's turn to speak, she only got a few words out. You could tell she wanted to explain that the landlord didn't respect her privacy or property rights, but Judge McCarthy stopped her right in her tracks with an outstretched hand.

"Ma'am, are you free tomorrow?" he inquired.

"Yeah, but you see—"

"How about three o'clock?"

"Well, yeah, but—"

Judge McCarthy put up his hand again and turned to the landlord. "You'll be there at three o'clock to make repairs?"

"Well, I have to get my men and—"

"Sir, three o'clock?" Judge McCarthy said in a way that communicated, I'm giving you what you want, so it's in your best interests to go along with me here.

Instantly catching on, the landlord said, "Yes, I will be there."

"Good. You'll be there at three," Judge McCarthy said, and then he turned to the tenant. "And you'll let him in. Thank you, people." He handed the file to the clerk. "Another one down. What's next?"

When the clerk called Kendra's motion, I was cleaning my eyeglasses with a chamois cloth. I quickly put the cloth in my pocket while rising from my seat, and then I walked over to the counsel table. I noticed Judge McCarthy looking at me with displeasure, and though in a way it seemed that he was putting on an act, I wasn't entirely sure. Kendra had her one-year-old in her arms, and her two children followed her as she slowly made her way past the legs of people seated in the gallery. In order to reach our counsel table, she had to pass through a narrow opening behind the landlord and his attorney who were already in position. A chair had been moved in her way, and she had difficulty trying to move it while balancing her baby in her free arm. I took a step in her direction to assist her, but Frank Green, the landlord's attorney, got there first and moved it for her.

Kendra and her children lined up next to me. Her five-year-old stood behind her holding onto her pant leg while her ten-year-old stared straight ahead, his jaw firmly set. My heart raced and my palms were sweating. Judge McCarthy instructed Frank to begin his argument. He crossed his arms in front of himself and said, "Your Honor, a few weeks ago the landlord and the tenant entered into an agreement for judgment. It was a non-payment of rent case, and the tenant owed three months. The agreement said the tenant was allowed to stay in the apartment if she paid rent going forward, and also if she made payments towards the arrearage, which the landlord was good enough to cut in half in the agreement. The first payment came due of eight hundred dollars and the tenant hasn't paid the landlord anything." Frank lifted his hands with his palms facing upward, as if presenting an offering at an altar. "He has to ask for possession."

Judge McCarthy looked at me. "Mr. Langley?"

"This is Kendra Clark, the tenant." I gestured towards her. "The reason she fell behind in rent is that the father of her three children suddenly just moved out of the apartment one day. He was just gone. He was the one working and making money for the family and paying the rent, and Miss Clark was taking care of the children. When he left, she found out that he hadn't paid the rent." During the first couple of sentences my voice felt like it was shaking, though I wasn't sure if it was noticeable, and after that I began to feel more confident.

"As for the arrearage," I continued, "it was cut in half because there were bad conditions like roaches. It wasn't just benevolently done. Miss Clark's children are one, five, and ten. If they're evicted, the oldest child will have his schooling disrupted and—"

"What are your defenses," Judge McCarthy interrupted. "Why should your client stay? I take it you're not challenging that she owes the money."

"No, Your Honor, I'm not. Miss Clark is expecting a welfare check within a week and she'll give that to the landlord. She just needs an opportunity to get things in order going forward, so she asks for more time to pay the arrearage. As I said, there is that check she can give."

"How much is the check?"

"Three hundred."

Judge McCarthy gave me a troubled look as if to say, that's not enough.

Frank Green jumped in. "No one disagrees that the tenant is in an unfortunate position. The problem is that the eight hundred was due two weeks ago, and now she's offering just three hundred in one week. Even if three hundred is paid, more than half of the rent will remain unpaid with the next month approaching fast. It seems like a situation that isn't going to ever get on track."

"He's right, Mr. Langley. The amount owed is eight hundred. You're only able to offer three hundred," said Judge McCarthy, his tone not unkind.

"Your Honor, Ms. Clark can pay the three hundred within a week, then we can revisit the issue. We're just asking for that week to pay the three hundred. Then we could come back here—"

"But the problem is that, as Mr. Green pointed out, it's eight hundred that's owed, not three hundred." Judge McCarthy looked directly at Kendra. "I'm sorry, ma'am, but I have to give the landlord the execution."

I dropped my head and heard a soft gasp come from Kendra. The clerk called the next case. I quickly gathered my things up from the counsel table and with a quick nod motioned to Kendra to go out into the hallway with me. She had a confused look on her face, as if she had just come out of the subway and had no idea where she was. After we exited the courtroom, I told her, "I'm sorry."

A tear rolled down her cheek. She wiped it away and then looked off to the side. "I don't know where we'll go."

"You should try some shelters," I suggested in a soft voice. "They may be able to help."

"I tried. I really did." She was slowly shaking her head back-and-forth while continuing to wipe away tears. "And now there's this."

"If you can get the money soon, let me know, okay? We can come right back here to ask the judge to let you stay."

Kendra nodded. But we both knew that she wasn't going to get the money and that she would be evicted. I looked over at her two oldest kids who were standing a few feet away. The five-year-old seemed oblivious to what was going on, and the ten-year-old had his head down and was looking at the floor. He knew what had just happened. With a somber, heavy feeling inside, I stood there as Kendra gathered her children together and left the court.

4

When I spotted Kevin Merola, the attorney for the Worcester Housing Authority, in the lobby I headed over to him. When I was just a few feet away from him, he abruptly turned in my direction with a surprised look on his face.

"Sorry," I said. "I didn't mean to startle you."

"No, no. It's all right. You sort of snuck up on me there."

I gave an innocent shrug. "Do you have a moment?"

"Sure."

"So how's your morning going?" I asked genially.

"Okay. Yourself?"

"So-so. I'm feeling a little wound-up. Too much coffee."

"Is that so?" he answered with a hint of amusement in his voice.

"I had a vente Starbucks Gold Coast blend. It's like friggin' rocket fuel."

Merola grinned. We had a strange relationship in that we sometimes got along well and sometimes pissed each other off. Once in a while, like now, I acted a little strangely towards him just to keep him off-kilter. More often than not, I enjoyed talking with him because he had a sharp mind and some interesting stories to tell from his many years as a lawyer. But when we were on opposite sides of a case, he could be tricky and manipulative. For instance, one time we had agreed to postpone a matter, and later he took the position that we had never done so. He would also on occasion push me hard on a point, and when I pushed back he would accuse me of being overly aggressive. I perceived it to be a tactic he employed to try to get me to back down, although I did allow for the possibility that he genuinely saw me that way, as a hard-hitting young upstart who overreached at times. Because he had many more years of practice under his belt than I had, I suspected that he thought I should be deferential to him.

"So how can I help you?" he asked.

"I'd like to talk to you about the Maria Roman case."

I was going to ask him about the case concerning the woman, Anna, whom I had just met, since as the housing authority lawyer he would be handling it, but I decided not to. Not yet having committed myself to representing her, discussing it with him could turn out to be a waste of time. Besides, he probably wouldn't give me any useful information and instead would turn the tables and try to get details from me that could help his case.

"Can we work out a probationary agreement?" I asked. "Like, say, the boyfriend doesn't stay overnight for six months. If he violates it, you get the execution. If she abides by it and everything goes smoothly, the tenancy gets reinstated."

Merola scrunched his lips together as if he was passing a difficult bowel movement and slowly began to shake his head side-to-side. "That won't work. This situation with the boyfriend really has to be addressed." He knew my case wasn't very strong, and I could tell that I wasn't going to get a very good settlement.

"What do you mean?" I asked him.

"He's been causing other problems at George Washington."

"Like what?"

"He almost got into a fight with another tenant's boyfriend a couple weeks ago. Supposedly, the two of them exchanged words and then your client's boyfriend threatened to beat the shit out of him." Kevin made the signal for quotation marks with his fingers when he said the words "beat the shit."

"This is the first I've heard of it. Which tenant's boyfriend? And did he really seriously threaten violence?"

Merola massaged his beard with his fingers, looking at me as though I was an innocent rube unaware of how the world worked. "The neighbor, Crystal's boyfriend. And he said he was going to beat the shit out of him, Mark, which I believe constitutes a serious threat of violence."

I gave an exaggerated sigh. "Sometimes people say stupid stuff and sometimes they're serious. My question is, which one is it?"

"I believe my witnesses will say that the threat was serious," he replied dryly.

"Was the boyfriend named Luis?" I asked.

"Yes, I think so."

"He's Crystal's boyfriend and he used to go out with my client. I mention this because I think, if it indeed happened, there might be more to the story. I think the boyfriend is still interested in my client. He may have been egging on her current boyfriend or who knows what."

"Whatever soap opera is going on involving your client, my understanding is that there was a threat, and the housing authority has to address that. They don't think a probationary agreement will take care of things."

"There was no actual violence, Kevin. And well, imagine that, someone in the projects talking trash. Who would believe it? How shocking!"

"That's the housing authority's position," he replied dispassionately. "We need the boyfriend out."

"With her being able to stay?"

"I'm not positive, but I think we can do that. Possibly."

I knew right then that would be the best settlement offered, if one was offered at all, and that Maria would need to take it. Her case was simply too weak to take to trial, and she couldn't risk losing her public housing just so that Jose could sleep over. Public housing was literally like gold for her, since her rent of $200 per month, calculated as one-third of her monthly income, was only about a quarter of the rent charged for a market-rate apartment in Worcester. But I knew that trying to sell the deal to her wouldn't be an easy task. In fact I dreaded the prospect of doing it, anticipating that she'd react with anger and think that I was giving in without a fight. As much as Merola could be a pain in the ass, he generally didn't puff in our negotiations, and I knew that trying to get more from him would be fruitless.

Thin, in his early-sixties, with fair skin and a gray beard, Merola had a slightly raspy voice that gave him a warm, avuncular manner. He and Frank Green were the top two landlord-tenant lawyers in all of Worcester County. While many lawyers in the region dabbled in that area of the law, he and Frank practiced it almost exclusively, so they knew the law inside-and-out. With other lawyers I could sometimes get away with posturing about the strengths of my case or the weaknesses of theirs, but that didn't work with Merola and Frank.

Since all of my cases in the past against Merola had settled, we had never gone head-to-head at trial. I figured I could probably hold my own against him, but doubted that I could match him evenly. He had a certain comfort level and polished speaking style in court that I lacked. His words flowed forth in cogent sentences, as if they had been drafted in advance. He was skilled in constructing arguments, able to communicate his position in just a few sentences and then go on at length to fill in the background. More than once after we had argued motions against one another, I left the courtroom thinking to myself, I wish I could've done as good a job as he did.

Merola was in a class with the most experienced Boston litigators I had seen in action. An ex-hippie and a product of the Sixties, he had started off his legal career years earlier as a public defender. After about seven years in that position, he opened his own law practice and over time moved away from criminal defense work to representing landlords and doing other real estate work. Criminal defense was an area that generally didn't pay well, at least compared to civil work, unless your clients were white-collar criminals or wealthy drug dealers. He landed the Worcester Housing Authority and a couple of other large federal and state-subsidized apartment complexes as clients and gradually limited his landlord clientele to them. Those were the best clients to have with respect to housing court work, since they paid their bills and provided a constant stream of business.

It was my belief that by representing those public and quasi-public entities, he considered himself to be furthering liberal ends. His clients weren't slumlords, as he saw it, but instead admirable purveyors of low-income housing. When we were adversaries in a case, he would sometimes portray his clients as being akin to saviors of the poor, as if they were doing God's work. In contrast he would imply, if not state outright, that my clients were degenerates who were intentionally trying to harm the mission of public and subsidized housing by failing to obey their lease obligations. In a way he was right. I certainly wouldn't have wanted to live next door to most of my clients. But, at the same time, he took too dim a view of them. They were just poor people who had problems, who had received a crappy roll of the dice in life, and aggressively evicting them wasn't always the right answer. Despite his posturing, I suspected that deep down Merola felt a little less than pure on an ideological level. He was, after all, a former public defender now seeking to evict poor people from their homes. I believed that this unacknowledged guilt fueled a little hostility on his part towards me, a legal services lawyer who was often his adversary, and a young one at that who hadn't been around during the Sixties like he had, who hadn't paid his dues. The hostility surfaced in odd ways, like how he would push me hard on an issue and then recoil with surprise when I pushed back.

"Kevin, just so we both understand, this alleged threat isn't part of this eviction case. If it's true, I understand your client's concern, though I honestly don't think it's as big of a deal as you seem to."

"But still—"

"I'll try to work with you on the situation, if you'd like. The boyfriend is here today, and I can talk to him. It makes sense to address any issues that are out there now instead of letting them potentially continue. But if we go to trial today, I'll object to any reference to it."

"On what basis?" he asked, jerking his head back. It was clear that he thought any objection I might have would be completely without merit.

"Because it wasn't alleged in the notice to quit, and I just got notice of it two seconds ago from you. This isn't trial by ambush. I haven't been able to conduct any discovery on the matter. And while you have witnesses here to testify about it, I haven't had any opportunity to call in witnesses of my own."

"If you want to bring in your own witnesses, we could continue the case for a week."

"That still won't cut it," I said, shaking my head. "You need to send a new thirty-day notice to quit. The notice to quit has to contain the grounds for the eviction and give a tenant proper notice of the allegations. Plus, like I said, I haven't been able to conduct discovery."

If Merola was required to send a new notice to quit, it would mean a delay, and we both knew it. A trial based on the threat allegations wouldn't occur for another two to three months. He'd have to serve the notice, wait at least thirty days, then file a complaint in the housing court, and a trial date would be set for about a month later. A delay was exactly what I wanted and what he didn't want. Of course, there was always the chance that Judge McCarthy might buy into Merola's argument and continue the case for another week—or worse, allow the trial to go forward today and let everything in. He was pretty unpredictable that way. But I was confident that my legal analysis was correct.

"I disagree," said Merola. "I think that the thirty-day notice I sent has put the tenant on notice that there has been a violation of the lease. After that, if the tenant chooses to violate the lease in new and innovative ways, it doesn't make sense for a landlord to send out separate notices and bring forth separate eviction cases for each violation."

"New and innovative ways," I repeated, shaking my head.

"Even if the judge technically doesn't allow the threats into evidence, he'll still hear them. This isn't a jury case where you can keep evidence completely away from the fact-finder. The judge decides what evidence gets in. I'll introduce it, you can object, but he'll still have heard it."

I maintained a poker face, but knew that he had made a powerful point. Even if not technically allowed into evidence, Judge McCarthy would still hear some testimony about the threats. And that testimony would marinate in his brain while he came up with his decision on the unauthorized occupant allegation. Judge McCarthy was a practical judge, and I doubted that he would totally disregard that kind of testimony.

I watched Merola go over to confer with his client, Jeannie Roberts, the manager of George Washington. Damn, I thought, he just bested me. I walked over to Maria and Jose, thinking, if this allegation about his threatening the boyfriend is true, he's just an idiot. It was bad enough that the housing authority was accusing him of living in her apartment illegally, never mind doing something like that. When I mentioned it to them, they vehemently denied that it had happened. I looked at both of them closely to detect signs of lying, but they didn't give any off. In part I believed them; after all, Jose was a pretty skinny guy who didn't look like a fighter. But, all in all, I was skeptical of their denial and left open the possibility that Jose had made a threat. When I first started as a legal services attorney, I probably would have taken Maria and Jose at their word, due to the conviction of their response. But having been burned so many times in the past by untruthful clients, I now did that much less frequently.

I noticed that Maria had her fists clenched, which worried me somewhat.

"So let me get this straight," I said. "Nothing at all happened with you, Jose, and the boyfriend? No fight? No controversy?"

"No," Maria answered resolutely.

"No way," Jose said. "You see, the only thing that happened was that Crystal was there at Washington with her boyfriend. And I told her she should stop causing trouble for Maria, and I said it in a real non-confrontational way. Then the boyfriend told me it was none of my fucking business, but I didn't do nothing. I swear. I didn't want to get involved with any trouble, since I knew Maria already was being evicted, so I just said, 'Whatever, man,' and I let it go. That's all that happened. I went right into the apartment after that. You just gotta know that these people have it out for Maria."

"And how come Crystal's boyfriend gets to live there," Maria challenged, "but I'm getting in trouble for Jose? You see what I mean?"

"Okay, okay." I raised my hands in the air. "Let's just see if we can settle this."

Ultimately Merola made an offer: Maria could keep her tenancy under a six-month probationary agreement, but on the condition that Jose would be permanently banned from her unit. That meant Maria would continue to live in her apartment, but if the agreement was violated she would face a speedy eviction hearing. If the six months passed without event, her tenancy would be reinstated. Merola insisted on a further condition—if Maria even saw Jose at George Washington, she had to notify both management and the police of his presence. I tried my best to dissuade him from this particular requirement, knowing it would be hard to get Maria to agree to it, but to no avail.

"You tell him, no way," Maria said angrily.

"Maria, you should consider it," I advised her.

"They're trying to run my life, not yours. Do you understand that? I have a right to my own privacy and to do what I want in my own apartment. They're favoring Crystal. They believe everything she says, and they let her boyfriend stay there and they don't even care."

Speaking softly and slowly, wanting to lower the temperature between us, so to speak, I explained that I had tried my best but the housing authority was inflexible and it was the best deal she could expect to get. I emphasized that it would allow her and her children to stay sheltered, which was the most important thing, and if she wanted to see Jose, she could always do so at some other place. I further told her that, in my opinion, if we went to trial she would lose, but it was her decision on how to proceed. I agreed with her that what was happening to her was unfair and said I'd be frustrated and angry, too, if I was in her shoes. I summed up by saying that while I couldn't change the law, I could try to secure the best deal possible for her, and that's what I had done.

Just one year ago, I wouldn't have taken that approach with her; I would have instead thrown my hands up in the air in frustration. But I had learned over time that it was very effective to empathize with clients and what they were going through. It was important to reassure them that I was on their side, and not just some bureaucrat giving them bad news.

I backed away from Maria in a way that physically signaled that the ball was in her court. She and Jose huddled together to discuss the matter, and I watched as she gestured angrily while he tried to calm her down. I sensed that he understood what she was up against and knew that she should take the deal. In the meantime, I talked with a lawyer I knew from a prior case, every now and then glancing over at Maria and Jose to see how they were doing. After a few minutes passed, she approached me.

"Fine, just take it," she said.

"Are you sure?"

"I just want to get this over with. Take it," she instructed, not looking me in the eye.

"Are you really sure?"

"Yeah, I'm sure. Just do it."

Merola and I sat down together on a bench and wrote out the agreement together.

"By the way," he said, "your client has to pay the one hundred eighty dollars in court costs that my client paid to file this case."

"What? You never mentioned that before."

"Your client was in the wrong, and my client had to pay to file the case, so your client should reimburse my client."

I sighed. "Kevin, we're agreeing to completely ban the boyfriend from Washington. I think we're giving up a lot."

"And you're getting a lot. Your client is getting to stay in her apartment."

"Don't make me do this, Kevin," I groaned, tilting my head back in a dramatic fashion. "It's just going to make things a lot tougher. If you keep backing her up against the wall, this might fall apart."

Kevin shrugged. "I'm letting her stay in her apartment. I don't think this is a high price for that."

When I informed Maria of this latest demand, there was no inflection in my voice. I was feeling tired of the back-and-forth and of being the guy everyone dumped on. If she wanted to scuttle the settlement, well, that was her choice.

"I'm not paying them money to file this case," she exclaimed. "No way!"

"I know it's upsetting, but try not to take it personally. That's all I can say."

"Don't take it personally?" she responded incredulously.

"Just try to look at it this way—it's one hundred eighty dollars and it saves your apartment. You pay two hundred a month in rent, and if you had a private apartment you'd be paying like eight hundred a month. That's all I can say, Maria. Again, it's your decision." I took a few steps away from her, again communicating that the ball was in her court. In a few moments, she came over to me and said, "Fine." Then she walked away.

After Judge McCarthy signed off on the agreement, I handed a copy to her.

"Thanks," she said in a cold and clipped manner. Then she brusquely turned her back to me and walked out of the lobby without saying a word.

Jose quickly shook my hand and said, "Thanks, man." Then he hurried after her. Well, I thought, at least it was nice that he did that.

5

Outside a cold wind was blowing, and it felt like the temperature was below freezing. I buttoned my coat, shoved my hands into my pockets, and began walking the five blocks back to my office. The winter weather in Worcester was absolutely brutal. The temperature was always a few degrees colder than in Boston, and Worcester received more snowfall because it was located inland and at a higher elevation. A number of times on my drive home from work, I navigated through six inches or so of snow and when I reached Boston there was only wet roads with no accumulation.

I walked along in a sort of tired haze, drained from the morning's events, intermittently thinking about Kendra's case, and not very aware of my surroundings. An image stuck in my mind of her with tears in her eyes, and I cringed at how helpless and scared she and her kids must be feeling. I wondered if they would be able to get into a shelter, and if so, what life would be like there. I had never visited one, even though I had a number of clients who went in and out of them. The actual physical environments of shelters had nothing to do with the legal work I performed, so I didn't feel a need to actually see one for myself. And I avoided seeing them out of the fear that it would be really depressing. I didn't want to have that in my mind when I represented clients in evictions.

I also wondered how Kendra's ten-year-old would turn out in the future, given that he had such a palpable anger. Certainly an event like today could only make things worse.

I stopped at Dunkin' Donuts to get a cup of coffee (there was no Starbucks in downtown Worcester) to help pick me up. I looked forward to slumping into the chair behind my desk, loosening my tie, and putting my brain on cruise control while working on the administrative tasks that had piled up during the week. I had about forty or fifty cases at any given time, so there was always a long list of things that I had to do.

I took the elevator, a rickety contraption that had broken down several times in the past, up to the third floor. The entrance area had posters on the wall advertising the WIC and food stamps programs for the poor. Set off to the left was the waiting room, a cramped rectangular-shaped area filled with old plastic and metal chairs like those in a public school classroom. The receptionist, Lucelia, an attractive young Latina with long dark hair, was on the phone at the front desk speaking in Spanish. Generally, she acted coolly toward me for no reason that I could discern, and she did so on this day by giving me only the slightest sign of acknowledgement when I walked past her to my mailbox. All I really knew about her was that she had a couple of kids and a boyfriend she was always breaking up with and then getting back together with again.

I went directly to my office, plopped down in my chair, turned on my computer, and started going through my mail.

The Legal Services Corporation was first established by Congress during the Nixon Administration to provide civil legal aid to the poor in areas of law that affect basic rights such as housing, welfare, disability, child custody, and domestic violence. There were three different practice groups in my office that covered all of these areas: Housing, Public Benefits, and Family/Domestic Violence. At one time there were two lawyers in the Housing Unit, but six months earlier the other attorney left to go into private practice, and so I was the only one left. Although my boss, James, the litigation director in the office, had posted a couple of job advertisements, no replacement had yet been hired. I suspected that he was waiting around to see if I could handle the workload by myself, which irritated me since it was substantial.

Back when I entered Boston College Law School, I had my sights set on getting a public interest job after graduation. Only a small percentage with similar intentions end up staying true to this cause, taking jobs as public defenders and legal services lawyers. Out of that group, only a small percentage remain in the public interest field for more than a few years. For most a change of goals occurs somewhere along the line, and they opt to take higher-paying positions in private practice. Who can blame them? The combination of law school debt and the high cost of living in metropolitan areas that appeal to young people like New York, Boston, Chicago, San Francisco, Washington D.C., and Los Angeles make it difficult to survive on the salary of a public interest lawyer.

During my second year of law school, I took part in the interviewing process for large law firms, even though I really wanted to be a public defender. My mother kept telling me, "Go see what they have to offer. It doesn't hurt to go on interviews. The practice of interviewing will be good for you." I knew what she really wanted was for me to land a high-paying job with a big firm. She was subtly trying to steer me in that direction, hoping that I'd get a job offer and she'd be able to brag about me to friends and relatives. All of my life she had pressured me to succeed: in high school it was with respect to academics, sports, and social status. When I entered law school, and ever since, her focus was on the salary and prestige of my job. It was fair to say that she was let down when I began working as a legal services attorney.

The hiring for public defender jobs was erratic, and not knowing if any positions would even be available when I graduated—or for that matter, if one would be offered to me—it seemed foolish to put all of my eggs in that basket. I ended up following my mother's advice, rationalizing that I could always work at a big firm for a couple of years in order to pay off my loans, then become a public defender later on.

Because I wasn't thrilled with the idea of working for a large firm, I didn't get nervous before the interviews as some of my classmates did. That attitude was probably what enabled me to perform well at my interview with Morgan & Reilly and ultimately receive a job offer. In the final analysis, how could I say no to Morgan & Reilly? They were among the best trial lawyers in the city, and working for them would be a good apprenticeship, not to mention a financially beneficial one, since in 2001 they paid a starting salary of $125,000 plus bonus. The fact that the firm defended corporations did not register that strongly with me at the time, because I was only focusing on the long view. I figured that I could live with the job for a couple of years and then move on. But once I started working there, I found the adjustment more difficult than I had anticipated. Eventually I got fired. I never told my parents about what really happened, as I didn't want my mother to find out the truth. I was afraid that she'd criticize me for what I had done—and worse, think that I hadn't been able to cut it at the firm. I pretended that I had never been fired and was still at the firm. When I got the legal services job, I told my parents that the reason for the job change was my desire to work in the public interest and make a difference. Better for my mother to believe that, I figured, than to know I had been fired.

I sat in my office, my tie loosened and my sleeves rolled up, drinking my coffee and reviewing the administrative matters that had piled up. Once again, I began to think about what had happened to Kendra. I was still bothered by it and I couldn't shake the image of her tear-filled eyes and her son's sullen look. I analyzed the argument I had made to Judge McCarthy and wondered if I could have presented it in a better way, a way that might have changed the outcome. Deep down I knew there was nothing that any lawyer could have done to prevent her from being evicted, but I couldn't help but scrutinize my performance.

A little while later, I went over to my colleague Alec's office a few doors over. I had gotten over my earlier tiredness and was a little revved up inside from court and felt like hanging out and talking to someone.

"Ah, back from the battlefield," he said as I walked through his door. "How was court?"

"Not so good."

"Oh yeah?"

I gave him the rundown of what had happened in both Maria's and Kendra's cases.

"These things happen and there's nothing you can do about it," he said. "As Frank Green once told me, you can't turn hamburger into filet mignon. But hey, you got a good result in the unauthorized occupant case."

I shrugged. "Yeah, I guess."

Alec was a few years older than I and had worked in the housing unit for a few years before I joined legal services. After getting married and having a child, he transferred to the benefits unit because it was a less demanding position that didn't require him to go to court as often. Alec's birth name was Alejandro. His family had emigrated from Argentina to Massachusetts when he was six years old, and he had grown up about twenty minutes away from Worcester in Framingham. Soon after I was hired at legal services, we struck up a friendship. We had a similar sense of humor and were both huge fans of Howard Stern and *The Godfather.* Since we were in the politically correct environment of legal services, we kept our Howard Stern interest quiet. Physically we looked nothing alike. I had the look of a clean-cut young guy who hailed from an upper middle-class suburb, while Alec looked more rough-and-tumble. He stood about five-feet nine inches tall, weighed about two hundred pounds, and had short-cropped dark hair and light brown skin. He also had one of the keenest minds and sharpest wits of anyone I knew.

"Every time I go to housing court I'm struck by how many people are just hanging on by a thread," I reflected. "Most people are just one paycheck away from eviction or some other catastrophe."

"Our country doesn't have much of a safety net."

"And sometimes justice is in short supply."

"There's no such thing as justice, my idealistic young colleague."

Alec leaned back in his chair. He absolutely loved getting into philosophical and political debates and was setting the stage for one now.

"Do you really believe that?" I asked, playing along with him.

"Yes, I do."

"Well, why do you work here if you don't believe in justice?" I asked, suddenly feeling that a good bullshit debate about higher principles might get me out of my funk from Kendra's case. It felt like the right thing at the right time. "The idea of legal services is to obtain justice, to help those on the bottom rungs of the ladder get a fair deal." I still believed this after two years in the trenches, but with the passage of time it seemed more and more like a difficult enterprise—the result of suffering numerous defeats at the hands of Judge McCarthy, and handling too many cases that were unsalvageable and out of my power to influence or control.

"I'm here because I have job security, reasonable hours, and I get decent benefits," Alec responded. "Besides, our mission is simply to provide poor people with representation in civil cases. That's not necessarily justice."

"I think that constitutes justice in a way."

"Setting up a level playing field isn't justice because bad results can still follow from it. For instance, if the Axis powers had had the same military strength as the Allied Forces that would be a level playing field, but would you call it justice?"

"I don't think that's an accurate analogy. In one instance you're talking about how a legal system is supposed to function and how it affects society as a whole, and in the other, you're talking about the brute force of world domination."

"The common denominator is that in either situation power is what is at issue."

I could tell from the glint in his eye that he was thoroughly enjoying himself. Frazzled from my morning at court, my brain not firing sharply enough to keep up with him, I relented. "You win," I said, ostensibly giving up, but my tone indicated that I hadn't really changed my position. "The world is just a Hobbesian power grab."

He chuckled. "See, I knew you'd come around." He put his hands behind his head. "So does the colonel still have you doing that CDBG stuff?" The colonel was the nickname we had bestowed on our boss, James, since he was not only our boss, but also a serious fellow. CDBG was an acronym for Community Development Block Grant, a federal program that funded local community development activities such as affordable housing, anti-poverty programs, and infrastructure development.

"Unfortunately, yes. Next Monday I have to go to a meeting with the community leaders." I leaned forward in my chair and rested my chin on my hands. "It takes up so much time. You don't know how many hours we all put in before even sending that simple letter. And I don't think it's a good case, if we were to file a lawsuit, that is. I mean, courts don't want to get involved with how local governments spend money."

"I agree."

Silence fell between us. I was always hyper-conscious of the moment when conversations were about to or did reach their end. This seemed like one of those times, so I tapped both of my hands on the armrests of my chair and stood up.

"Leaving?"

"I don't want to interrupt you any more than I already have. I know you're a busy man," I said in an exaggeratedly deferential manner.

Alec extended his hand, palm facing upward, in the direction of my chair. "Please, stay. It's no interruption at all. An esteemed colleague like you is welcome in my office any time."

"You are the esteemed colleague, and the pleasure has been mine, really. In any event, my tasks beckon, so I'll return to my office. But perhaps we can converse with one another at some point in the future?"

"Of course," Alec responded. "It would be my pleasure."

6

D riving home that evening on the Mass Pike, I welcomed the sight of the Prudential and Hancock buildings in the distance, and further beyond them the tall office buildings in the financial district. It felt good to return to Boston. It was eight o'clock when I arrived in the Back Bay section where Sara and I lived, and I got a parking spot at a meter on Commonwealth Avenue across the street from my apartment. Resident spots were nearly impossible to get after about 4 p.m., but metered spots were usually available in the evenings because the meters shut off at 6 p.m. and reactivated at 8 a.m. That wasn't a problem for me since I had to leave for work by that time.

We lived in a one-bedroom apartment in a brownstone with hardwood floors, white walls, old steam radiators in the corner of each room, and a bay window that overlooked the street. It was a classic Back Bay apartment. I put the key in the front door lock, wondering if Sara would be home, and if so, whether or not there would still be tension between us from last night. I just wanted to relax after a long day, maybe watch a little TV and later on read in bed, and I wanted things to be okay between us. I had already experienced plenty of combat that morning in court and didn't want any more of it. Instead I was seeking softness, a soft and warm place to fall.

While I wasn't the type of person to hold a grudge for very long, Sara was. I knew that I'd be able to tell how she was feeling by the look in her eyes when I first saw her. She had such wonderfully expressive bluish-gray eyes. They were her most striking physical feature, like cat's eyes, rounded in the middle and slanting towards the corners.

I entered the foyer, closing the door behind me, and could hear the sound of the TV from the living room. My first thought was, she's here, followed by, she's watching TV *again*. I walked in the direction of the kitchen and Sara almost collided into me as she exited it. Her eyes opened wide and she put her hand to her chest. "You scared me."

"Sorry." I paused while she composed herself. "Hi," I said softly.

"Hi," she said in a kind of amused way because of our near collision. She walked past me and sat down on the couch. I could tell that she wasn't angry, and that made me feel relieved. She might still feel a little resentful about last night, but she wasn't angry.

"You look nice," I told her. Her dark brown hair, usually parted in the middle and falling down past her shoulders, was tied back in a ponytail. She had a toned, athletic figure that she kept in shape with aerobics classes. She had a small bust and was curvy in the hips, but at the same time was trim, wearing a size two.

"I look terrible today," she replied, looking at me as if I had two heads.

I could tell right then that things were at least somewhat okay between us.

I changed into more comfortable clothing, a pair of blue cotton lounging pants and a long-sleeve shirt, and sat down next to her on the couch. She had on comfortable clothes too: a pair of red cotton sleeping pants and a light blue, long-sleeved shirt with drawings of seashells in the front. It was an outfit she wore a lot inside the apartment that I affectionately referred to as red pants and seashell shirt. She was watching "Sex and the City," one of her favorite programs. In a slightly cool tone, she asked me how my day had gone, and I told her about my morning in housing court. She seemed to genuinely feel bad for Kendra. She also gave me some perspective on Maria Roman, telling me that she probably had lived a tough life and had acted as she did as a defense mechanism.

A few moments passed in which we didn't say anything and then I told her, "I'm sorry we fought last night."

"I'm sorry, too."

"You had trouble sleeping, didn't you?"

"Yeah, I hardly slept. I've been really tired today."

"I'm sorry. I had trouble sleeping too."

"You did?" she asked incredulously. "You never have trouble."

I shrugged. By making an apology, I felt I had cleared the air between us, at least somewhat. More could have been said, of course. Typically, I would've proceeded to review the argument with her as if I were football analyst going over an instant replay, unearthing the cause of it and trying to find a remedy. But it just didn't seem right this time. After a few moments passed, she proceeded to tell me about her day. Only a couple of people had come into the real estate office, and they had gone to look at apartments with other agents. It was dispiriting to her to sit there all day and have nothing happen. The owner of the office, Jeff, was caught up in a crusade to get a Republican appointed to the Boston City Council. Jeff came from old money and his father had set him up in the business, but he was uninterested in real estate. Instead he seemed intent on stirring up the political waters in the Beacon Hill neighborhood as a frustrated Republican in a liberal enclave. Not infrequently, he wrote letters to the editor of the *Beacon Hill Times* that were full of vitriol, not to mention a little wacky, though they were well-written from a technical perspective. His right-wing politics annoyed Sara and he often goaded her into debates that only left her frustrated.

"He's just so thick," she said. "He blames the Democrats for everything, even the problems with the Big Dig. And I'm not much better since I engage him in these arguments. Afterwards, I ask myself, why do I even bother?"

I chuckled. "That's a good question. You'll never change him."

"I know," she said, shaking her head.

"Hey, I know I'm changing the subject, but what do you want to do for dinner?"

"I'm not really hungry."

"Are you sure?"

"Yeah."

"I was thinking we could order some food together. Like a pizza or something."

"You can order for yourself, but I'm not going to have any."

"Sometimes you get hungry later at night, though."

"I'm not hungry *now*," she responded, a hint of a smile appearing on her face.

"Okay."

There was only one good pizza place near our apartment—Boston was horribly lacking when it came to good pizza—but it didn't deliver, so I called up one of the crappy ones that did, and ordered a small sausage with roasted red peppers. While waiting for the food to arrive, I sat on the couch reading *The Boston Globe*. After "Sex and the City" was over, Sara began watching "Will & Grace," another show that I had no interest in. When the pizza arrived I had no choice but to watch the program as I ate. We didn't have a kitchen table, so we took all of our meals at the coffee table while sitting on the living room couch. During a commercial break, I picked up the remote control and asked Sara if I could scroll through the guide.

"I guess so," she replied, obviously not thrilled by the idea.

I flipped through it and saw that *A Few Good Men* was on. "So, you want to watch 'Will & Grace,' huh?" I asked a little sheepishly.

"Yes, I do."

"So that means you don't want to watch *A Few Good Men*?"

"That's exactly what it means." She shook her head while wearing a slightly amused smile.

After a few minutes passed, I noticed that she was eyeing my pizza. "That looks good," she remarked.

"It's okay. You know how the pizza places are around here."

"I just got hungry."

I pointed at her playfully. "See, I knew you would."

I took a bite of pizza while she sat there looking at me. I knew she wanted some, but figured I would wait for her to ask for it rather than offer it to her, given that she was reluctant to change the channel.

Finally she asked, "Can I have a piece?"

In a dramatic fashion, I looked up at the ceiling, then lowered my gaze to the floor, and finally pressed my lips together as if I was grappling with a tough issue. "Hmm, I seem to recall asking if you wanted to order pizza, and you said no. Therefore, I only ordered a small pizza rather than a large. You know what a big appetite I have."

"But I got hungry."

"I guess we find ourselves in an interesting situation."

"How's that?"

"Well, on the one hand, I have the pizza, which you want—"

"You're so cruel!" she said, laughing.

"On the other hand, you have control of the TV, which I would like to change the channel on. It's quite an interesting situation." I took a generous bite of pizza and then closed my eyes as if the taste was heavenly. "My goodness, this pizza is good."

"I thought it was just okay."

"I wasn't appreciating it fully before."

Sara shook her head. "You're ridiculous."

"I'm just kidding. You know that. Have some." I gestured to the pizza box and Sara extracted a slice.

"This is really an opportune moment for you to make a benevolent gesture," I remarked, "by switching the channel."

"Fine," she responded with a sigh. "Switch the channel."

I felt a little guilty that I'd be getting my own way, and asked her two more times if she was sure it was okay. Each time she insisted it was, so finally I put the movie on.

7

An initial client meeting is not unlike a first date. You ask questions to learn about the person's history. You try to get a sense of her character. You try to discern whether she is trustworthy or someone who could turn out to be trouble. You gather facts and make judgments in order to decide whether or not you want things to go forward between the two of you.

Even though I kept all of those lines of inquiry in my mind during initial client interviews, I nevertheless took most of the cases that came my way. The exceptions were drug eviction cases that lacked compelling evidence in support of the tenant, simply because they were so difficult to win and the housing authority usually settled for nothing less than an immediate move-out date. When Alec was in the housing unit, he was much more selective than I was. He joked that I was as choosy when it came to taking new cases as a drunken sailor in a bar at 2 a.m. trying to pick up women. Our different approaches resulted from our divergent philosophies about the role of legal services. He wanted our office to operate more like a boutique law firm, putting a lot of time and attention into a small, select stable of cases that addressed larger, systemic issues facing poor people, such as housing discrimination in large apartment complexes and predatory lending. In the end, he wanted to take on fewer of the small cases that I handled on a day-to-day basis at housing court, which had historically been the bread-and-butter of legal services work. I was interested in working on big cases, too. You could make a difference with them for many people, and they were also more intellectually challenging. At the same time, I wasn't prepared to abandon eviction clients. The stakes for them were just too high. And besides, to my mind, representing them was what legal services was all about.

When I greeted Anna in the waiting room, I noticed that she was wearing the same black winter coat that she had on at court. Her demeanor seemed a little more pleasant and relaxed. We sat down together in the conference room and she placed a large envelope on the table.

"So your son isn't here," I said.

"No, I couldn't get in touch with him. Anyway, I brought some papers." She began extracting documents from the envelope in a very careful manner. "I got a notice to quit and my lease. I got the court complaint you saw yesterday."

Before looking at the papers, I obtained some personal information from her. Her full name was Anna Rivera, she was thirty-eight years old, worked part-time as a clerk at Wal-Mart, and received monthly SSI benefits. SSI was an acronym for Supplemental Security Income, a governmental program that provided financial assistance to disabled persons with little or no income. She had been on assistance for some time because she suffered from anxiety and depression. She was now in a trial period that allowed her to continue receiving benefits, but at a lesser amount, while she tested whether or not she was able to return to the workforce.

I picked up the notice to quit from the table and began reading it. It was dated January 8, 2004 and alleged:

> You, your household members, or guests engaged in illegal drug activity in violation of section 6(g) and 7(b) of your lease agreement when: your son, Miguel Rivera, engaged in the illegal sale and distribution of a Class A substance (heroin) on or about January 5, 2004. Mr. Rivera was a passenger in a vehicle when he was arrested by the Worcester Police Department for selling and/or distributing a Class

A substance at or near the Rite-Mart convenience store on Worcester Center Boulevard.

Just as I had anticipated, the notice was signed by Kevin Merola. I had a vague sense that something wasn't quite right about it, but I didn't know exactly what. I read it again starting from the top where it stated, "Fourteen (14) Day Notice to Quit," and then it hit me—Merola had used the wrong type of notice. That was an error that could warrant a dismissal of the case.

A fourteen-day notice to quit must be served on the tenant prior to the commencement of a non-payment of rent case, but a thirty-day notice must be served in eviction cases that allege tenant misconduct, including illegal drug activity that occurred off the premises. It puzzled me that a smart, experienced lawyer like Merola would make such an obvious mistake.

I went to section 6(g) of the lease which stated:

> Any criminal activity that threatens the health, safety, or right to peaceful enjoyment of the premises by other tenants or any drug-related criminal activity on or off such premises, engaged in by a public housing tenant, any member of the tenant's household, or any guest or other person under the tenant's control, shall be cause for termination of tenancy.

I moved on to the next lease clause implicated by the notice, section 7(b), which stated in relevant part:

> … if a tenant, any member of the tenant's household, or guest is alleged to have engaged in any drug-related criminal activity on or near the premises, the tenancy may be terminated by a fourteen (14) day notice to quit.

Never before had I seen this particular lease clause in any of my other drug eviction cases. I figured that it had recently been put into effect. By serving a fourteen-day notice, Merola was quite obviously operating under the theory that the Rite-Mart was located near the premises.

"You may have already told me this at court, but how old is your son, Miguel?" I asked Anna.

"He just turned nineteen."

"I see he's on your lease."

Maria nodded. "Yeah."

"Has he been arrested before for drugs?"

"Like when?"

"Any time."

"Once before."

"For what?"

"Marijuana."

"Dealing or possession?"

"Just possession. I don't think it was much."

"Do you know how much?"

Anna pursed her lips together and looked off to the side, then slowly began to shake her head. "No. He was a kid back then. I don't know."

"Do you know how old he was?"

Anna rolled her eyes upward. "Sixteen, maybe."

"What happened in court? It went to court, right?"

"He didn't go to jail or anything."

"Do you know specifically what happened to him?"

"No, I'm sorry. I don't."

"Has Miguel been arrested for anything else?"

She paused for a moment. "One other thing. Him and some friends took a bike, a moped I think it was, that belonged to someone else. It was around that same time as the marijuana. They took a joy ride, you know, and the police caught them. They said they planned on giving it back."

Sure, I thought. Of course, they were going to return the moped. "Do you know what happened to him in court?"

"No."

Her lack of knowledge about her son's criminal history didn't surprise me. In fact, most of my clients in drug eviction cases were similarly in the dark when it came to their sons' activities.

"Anything else?" I asked.

She shook her head. "No."

"Does he live with you?"

"No. He used to stay with me sometimes, but he doesn't live with me. You know, it was maybe once every one or two weeks, like when he wanted to shower and get some food. That's it."

I clasped my hands together and placed them on the table. "Okay. Well, if he didn't live with you, why didn't you take him off your lease?" I asked in a way that I hoped didn't sound judgmental.

"I just didn't think of doing it. When it was my lease renewal time, I just signed it. I didn't think to take him off."

"Did you not take him off because of your anxiety or depression? Like you forgot or you get overwhelmed by tasks, anything like that?"

"No."

That meant that I could not allege a psychiatric disability as a defense to the eviction action. In other words, I could not claim that if it was not for her disability, Anna would have taken her son off the lease.

I shifted my focus to the drug arrest. According to Anna, Miguel's friend had picked him up at his girlfriend's apartment to go to the mall, and while they were on the road, the friend decided to stop at the Rite-Mart. After they parked, some guy came up to the window and within seconds a heroin deal went down with the friend selling and the guy buying. Miguel had no idea that it was going to happen, or, for that matter, that his friend had drugs in his possession. The police were on them so fast that he thought it had to be a sting.

"I don't see how I can be evicted for what my son did," Anna said. "That's not something I did."

"I'll explain. I'll go over that with you. But first, who was this friend of his?"

"Just some friend. I don't know who he is."

"You don't know his name?"

"No."

"So is Miguel in jail?"

"He was, but he's out now."

"Does he have a criminal lawyer?"

"Yeah."

"Do you know who the lawyer is?"

"No."

"Did you have any knowledge before the arrest of your son being involved with drugs?"

"Didn't you just ask me that?"

"I asked you if he was arrested for drugs. Now I'm asking if you had any knowledge of him being involved with drugs."

Anna shook her head. "No."

I concluded that her case was a loser. All that the Worcester Housing Authority had to do in order to prevail was show by a preponderance of the evidence that Miguel had been involved in the drug deal, and it would not be a terribly difficult feat to accomplish. Miguel's apparent excuse—that he and his friend were going to the mall and he was unaware that a drug deal was going to occur—didn't strike me as particularly compelling. No doubt, it would seem even less compelling after Merola finished cross-examining him about his prior criminal activity. Moreover, Anna apparently knew very little about her son's activities, and in my experience, that was not a good sign.

But I was nevertheless intrigued by the case based on a procedural aspect. There was a colorable claim that the notice to quit was defective which could possibly get the case dismissed. If I lost that battle, I would have to try what was essentially a losing case, but if I won, I would get Anna more time in her apartment and in the process keep Merola and the housing authority in line. They might think twice next time before using a fourteen as opposed to a thirty-day notice. The case posed a challenge, as opposed to being a routine matter, and it appealed to me for that reason.

I explained to Anna that she could, in fact, get evicted if her son was found to have engaged in illegal drug activity, and I cited the Supreme Court decision.

"How can that be the law? That's so unfair."

"I agree. But it's the law." I shrugged. "I think you have a very tough case, but I also think that on technical grounds the housing authority is not following the lease. I think an argument can be made that the Rite-Mart is not near George Washington and they should have given you a thirty-day notice." I explained the lease requirements for using a fourteen as opposed to a thirty-day notice. "I can't tell you that I can stop you from getting evicted. I just think that there is a chance I can get the case dismissed because they used the wrong type of notice. Even if I'm right, though, the housing authority can still turn around and file another case against you. And if that happens, your prospects won't be very good in my opinion. These are just very tough cases, and the facts as I understand them aren't in your favor. But anyway, if I'm lucky, I might be able to buy you more time."

"Have you ever had these cases go to court?"

"Oh, yes."

"Have you ever won?"

"No, I haven't."

Anna looked down at her lap. "I'll have to move back to Puerto Rico with my son if I lose. I have a son, David, who's in high school."

"Another son?"

"He's a senior. He's got a scholarship to go to U. Mass. in Amherst. You know, I'm so proud of him for that, but if we have to move maybe he won't get it."

"A scholarship?" This was highly unusual given that none of my past clients had children who went to college, much less children who had received scholarships.

"Yeah, he got a scholarship through the state. But if he's not living here any more and not going to the high school, then he probably can't get the scholarship. He needs to graduate from here."

"The scholarship is through the state?"

"Yeah, David got good grades and he got high scores in that test."

"The MCAS test?" The MCAS was a standardized test that Massachusetts students were required to pass in order to graduate from high school.

She nodded. "Yeah, that's it. He's in the honors courses and everything."

"Well, that's fantastic that he received it." I paused. "Let's just see what happens with your case, okay? I want you to know what you're up against, but don't stress out and jump to any conclusions just yet. It won't do you any good. We don't know exactly what will happen yet. What I'm going to do is to file papers with the court answering the eviction complaint. That will ensure that your case will be continued for at least two weeks, maybe longer."

Anna suddenly brightened, as if a light had turned on inside her. "You don't know what this means. I mean, I've been so nervous since I got this notice. Thank you so much."

"I know. It's very nerve-wracking. But we'll just take it one step at a time."

"Okay."

"Also, I'll need to meet with Miguel."

"Okay, I'll tell him next time I see him."

"You should try to contact him soon because I want to meet with him sooner rather than later. I'll want to speak with his criminal attorney, too, to get the police report and whatever records he has."

I took Anna's paperwork from her and tucked it away between the pages of my notebook. We both rose from the table and shook hands, and then I escorted her out of the conference room to the lobby. Lucelia was at the reception desk, looking quite pretty with her hair down, flowing past her shoulders, and I stood in front of her desk as I watched Anna walk out the door to the elevator. I wondered what caused her two sons to take such different paths in life and hoped I might gain some insight into that as her case progressed. I glanced at Lucelia and sensed that she was a little annoyed that I was hanging around her desk, so I returned to my office.

8

St. Mary's church was a dark red brick structure with tall front doors made of vertical wooden slats and curved in a half-moon shape at the top. Its gray steeple jutted sharply into the sky and towered high above the neighborhood with thin greenish-gray colored strips traveling from its base along each edge up to the tip. St. Mary's had a distinctly medieval appearance. When I was a kid and my family drove up to it on Sunday mornings, I'd get the feeling that I was traveling back in time to the age of King Arthur.

I pulled up to the curb in front of the church and spent a few moments just looking at it before getting out of my car. My eyes traced its height from the doors up to the tip of the steeple, and then I silently cursed the colonel for sending me on this mission. Back in high school I had been very involved with the St. Mary's community, but after I went away to college, I stopped attending mass and disassociated myself from the church. Father Kelly knew that I returned home for holidays and other times as well; he was aware of my absence. Now he was the one who was spearheading the CDBG meetings I had been attending, and each time I went to one I felt a little uncomfortable due to my history with him and St. Mary's.

I got out of my car and hunched over a little in response to the cold, jamming my hands into my pockets. Taking small, careful steps I managed to navigate the hard-packed snow and ice on the walkway. In the summertime weeds sprouted from the cracks between the cement blocks, and an image came into my head of the end of mass on those summer days when I was a teenager, when Father Kelly would stand on the front steps and greet parishioners as they exited the church, always giving me a knowing look when he saw me.

I went around to the side entrance of the church and down the stairs to the basement. After passing through a narrow hallway with a low ceiling, I entered the small conference room where the meeting was being held. People were seated around a rectangular table with metal legs and a fake wood-grained surface. Father Kelly was at the head of the table. I was the last person to arrive and felt self-conscious when everyone turned to look at me. I noticed that a new person was in attendance, a Hispanic woman in her forties who was a little on the chunky side and wore a lot of makeup.

Once I took my seat, the meeting got underway with Father Kelly introducing the woman. "This is Gloria Ortiz. She's the new director of the Worcester Hispanic Center, and she's going to be joining us." To Gloria he added, "Mark is a lawyer with legal services." Then to the rest of us he said, "I'm going to start off by giving Gloria an overview of what's happened thus far."

I was familiar with the Hispanic Center, as they had previously referred clients who were facing eviction to my office. Father Kelly explained to Gloria that each year HUD distributed funds to Worcester and other cities with populations over fifty thousand under the Community Development Block Grant program, otherwise known as "CDBG." The amount of money that each city received correlated with its population and poverty level, and in the last calendar year, Worcester received seven million dollars. According to federal regulations, CDBG funds were to be used for the purpose of providing decent housing and expanding economic opportunities for low and moderate income citizens. Examples were the rehabilitation of existing housing, the construction of new housing, mortgage down payment assistance, and rental assistance. In fact, before receiving CDBG funds, eligible cities had to prepare a plan describing the intended uses for the funds, and the public had to be given a chance to comment on it at public hearings.

I was impressed by Father Kelly's knowledge of the subject matter. He really knew what he was talking about. He knew more than I did.

Father Kelly explained that over the past few years not all of the CDBG funds that had been distributed to the city of Worcester had been spent, and so a slush fund of about one million dollars had accumulated. Recently, the city manager and city council, acting together, had authorized the distribution of the funds to pay John Miller's construction company to build a skywalk between the downtown sports arena and an adjacent hotel. John Miller was a well-known developer and landlord in the city; in the past I had represented his tenants in eviction cases. The remainder of the cost of the project was being financed by private sources. In entering into this arrangement, Father Kelly said, the city had bypassed the public comment requirement and, more importantly, had put the funds to an improper use.

"The funds aren't being used for the benefit of poor people, as is the objective of the CDBG program," he said. "The only argument the city could make that a skywalk in the downtown area would assist the poor is that it would create jobs for them, which is a permissible use of CDBG funds under what's called the 'Jobs Benefit Test.' But the city would have to show that the skywalk would involve the employment of low-income people. For instance, it would need to show that they'd be employed in the construction process or afterwards by the hotel or the arena. But we think that type of argument is a stretch. The people employed for the construction would be the workers employed by Miller. And it's not likely that a skywalk would create new economic opportunity once it's in place." Father Kelly briefly paused and looked around the room. "The question now is what steps to take."

Lawrence Geuss, the fiery, sometimes wild-eyed director of the South Main Neighborhood Center, was seated across the table and to the right of me, and his clenched fist was resting on the table. The South Main area was the poorest area of the city, a center of drugs and prostitution. Having been a fixture there for the past twenty years, he had earned street-cred among social services people, but at the same time they considered him abrasive and self-righteous, as well as a little crazy. He had a history of pushing hard for his agenda, without any regard for those he might offend in the process. Sometimes his approach helped him get results; sometimes it did the opposite. Every time I saw him he was dressed in jeans and a plaid work shirt. He had a kind of electric craziness that reminded me of Doc Brown from *Back to the Future*.

"I say we take it to them," he said. "The way I see it, this is like a robbery. They're reaching their hands into the pockets of the poor and handing it over to the rich. It's like a robbery."

"It's like a skyway robbery," I remarked dryly.

I looked around the table and saw a number of blank expressions, with the exception of Father Kelly who gave a muffled laugh. "You know, there's the expression highway robbery, but this involves a skywalk, so it's like skyway robbery." I looked around the table. "No good?"

Ignoring me, Lawrence suggested, "I say we picket city hall, since the city council and the city manager are the ones who hold the purse strings. That'll get their attention real fast."

"I understand the desire for action," Father Kelly responded diplomatically, "but I think we should try some other less confrontational methods first. Community groups and non-profits have to go to the city council with their hands out each year to get funds, and if we rub them the wrong way, it could make it difficult for us in the future. That's the political reality we face. That's not to say at some later point we might want to take a more aggressive stance, but I think we shouldn't escalate things at this point."

"But we sent the letter to the city manager and city council, and we didn't even receive a response," Lawrence countered. "At some point we have to act. We may have pissed them off already, anyway." He looked around the room as if trying to stir up agreement, but no one responded.

"True," Father Kelly said. "But my disagreement is based on the fact that I don't believe now is the time. I think if we continue to let them know this is a concern for us, we might be able to get some traction. If not," he turned to Lawrence, "we could always try something else. I'm not suggesting we take your idea off the table, but rather that we should wait."

Nancy Brightman, the director of a domestic violence outreach center, was the next to speak. "I think publicity would be a good next step. It could put pressure on the city council if suddenly, say, just as an example, they were in the newspaper being accused of impropriety. Or, if we were to hold meetings highlighting this issue, it might grab their attention."

I had stolen a few glances at Nancy during the meeting. She was an elegant and attractive woman in her early forties with a slender figure and loose, curly brown hair that fell just past her shoulders. I had a little crush on her—a harmless one, given that she was married with two children and I was in a relationship. The crush was no doubt fueled by the fact that the romance had faded between me and Sara. I could count on one hand the number of times that we had sex during the past year.

"I have a question," Gloria said tentatively. "How are both the city council and the city manager involved with this? What are their respective roles?"

"We're not entirely sure," Father Kelly responded. "We know the city council had to authorize the funds. The city manager can't do that on his own." Father Kelly looked around the table to see if anyone else had anything to add before continuing. "Again, I hear what Lawrence and Nancy are saying, but I remain concerned about taking on the city council."

Lawrence Geuss shrugged and then leaned back in his chair.

"I think we should try to schedule a meeting with the city manager and the city council," Father Kelly suggested.

"I agree," I said.

"I think it'll make us look weak and pandering," Lawrence said, "but if that's what you want to do…" He lifted his right hand and then let it fall on the table.

After a little more discussion our group agreed to give Father Kelly's idea a try, concluding that the worst that could happen was that the city would refuse the meeting—or that if it was held, nothing would come of it. His was the conservative approach that might yield gains but would not cause us to suffer any losses. If it didn't work, it wouldn't foreclose the other options that had been mentioned.

After the meeting was over, we all briefly mingled in the conference room. Then people began to take their leave until finally Father Kelly and I were the only ones left. It dawned on me that it was the first time we had been alone together since I was in high school.

"How is your work going?" he asked me.

"It's okay."

"So are you more fulfilled than at your last job?"

We had never talked about my last job, so I figured that my mother must have told him about it.

"Yeah. I'm helping people, which I didn't get to do before. I guess on the downside, though, the work can be tough. Most of my clients have bad cases and are in dire straits. Sometimes you just can't help them. Or sometimes you can help them, but due to their problems, they end up in the same situation again. But putting that aside, I like it."

Father Kelly smiled and then crossed his arms in front of himself. "Working with the poor isn't easy, but it's a worthwhile thing to do with one's life."

I nodded. "Yeah, it is." I felt a little nervous and uncomfortable. It seemed that Father Kelly was leading me somewhere with the conversation, but I couldn't quite figure out exactly where.

"So is there any chance of your moving back to these parts or are you a Bostonian now?"

"I like Boston. There's more for me to do there than here."

"Well, it's nice to have you involved with this. I was just talking to your mother about it after mass last week, as a matter of fact. You know, she always speaks of you with such pride."

I shrugged indifferently. "She's not enthused by the fact that I'm a legal services attorney. She'd prefer it if I were at a private firm making more money."

"Well, she wants what's best for you in her own way, but she's still proud of you."

"Her own way being the key words." Wanting to change the subject, I said, "I understand the approach you want to take with CDBG. I think we do have to make certain overtures at this stage and appear diplomatic. Having said that, to be honest, I'm not terribly optimistic that anything will come from a meeting."

At this point we had drifted into the hallway and were making our way toward the side entrance. Father Kelly had been at St. Mary's for three months when I first met him. I was fourteen years old and my best friend's father had died in a car accident. Even though he didn't know the family, Father Kelly had sat with them at their kitchen table until late into the night. That gesture gained him the trust of many people in the parish, and it was then that I stepped up my involvement with the church. Father Kelly spurred the youth group into action after years of inactivity. I became very involved in it, finding it a welcome refuge from a high school environment where I had a tough time fitting in. I wasn't a total geek or anything, but rather an awkward kid with lackluster social skills who tried too hard to be liked.

After leaving home for college I drifted away from the church. In my sophomore year I took a philosophy course in which we read Nietzsche's *Genealogy of Morals,* which blew me away. It was my first introduction to any substantive critique of Christianity, and reading it made me feel like one of Plato's cave dwellers suddenly taken out into the light. At the time, I was smoking large quantities of marijuana and experimenting with LSD, and that, together with my philosophy readings, sent my mind hurtling in new and exciting directions. After that semester I became a philosophy major, approaching my studies as if each new book held the key to understanding life. And I came to view religion as a meaningless collection of myths, something that fooled people rather than exposing the truth. It was a point of view that did not sit particularly well with my mother. She thought I had become a little "weird," as she once put it. I had grown my hair a little longer and returned home with new and controversial ideas about life. I was a different person from the Mark she had known for the first eighteen years of my life. And her reaction to me caused me to dig in my heels even more, refusing to even go to mass on Christmas and Easter.

Just as I was about to exit the church, Father Kelly said, "By the way, I have something in mind for the CDBG money, but I haven't shared it with anyone yet."

"Oh yeah?"

"There's a building for sale in South Main, near Clark University, that I think could be bought for less than a million dollars. It needs work, but it could hold between six and nine apartments. I was thinking it could be made into transitional housing for single mothers and their children, specifically those women who need to get away from domestic violence."

"That sounds like a good idea."

"Well, we'll see. We have a long road ahead of us." He smiled warmly. "Take care, Mark."

9

That evening my mother prepared chicken pot pie for dinner, her signature dish that she was famous for with our relatives. Whenever she brought it to family gatherings, people made a bee line toward it. It was comfort food at its best, with tender chunks of chicken, carrots, and potatoes encased in a soft and flaky crust. For unexplained reasons, she rarely made this dish at home. So when I arrived at my parents' house and found out that she was preparing it, I felt certain that she was sending me a message—I didn't visit often enough. It had, in fact, been over a month since I had last been home.

Seated at the kitchen table, I felt my stomach rumble as she took the chicken pie from the oven, the thick brown gravy bubbling up from underneath its crust. It felt like ages since I had last had a nice home-cooked meal. Because Sara and I each possessed only rudimentary cooking skills, we cooked at home infrequently, and when we did, we usually made simple things like hamburgers and pasta.

"Have you finished setting the table?" my mother asked me.

"I haven't started it," I responded.

My father was sitting next to me at the table and we were both drinking red wine. He usually drank two or three glasses in the evening after work. It was somewhat of a sore spot between him and my mother, who was of the opinion that he drank too much. She often brought it up in a bitter way when they had little spats.

"Well, we're going to eat soon, so let's get a move on," my mother said good-naturedly.

"Since I don't live here anymore, technically I'm a guest in your house," I joked. "The polite thing would be for you guys to serve me."

My mother laughed.

"Is that what you think?" my father said, raising an eyebrow.

"It's not what I think," I said. "It's what I know."

My father smiled just a little, while my mother laughed.

At home when we ate, we kept to the same assigned seats that we had back when I was a kid: clockwise from the seat closest to the kitchen it went my mother, sister, father, and then me. My sister was two years younger than me and lived in Sterling, a small town fifteen minutes north of Worcester. She was married with a five-year-old daughter and a three-year-old son. My father and I both got up from our seats and helped set the table. Soon my mother served the chicken pie and we all sat down to eat.

"So it must be nice to have a home-cooked meal?" my mother asked.

"It is. Especially your chicken pot pie," I said, giving her the compliment I knew she was looking for.

"Thank you. I made it because you were coming over for dinner. We hardly see you anymore."

Just as I thought, I told myself. Now comes the guilt trip. "I know. I guess that I usually just instinctively head home after work."

"You could always stay overnight here once in a while," my mother suggested. "You wouldn't have to do such a long commute."

"I am staying over tonight."

"Or you could move back home with us," my father joked. "I'll get you working on chores right away."

"Great, when can I start?"

My mother smiled. "We just miss seeing you."

"C'mon, don't try to make me feel guilty."

"I'm not trying to make you feel guilty."

"I'm just busy. I have stuff going on at work. I have to see Sara, too."

"Well, you two are together quite a lot," my mother said in a slightly negative tone.

"I don't want to get into it, Mom," I responded. My mother was not a big fan of Sara's and hadn't been since the early days of our relationship. We were staying overnight at my parents' house for Thanksgiving, our first one as a couple, and were in my bedroom and got into an argument and Sara began yelling at me, and my parents heard it. From that day forward, my mother branded her a wild and out-of-control person. She never said it outright, but I was certain that she didn't want the relationship to last.

"Anyway, let's change the subject," my mother said. "You said you saw Father Kelly at St. Mary's. How was that?"

I made an effort to keep my irritation in check and keep the conversation going in a pleasant manner. "It was fine. There are a lot of meetings, though, with this particular case, so things are moving kind of slowly. But it was good to see him. It's always a little weird, though, since I don't go to church anymore."

"Well, you should go, at least on holidays," my mother said.

"Yes, I know, mother," I said in a tired tone. "Any more instructions for me tonight?"

My father chuckled. "Kind of touchy tonight, isn't he?"

My mother changed the subject by saying, "Well, your sister is doing fine. She visited last weekend. You should see Nora and Ryan, they're so cute. When was the last time you saw them?"

"I don't remember exactly. A few months ago, maybe. I need to see them again."

"Ryan is such a character," my mother continued. "We were watching TV the other day and there was a picture on the screen of a big snow-capped mountain, and he said, 'Boy, there are so many things I haven't seen before.' It was adorable."

"That's funny," I said.

My mother mentioned that a new store was opening at the Greendale Mall and it was having a sale; its name went in one ear and out the other. She was something of a shopaholic, spending quite a bit of her free time at the mall. "Do you need any dress shirts for work? They're having a forty-percent off grand opening sale."

"Not really. I just wear them for court, so I don't wear them every day. And I already pretty much have enough."

"Forty percent off is a good deal."

I took a bite of food and while chewing told her, "Don't bother. You don't have to get any for me."

"It's no trouble. You need good shirts. You want to look nice for court."

"I have some from my last job. I'm really all taken care of."

"But that was two years ago."

I chuckled at her persistence. "I don't want you to go to the expense. Plus, trust me, the Worcester Housing Court is no beacon of fashion."

"Well, you never know where you might be in the next few years. You might have another job."

"All right, Mom."

In a short while I noticed my father gazing over my shoulder through the window at the backyard. Except for a small area illuminated by an exterior light, everything out there was covered in darkness.

"I'm going to put new mulch in the backyard this spring or summer," he said dreamily, and then he looked over at me as if expecting a response.

"Okay," I said.

"I may even put in some new shrubbery." He paused for a moment, as if lost in thought. "I broke the shovel last year, so I'll have to get a new one." Again he looked at me for a reaction but I had nothing for him.

Soon we finished eating and cleared the table. When we were done, my parents invited me to watch TV with them, but I decided to go upstairs to my room instead. I carried my overnight bag up there and put it down on the floor, then stood there and took a look around. I hadn't been in my old room in a while, and it seemed strange and unfamiliar, as if it belonged to someone else. It hadn't really changed much from when I was in high school which all of a sudden I found a little unsettling. On top of my bookcase was an old boom box that for some reason no one had ever thrown away—the type that people carried around on their shoulders in the 1980s and required eight D batteries. Seeing it made me remember that my old cassette tapes from that time period—an expansive catalogue of Van Halen, Def Leppard and Led Zeppelin—were stored in a couple of shoe boxes in my closet. I should really throw all of that stuff away, I told myself. When the hell am I going to listen to a Def Leppard cassette?

I took a few steps forward and bent down in front of my old desk to look at a framed 5 x 8 inch picture of myself when I was ten or twelve with my pet chocolate lab, Maggie. She was sitting on her hind quarters with her tongue out, and I was on one knee with my arm around her. She died when I was fourteen, which really broke me up at the time. Next to it was a picture of me and my family together at my high school graduation. I marveled at how young I looked, my facial features soft and smooth. It was strange to me, upon reflection, that I had only a few clear and distinct memories from high school. They were separate and disassociated from one another, like different colored patches on a quilt.

My next clear memory after high school graduation was of my parents taking me to college for my freshman year. My mother stayed up late the night before we left, long after I had gone to bed, packing my stuff and even baking chocolate chip cookies for me. When my parents finished helping me set up my things in my dorm room, I walked them to their car to see them off. Hugging them goodbye and watching their car drive away, I felt a sense of desolation at being on my own for the first time in my life. But I was also excited at the prospect of it. I ended up eating only half of the cookies and felt guilty a few days later when I threw the rest away.

10

The following Monday morning, the colonel called me into his office to do a case review. It was an exercise that I wasn't particularly fond of. He would ask me detailed questions about my cases and I'd feel pressured to answer them off-the-cuff. Analyzing cases was the part of being a lawyer that he enjoyed most, and while I enjoyed it, too, I didn't like being peppered with questions by him.

For the past ten years, since graduating from Columbia University Law School, the colonel had been a public interest attorney, starting off at Mental Health Legal Advisors in Boston and two years later coming to our office in Worcester. After only one year as a staff attorney doing my job representing tenants in housing court, he was elevated to the position of litigation director. That put him in charge of the more complex cases that came into the office, such as those involving housing and employment discrimination. Rumor had it that his promotion resulted from his cozy relationship with the executive director, a largely absent figure who was often off attending conferences and engaging in lobbying efforts. For a relatively young and inexperienced lawyer, it was a rapid rise in the hierarchy. But he was a very smart guy and a good lawyer, and as time passed, the executive director more and more left the day-to-day operations of the office to him.

One thing always struck me as a little odd. Although he was the litigation director of the office, the colonel had only tried one case in his entire career. It was an eviction trial, and I never learned the specifics of it or whether he had won or lost. As litigation director, he had a stable of good cases that he worked up well, and the defendants tended to settle. The crappy cases that I routinely handled were the ones that often went to trial.

As usual the colonel and I got down to business without any small talk—not even a perfunctory question about our respective weekends. I didn't have much to tell him anyway, given that I had spent the weekend alone. I had only left the apartment to go to Starbucks in the mornings to read the newspaper and drink a cup of coffee and to go out jogging in the afternoons.

Last Tuesday, Sara had mentioned that she might visit her parents for the weekend by herself. She always visited them without me, and like many times in the past, I made an issue out of it. I claimed that she wasn't proud of our relationship, that it didn't mean enough to her to make her stand up to her parents and tell them that her visits would have to include me coming with her. Things escalated from there into an argument and she stuck to her decision to go without me.

"You don't understand my relationship with my parents or the position I'm in," she said to me in an impassioned voice.

"What's there to understand? They want you to visit them without me and you comply."

"Yeah, because they're crazy and they're not nice. I hardly see them, so I just go along with it because otherwise I wouldn't see them at all."

I never fully understood why her parents didn't want me to visit with her. I had been out to dinner with them a handful of times and it had always been pleasant. But apparently behind the scenes they didn't want their contact with me to extend beyond that. Sara always chalked it up to their being crazy and unreasonable, and not anything personal having to do with me, saying that they had always acted that way with her boyfriends. But she never spelled it out for me beyond that.

In part I understood the point Sara was making—that she was between a rock and a hard place—but I also couldn't help feeling wounded by her actions. I couldn't help thinking that in her shoes I would've taken a stronger stand. After seven years together, weren't we supposed to come first in each other's lives?

The colonel began by inquiring about what had happened at the last CDBG meeting. I briefly paused to order my thoughts. My general approach with him was to reveal limited information, but not to mislead him, which was a delicate balance to achieve. I cleared my throat, then told him that Father Kelly had made a convincing argument that we should propose a meeting with the city and that was the direction we were going in.

"Has anyone mentioned filing a lawsuit?"

"No, not seriously."

"Well, keep me posted, okay?"

"Sure."

We moved on to talk about other cases. I felt glad that the discussion about CDBG had been brief. It was a little pet project for the colonel that he liked to watch develop from afar. What interested him about it was that it had a political dimension, high stakes were involved, and he viewed it as a chess game where each move had to be carefully chosen. The colonel was a skilled legal tactician. If presented with a legal issue, he had an impressive ability to give a snapshot analysis of it and recommend the best immediate course of action. He was, in fact, my superior in that regard, given his considerable intellect and years of legal experience. But when it came to legal strategy his abilities were a little weaker. Legal strategy was different from tactics, because it encompassed seeing the big picture of the case and engaging in long-range planning. Uncertainty caused the colonel to waffle at times, and he tended to err too much on the side of caution. If he saw a weakness in his case—and nearly every case has at least one—he would allow it to cast a big shadow over how he approached the case as a whole. His doubt made him tread cautiously at times when he should have marched forward. For instance, if he thought his client wouldn't be a strong witness, he'd become convinced that the case couldn't go to trial. It did not matter that the witness wasn't really that bad, or that other witnesses could pick up the slack, or that the other side may have had even more serious flaws with its case. Consequently, he'd take less in settlement than he might otherwise have gotten if he'd been more hard-charging.

The colonel's phone rang and he picked it up on the first ring, giving me the "one second" sign by sticking his finger in the air. When he began speaking in a soft voice, I knew he was talking with his wife. I looked to the side at his bookcase, pretending not to listen but eavesdropping all the while.

"I don't want them to think it's due to me." He paused. "Yeah, but if you say that, then they'll automatically think it's me." Thirty seconds later he hung up the phone. He leaned back in his chair and touched his fingers together. "So what else are you working on?"

"Just cases," I responded with a shrug. "Same old stuff."

"What's new that you're working on?"

Somewhat reluctantly, I told him about Anna's case. When I finished he looked at me with an amused smile.

"What?"

"You really took this case? You know it's a complete loser, right?"

"It's weak, yeah, but it has an interesting legal issue with the notice to quit—whether the drug activity was on or near the premises."

"But you're still going to lose in the end. Even if you get it dismissed, the housing authority will just bring a new case with a thirty-day notice. With these facts, Judge McCarthy will definitely find that the son was involved in drug activity. He was arrested in a car that heroin was sold from. In the end, the client will be out."

What he said was true. I was putting my stock in one particular argument that would probably go nowhere and then I would be left with a very weak case. "I know, but if we don't stand up against this type of shortcut with the notice to quit, Merola will keep doing it. It's a worthwhile issue to pursue."

The colonel considered my statement. "You have a point. But you do know that Judge McCarthy is going to deny your motion to dismiss, right?"

"Maybe he'll research all of the relevant Massachusetts law and write a lengthy, well-reasoned decision in my favor."

"Yeah, right." The colonel chuckled. The only time he ever laughed at jokes was when they were of a legal nature. "So when is the trial date?"

"I don't know."

"You filed an answer and discovery request, right?"

"Yes."

"Well, that means the trial date is automatically kicked over two weeks from the original date, right?"

"I made a request for a jury, so I haven't been assigned a trial date." The words escaped my lips quickly and without inflection. I knew they weren't going to make him happy.

"You what?"

Although tenants in Massachusetts had a right to a jury trial in eviction cases, juries were never requested by our office, or by other private lawyers who practiced in the Worcester Housing Court. There were reasons for this. A jury trial took more time, expense, and preparation than did a case tried in front of a judge. Landlord-tenant cases, which were almost always small and uncomplicated affairs, generally did not warrant the investment of time and resources that were required. And although Judge McCarthy certainly had his faults, the general consensus was that for tenants, he was preferable to a jury in conservative Worcester County. Most people in the jury pool were property owners who believed that landlords should have a sovereign right over their property. They had also been tainted by stories promulgated by the media and through word-of-mouth about landlords who were unable to evict deadbeat tenants for months and months. For the most part, the stories weren't true. When tenants failed to pay rent in Massachusetts, landlords could get them evicted pretty quickly, usually in about a month. But the stories were out there and people heard them.

A third reason, and the most compelling one, was that Judge McCarthy simply didn't want jury trials to occur in his courtroom. Jury trials took the ultimate decision-making power out of his hands, and they were also more work for him. They required him to go through the jury selection process and to charge the jury at the conclusion of the case. Over the years he had reportedly made this preference quite clear to lawyers by beating up on them in front of juries, making it tougher for them to win.

The colonel said, "You know Judge McCarthy is going to come down on you for requesting a jury trial, and it's also going to take up much more of your time. And it'll all probably be for nothing. You should've asked me first."

"I know. I'm sorry."

He paused, shaking his head. "Why are you requesting a jury, anyway?"

"Because of the son. I think if a jury knows what's at stake with regard to the scholarship, they might not evict the family. I think this is one instance where a jury, even in conservative Worcester County, is better than having Judge McCarthy hear the case."

"I don't think you can get into evidence that if your client is evicted, her son won't get a scholarship. It's not relevant and it's prejudicial. If I were Merola, I'd object to it."

"I know. It's a problem. But maybe I can slip it in."

"Slip it in?" the colonel said incredulously, shaking his head like a scolding parent. "Well, it is what it is. From now on, I want to know before a jury trial is requested."

"Sorry."

I left his office feeling freer inside, since I could now run with Anna's case and conduct my first jury trial. Although I chafed under his authority, his take on the case confirmed my own doubts. I was probably going to lose.

11

I began to focus more intensely on Anna's case. Even though I had never met her son, David, I was motivated by his story and what was at risk. It was upsetting to think that a kid from the projects who had performed well in school and earned a college scholarship could lose it through no fault of his own. It struck me as exactly the type of case that had compelled me to go to law school in the first place.

My first step was to research whether, under the law, the Rite-Mart parking lot could be considered "on or near the premises" of George Washington. If I could convince the judge that it was not, I could possibly get the case dismissed on the grounds that the use of the fourteen-day notice was improper. I went on Westlaw (an online legal research service) and discovered that Massachusetts courts had not interpreted that phrase in the context of residential leases. But I did find something else that I thought might be helpful. There was a Massachusetts law which provided that the sale of a controlled substance within 1000 feet of a school was considered to be "near" the school. That law could be persuasive because it used the term "near" in the context of drug sales and set forth 1000 feet as an outer distance. Of course, the Rite-Mart would have to be more than 1000 feet away from Washington in order to analogize to the case.

Next I researched court decisions from other states that concerned the eviction of public housing tenants due to illegal drug activity. I found one that was helpful, issued by the Connecticut Superior Court, holding that 0.3 miles away was too far away to be considered on or near the premises. A Pennsylvania Supreme Court decision determined that 0.9 miles was also too far away to be on or near the premises. Since they were decisions rendered by out-of-state courts, they would also be persuasive and not binding.

With the legal research out of the way, my next step was to get out of the law library, so to speak, and drive out to Washington and measure the distance to the Rite-Mart. One day Anna called me to ask if a trial date had been scheduled to which I responded, not yet. When I informed her of my plan, she suggested that I pick up David and have him accompany me. Really, there was no point in having him come with me, since it was a simple task that I could do on my own. But I agreed to it, as I was curious to meet him. I also figured she probably wanted him to meet a male who she thought would be a good role model, and I was happy to oblige in that respect.

It was about forty degrees outside, and the sun was peeking through a gray, overcast sky when I drove through the front entrance of George Washington. I was entering a world of dilapidated buildings and colorless concrete and steel, and it felt as if I was leaving the rest of the world behind and entering a dangerous place. My insides tightened up a little. I had never driven in there before, despite having represented many of its tenants.

Directly ahead of me were three high-rise towers clustered together, encircled by a ring of four-story buildings. The buildings were constructed during the Fifties and had a box-like architectural design that reminded me of pictures of the Soviet Union during the Cold War. The towers were the center of crime at Washington. Reportedly, a gang would commandeer an apartment in one of them and use it as a headquarters for its drug operations. When the housing authority, working in conjunction with the Worcester police vice squad, performed a sweep to stop the illegal activity, the gang would end up commandeering a different apartment.

The streets all had patriotic names like Constitution Avenue and Hancock Lane, the result of some ridiculous, over-the-top form of social engineering. Name the project and the streets in it after the founding fathers and you'll get a patriotic, civic-minded population.

As if it was that easy. The streets were nearly empty, probably due to the cold. In contrast, during the summer throngs of people reportedly hung out on the front steps of buildings and in the streets in order to escape the heat in their apartments. Violence occurred on those summer nights, when somebody would talk shit to somebody else, or a young guy would accidentally bump into another young guy who was just looking for trouble. Then out would come a weapon and blood would spill. The previous summer, a seven-year-old girl who had been leaning out her window died from a gunshot wound to the face when a gang member, shooting at a rival gang member, missed his target. You heard all the time about that type of senseless violence happening at Washington.

There were no stores or restaurants located inside Washington. No churches. In fact, there were no other neighborhoods located nearby. It was a densely populated housing project that was isolated from the rest of the city. People on top of other people with no other distractions.

I drove by an old Dodge Aries that was elevated on jacks and stripped of its tires and pulled into a spot outside of Anna's building, one of the low-rises. The exterior had spray paint on it and there were a few broken windows covered with boards. I felt nervous getting out of my car, even though no one was around. Warily, I walked up to the front door of the building, and when I buzzed Anna's apartment the buzzer seemed dead. I fished around in my briefcase for her file to get her phone number and then called her on my cell phone.

"It's Mark. I'm outside."

"Oh, I'm sorry," she apologized. "I forgot to tell you about the buzzer. It don't work. I'll be down."

I turned around in order to keep an eye on my surroundings. The cars in the parking lot were mostly older models. A basketball court was directly across the street and the rims on both ends were bent and without nets. After a minute went by Anna appeared at the front door wearing jeans and a red sweater. "Come in. It's cold out. David is inside."

I followed her up a flight of stairs and through a dimly-lit hallway, its gray concrete walls splotched with spray-paint graffiti.

The apartment doors were painted an outrageously bright red. Entering her apartment, I saw a small kitchen set off immediately to the left that was in worn and tattered condition. It had an old, deep basin-style sink with rusted pipes underneath, and some of the kitchen cabinets hung in misalignment and were covered with scratches. The brown linoleum floor was ripped up in a few places revealing off-white flooring underneath. Beyond the kitchen there was a small dining area with a square table, and beyond that was a living area. Off to the right a hallway led to the bedrooms and bathroom.

A slender, good-looking, young Latino kid was standing in the living area. He was about five-feet-ten and thin with a shock of dark hair that fell over his forehead. Anna practically took him by the arm and led him towards me. "This is David," she said. Up close I saw that he had high cheekbones, full lips, and placid brown eyes. I extended my hand to him, and he shook it in a shy yet polite manner, his grip neither firm nor weak.

"So I hear you won a scholarship to U. Mass-Amherst."

"Yeah," he answered.

"That's great. Congratulations."

"I'm so proud of him," Anna said with sparkling eyes. She affectionately tugged his arm. "My son. Going to college. Who figured?"

Hopefully going to college, I thought to myself. Hopefully.

"All right, Mom," David said good-naturedly but with mild annoyance. I sensed that his mother had fawned over him hundreds of times in the past, and it was something he disliked but had resigned himself to having to tolerate.

"So how long have you guys been living here?" I asked.

"Fifteen years," Anna answered. I suddenly recalled that she had told me that in housing court the morning I first met her.

Standing there with my briefcase slung over my shoulder, I took another look around the apartment. The kitchen table was surrounded by four green plastic chairs. In the living area was an old TV with a wood-paneled frame, a shabby brown couch with a plaid design, and a wood coffee table with a full ashtray on it. Not quite blending into the picture was a very basic wooden chair, like one you'd see at Starbucks or in a school classroom, set off by itself and angled directly at the TV.

"It's cold in here," I observed. "What's with the temperature?"

"This is how they keep it," Anna responded.

I noticed that both Anna and David were wearing sweaters.

"One of the windows in here is drafty, too," David explained. "There's like a two-inch gap on it. The cold air just streams through. When it's windy, it's bad."

I went over to the windows, which looked out over the parking lot, and saw that the metal frame on one of them was bent so that it could not shut completely. When I placed my fingers at the bottom of it, I felt a cold draft.

"What else is the matter with the apartment?" I asked.

"A lot," Anna said. She led me into the kitchen and pointed at the oven. "Our oven doesn't work. The burners on the top, they work, but the oven part don't."

"How long has it not worked for?" I asked.

"About a year."

"A year? Did you complain about it to the housing authority?"

"Yeah, but they don't do nothing about it. They don't care."

"Did you complain in writing?"

"No, I told them sometimes when I paid the rent."

"Did you complain about the heat and the window?"

"Yeah, I complained about that, too."

"Verbally but not in writing?"

"Yeah."

Anna pointed out the condition of the kitchen floor and cabinets that I had noticed upon entering the apartment.

"Is there anything else wrong in the apartment?" I asked.

"The bathroom," David said.

The bathroom door was constructed of thin, flimsy wood that was nicked in many places, and there was a three-inch hole near the doorknob that was covered with duct tape. Bending down at the side of the old, white porcelain tub, Anna pointed out how the faucet constantly dripped. She could hear it at night unless she closed her bedroom door. I noticed that the shower walls had some spots of gray mold; there were no windows in the bathroom and when Anna flipped the switch for the exhaust fan there was no effect.

I took a notepad out of my briefcase and began recording the bad conditions.

"Mice," David said. "We have mice, too."

"Everyone has mices and the housing authority knows it," Anna told me, "but they don't do nothing."

"How often do you see them?" I asked.

"Two a day on average," David said. "Mostly you can hear them at night. Like the other night I came into the kitchen to get a glass of water and turned on the light and I saw two of them in the sink. Then they just ran."

"They've gone into our food," Anna informed me. "Like, if you leave bread on the counter, forget it. They get right into it. And you can see their stuff around. The little brown pellets."

"All right," I said. "We're going to get these conditions fixed. I'm going to address them with the housing authority lawyer. Did you ever call the Board of Health to have them perform an inspection?"

"I tried to call them once," Anna responded, "but they won't come and inspect. They said that the housing authority should take care of it and to contact them."

"That figures," I said. Unfortunately, that response was all too common from the Board of Health when it came to complaints of bad conditions made by public housing residents. The Board of Health assumed that since the housing authority was a governmental agency, it would properly address tenant complaints and make repairs. It didn't consider that the housing authority might not do its job and might allow persistent bad conditions to exist in its projects. Of course, a consequence of this unwritten policy was a lightened workload for the Board of Health inspectors, not to mention that they were spared having to enter a dangerous place like George Washington.

The three of us exited the bathroom and went into the living room.

"What if they say no?" Anna asked me. "They haven't fixed these things so far."

"Then we'll go to court and ask for an order forcing the housing authority to make repairs. But I don't think it'll come to that." I looked over at David. "All right, well, do you want to measure the distance to the Rite-Mart with me?"

He nodded and said sure, then told me he had to go to his bedroom to retrieve his coat. I stood there with Anna waiting for him, my hands clasped together in front of me. When my eyes met with Anna's, I smiled politely as if we were strangers in an elevator. I couldn't think of anything to say.

"Don't you want to see David's room?" she asked me.

"Why? Is there something wrong in it?"

"No, I mean if you want to see his room to see where he lives."

"Nah, I'm okay."

She gave me a little nudge. "Go ahead. Go see."

It seemed like a funny thing for her to suggest to me, but for whatever reason she apparently wanted me to see his room, so I decided to go along with her. But first, wearing a hint of a smile, I said, "You don't want me to stay and talk to you?"

"No, go talk to him," she instructed, not picking up on my humor.

David was standing in the center of his room holding a dark green wool coat in his hands, looking ready to go. Hanging on his wall was a Red Sox poster and the famous poster of Che Guevara wearing a beret. In the corner of the room there was a twin-sized mattress covered with a red bedspread, low to the floor on a box spring. A few books were stacked on top of a shabby bureau. The room was badly in need of a paint job.

"Are these your school books?"

"Yeah."

"You're reading *The Great Gatsby*?" I picked up the book and looked at its famous blue cover with the visual reference to the eyes of Doctor T.J. Eckleburg.

"I haven't started it yet."

"The writing is beautiful. Fitzgerald has a very lyrical style."

"What do you mean, lyrical?"

"Poetic and flowing."

He nodded. "So what's it about?"

I paused to try and remember the book more clearly. I had first read it in high school, then again in college, and read it a third time a couple of years after college, right before entering law school. Because my last reading of it was about eight years ago, my memory was pretty hazy. "It's basically about the death of the American dream and the corruption of things innocent. And it's about a hopeless love that's not based on anything real. You should read it. You'll see what it means to you." I looked down at the cover again. "Actually, there's a gay scene in it, you know. They don't teach you that in high school, but it's there."

"There is?"

"Yeah." I began flipping through the pages to find it. It took me a little while but I finally located it at the end of Chapter Two. "See, the protagonist, Nick, is standing beside this guy who's in bed in his underwear. Since it was written in the 1920's, it's all very vague and indirect, but it's obviously a gay scene. You know, my high school teacher never told us that. I only learned it in college."

Then it hit me all at once—as if I had been in a darkened room and the lights were suddenly turned on, my eyes forced to adjust to the change in an instant—that I had just created a rather awkward and inappropriate situation. I was a thirty-two year old man alone with a teenage boy in his bedroom pointing out a homosexual passage in literature. I might as well have also asked him if he liked movies about gladiators and if he had ever been in a Turkish prison. Gladly, I didn't sense that David thought I was acting inappropriately. It was time to change both the subject of the conversation and the scenery.

"Uh, we better go," I said.

As I drove out of George Washington, I reset the odometer and headed in the direction of the Rite-Mart. I felt a little anxious inside. This would be the moment of truth, when I found out if my motion to dismiss would have any teeth to it.

David sat serenely in the passenger seat, alternately looking straight ahead and out the side window. I tried to think of something to say to him, but nothing came to mind. I wasn't the greatest conversationalist in the world, although when a conversation was flowing with a person I felt comfortable with, I generally did pretty well. My biggest hurdle was initiating a conversation. I could think of many different topics to talk about but had no idea where to begin. I was like a shopper who goes to a huge department store, looks out at the maze of aisles, the yards and yards of merchandise, and is totally perplexed about which direction to go in. In this particular instance, I had absolutely no clue what conversation topic might interest a high school student. I knew high school kids liked rap music, but the only rappers I knew of were Puff Daddy, or whatever his name was at the time, and Jay-Z, and I had never heard any of their songs. Suddenly David's brother, Miguel, came to mind. Everything I knew about him had come from Anna, so I figured that this would be a good opportunity to find out more.

"Have you spoken to your brother about the case?" I asked.

"No, he hasn't been around."

"Do you know how to get in contact with him?"

"Nah, he just comes around when he feels like it."

Up ahead I could see the Rite-Mart parking lot. According to the odometer 0.2 miles had elapsed and I prayed that I could squeeze out another 0.1 so that I could use the Connecticut decision. Significantly, I had cleared the requisite distance for the Massachusetts school drug law to apply.

"Are you and he close or not that close?" I asked David.

"We're not really close. We sort of live in two different worlds."

"What do you mean?"

"Well, he's out here on the street a lot, you know?"

"Is he involved with drugs?"

"I don't know."

I pulled into the parking lot—the odometer having just registered 0.3 miles—and took a parking spot in the rear away from the other cars. Good, I thought. Good.

"Does he associate with gangs?" I asked.

"Nah, Miguel isn't in a gang."

"How do you know?"

"I just know. That's not who he is. He's more on his own."

"You and Miguel being in different worlds—how did it happen, if you don't mind me asking?"

"It's always been that way," David answered with a shrug. "Me and my Mom are closer. She was always stressing school to me, making me study, talking about college. I think Miguel was just out and about and out of her grasp that way. I don't know, it was just different. And when our father died he was a little older and it affected him more. I don't know, maybe that has something to do with it."

"I'm sorry."

"Yeah, well, …" David's voice trailed off, and there was a far off look in his eyes. "Miguel is smart, too. People don't know that but he is."

I explained the significance of the 0.3 miles to David. He didn't get too excited about it, but getting excited didn't seem to be in his nature. On the drive back to Washington I was curious about what had happened to his father, but as much as I wanted to find out, I decided not to ask.

"I'm going to need to talk to your brother, so if you see him have him give me a call."

"Okay. So, about the case, do you think we can win?"

"We'll have to see what happens. All of the facts haven't been developed. For instance I haven't even talked to your brother yet, so it's difficult to say. I think today was a good day, however." Even though I had explained the significance of the 0.3 miles to him, I didn't feel comfortable getting too deep into the merits of the case with him, since he was a minor. To change the subject, I asked him how he got the scholarship.

"It was my grades and MCAS scores."

"So what do you want to study in college?"

"Biology."

"Why biology?"

"I want to become a doctor."

"That's great. What kind?"

"I'm not sure yet."

"Well, you have lots of time."

We were silent for a few moments and then he asked, "How about you? Why did you want to become a lawyer?"

I activated my blinker and turned into the entrance to Washington. The question seemed sort of comical to me, because I felt about a million miles away from where I had been seven years ago when I entered law school. I delivered a somewhat stock answer that I had always had an interest in history and government, enjoyed writing and argument, and had wanted to represent the underdog. It was exactly the kind of answer I would've given on a job interview, and it made me feel disingenuous. But I had nothing else to give him.

"It seems intimidating to have to argue in court," David said. "That wouldn't really suit me."

"It can be."

I pulled up in front of his building. An overweight black woman bundled up in a long, light-blue-colored winter coat slowly walked by pushing a shopping cart.

"Well, I'm sure I'll see you again," I said. "It was nice meeting you."

"Yeah, you too."

"Tell your Mom I'll be in touch, okay?"

"Okay."

"And the conditions will get fixed."

David smiled. "Okay, good."

After he got out of the car, I waited a few seconds until I shifted into reverse. He looked slight and vulnerable as he walked up the front steps to his building, the towers looming above him in the background.

12

Father Kelly and Nancy Brightman attended a meeting with the city concerning the use of the CDBG funds. I didn't go with them because at this stage I thought it would be best for them not to show up with a lawyer. A lawyer would sound off all sorts of bells and whistles. Unfortunately, the meeting was essentially a waste of time. Only the city manager attended, and while on the surface he appeared receptive to their concerns, he clearly indicated that there would be no change in plans. In fact, he actually tried to sell them on the idea that the skywalk would be a boost to the downtown and would help the city become a more attractive place to go on nights and weekends. It would employ poor and working class people during the construction process, and would also create jobs afterward by connecting the hotel to the arena. It would be a win-win situation for everyone.

Why people would want to go downtown outside of work hours, just because a skywalk was in place, was left unexplained.

When our group next met our collective mood was one of irritation for not having been taken seriously. It was our belief that we were perceived as annoying, clamoring liberals who were too naïve and idealistic to understand how things worked in the real world. It didn't take much deliberation for us to agree to go one step further and try to publicize the matter. A couple of days later, Father Kelly, Lawrence Geuss and I sat down with a reporter from the *Worcester Telegram* to tell our story. The reporter was a clean-cut, serious guy in his twenties who seemed ambitious, as if Worcester was just a stopping point in his career on his way to a more prestigious newspaper in a major market. This gave me hope that he wouldn't pull any punches, like an older, entrenched reporter might do. A week later he published an article about our efforts:

Community Groups Fight City for Federal Funds

The Worcester City Council has plans to allocate approximately $1,000,000 of federal funds for the creation of a skywalk in the downtown connecting the Regency hotel with the DCU Center. But community groups representing low-income city residents are fighting against it, claiming it would be a violation of federal law.

The funds are leftover from years of annual grants to the city under the Community Development Block Grant program, known by the acronym "CDBG." CDBG annually distributes funds to cities with populations over 50,000 with low-income residents. According to federal law, the CDBG program is intended to revitalize urban areas and provide safe and affordable housing for the low-income population.

In 2004 Worcester received approximately seven million dollars from the program.

The proposed skywalk is planned to be developed with a mixture of the residual CDBG funds accumulated over the years and financing from private sources. Local developer, John Miller, is slated to receive the contract for the construction work.

"The funds should be used to help low-income families," said Mark Langley, a legal services attorney

in Worcester. *"Federal regulations require that. It's not a bank account for private developers."*

In prior years, CDBG funds have been used for purposes such as the rehabilitation of abandoned buildings in the South Main area of the city, and a recent grant was also applied to the lead paint prevention program at the Board of Health.

The city manager, Christopher Belliveau, supports the plan. "The skywalk will create much-needed jobs in the city of Worcester," he said, "which is a legitimate use of CDBG money. It will also be an important part of a larger process to help draw people to the downtown area which we are trying to revitalize. This is good for both low-income residents and for the city."

According to federal regulations, a proper use of CDBG funds is to use them to create jobs for low-income people, but community leaders claim there is no evidence that this will be the result of the skywalk project.

"No one has given any hard evidence that jobs will result or that they will be given to low-income people in Worcester. It's all speculation," said Lawrence Geuss, executive director of the South Main Neighborhood Center. "And the amount of money at stake is much greater than any benefit to the poor that would result from the project."

Construction is slated to begin in the fall. For several years city officials have been trying to implement plans to give a boost to the flagging downtown. The last project was the Worcester Commons mall located downtown which has recently seen stores close due to a lack of business.

The day it came out, I read the article over a few times. I had never before been quoted in a newspaper, and it gave me a bit of a rush to see my name in print. On the whole I considered it to be a decent article, though I was of the opinion that the issues could have been more fully explored. I also thought that the ending made it seem like something had to be done to rehabilitate the downtown area, thus kind of legitimizing the use of CDBG funds for the skywalk. True, the downtown was flagging and had been for years, but to my mind, it hadn't reached the point that CDBG funds needed to be used immediately as part of the solution. And I still didn't see how building a skywalk would satisfy that objective.

I was seated at my desk drafting a set of interrogatories in an eviction case when the colonel came into my office with the newspaper in his hand. "Why are you quoted here?" he asked.

"We met with the reporter and he quoted me. I told you we were meeting with him."

"Yeah, but I've told you that I want the office to keep a low profile with this."

I was a little taken aback, thinking it should have been obvious to him that meeting with a reporter meant that I might get quoted. "We met with the reporter and we all explained the situation to him, and I got quoted. It just happened. I had no intention of putting the office in an awkward position."

He took a seat across from my desk. "All right," he said, as if recognizing that he had overreacted a little. He lightly tapped the newspaper against his free hand. "At any rate, the article was pretty good up until the end."

"I agree."

"It's like the journalist is saying that something needs to be done to the downtown. So someone reading this could think, well, maybe it's not so bad if CDBG money is used to help out."

"I know. My thoughts exactly. And it's just a walkway between two buildings. It's not like the Eiffel Tower or something."

"You didn't do anything wrong. I don't want you to think that's what I'm saying. My point is that if we ultimately don't get involved, then this article won't exactly help us. We're still a non-profit in this city. We're not insulated from politics. The council will read this and know we've been involved."

"Well, the thing is, we signed the letter before, and right now I think we are involved. I've been to so many of these meetings that if we back out now, I think it'll hurt us on the other end with the community groups who work in our same circle."

"Yeah, you're probably right," the colonel replied. Suddenly he seemed lost in thought, leading me to suspect that he had thus far only considered possible repercussions with the city and not with the community groups.

When I arrived home that evening, Sara was sitting on the couch reading a book with her legs curled up underneath her, Phil Collins playing in the background. It was a large couch, and at five-feet six and 110 pounds, she looked rather petite on it with her legs curled up. Without her noticing, I observed her from a side view. Her hair framed the side of her face, highlighting how her jaw line was free of any fat or loose skin.

She turned and saw me. "Hey there," she greeted me.

"Hi."

"Were you just standing there looking at me?"

"Yeah."

"Don't. You know I don't like that."

"Why not? I like looking at you. You look pretty."

"Yeah, right," she responded with an incredulous laugh. "You know I don't like it."

"Anyway, check this out." I handed her the newspaper article. "The CDBG project made the newspaper."

"Really?"

When she finished reading the article she said, "Wow, that's exciting. You were quoted."

"See how important a person I am," I joked.

"You are."

I laughed. "You're funny."

"Look at you, changing things in that city." She looked up at me lovingly and like she was really impressed.

I sat down next to her. "I don't know about all that. It doesn't seem like anything is getting changed. But I guess it's something. We'll see how it goes."

She mentioned that I should clip the article and save it which hadn't occurred to me.

"So what are you reading?" I asked.

She showed me the cover of the book: *Interpreter of Maladies* by Jhumpa Lahiri.

"I heard that's good," I commented.

"Yeah, it is. I just started it. My friend Ayesha recommended it."

The evening passed as it usually did with us—we had dinner together, watched some TV and read before going to bed. After turning off the lights and settling in to go to sleep, Sara said, "I'm worried about my Mom. She seems depressed."

"Did you notice it when you visited?" My irritation at her visiting her parents without me had for the most part dissipated.

"Yeah. She basically told me that she is."

When Sara was between the ages of five and ten, her mother was an alcoholic. When sober, she had been a fun and loving mother, but when she drank she would turn into a different person, one who was angry and destructive, even breaking and smashing fixtures in the house on occasion. More than once her father had been forced to physically restrain her mother. After going away to rehab for a month, a time when Sara's grandmother moved in to take care of her, her mother was able to quit drinking. But ever since, according to Sara, it was like a switch had flipped inside her mother, and she had become a quiet and depressed.

"Well, she doesn't really do that much, you know?" I said. "Maybe she'd benefit from volunteering or getting involved with the community or something? And certainly it'd be good for her to go to therapy."

"Yeah, I know. I think my father should be more attentive to her. He should be helping her, but he isn't. And he's a doctor."

"Well, their relationship is what it is. You know how your father is."

"Yeah, I do. I feel like there's something more I should do, but I don't know what."

"Well, you visited just recently."

"Yeah, but that's nothing special. I should be seeing them more than I do."

"Well, you do a lot for them. They don't come up here to visit you."

"I know, but it's different for them. They're older and more entrenched in their ways. They're not as mobile as they used to be."

I paused for a moment. Then I rolled over so that I was facing her in the dark. "I think things are a bit one-sided, to be honest."

Sara propped herself up on an elbow. "What do you mean?" she asked in a tone that indicated I should be careful what I say.

"It's always you running to help your mother, but quite honestly, your parents didn't do a lot for you when you were growing up. For some reason you feel the burden is on you, but it shouldn't be."

"I don't run to help my mother," Sara said defensively. "You're not listening to me. The point I'm making is that I'm not helping her enough."

"Okay, fine. I'm just trying to help."

"You don't know my situation. People in your family aren't depressed."

"Yeah, they are. They just don't know it."

Sara sighed. "Sometimes it's just impossible talking to you. My mother has problems. You don't understand these types of problems because you've never had to experience them."

"I represent poor people every day who are facing terrible things in their lives and have all sorts of problems," I countered.

"Yeah, but you don't know what it's really like for them. You see them in court and in your office, but you don't really know them."

Neither of us said anything more. We lay there with our backs to one another. We were both still awake and each of us knew it. I realized that what Sara had just said was true. I didn't really know what my clients' lives were like. I just tried to help them solve their problems—their legal problems, that is.

13

After what seemed like weeks of gray and overcast skies, the sun finally came out of hiding and the temperature rose to the mid-50's, higher than it had been for months. It was Saturday afternoon and I decided to go out for a jog. I took my usual route, heading west on Commonwealth Avenue past Massachusetts Avenue and then past Kenmore Square into Brookline, finally turning around at the St. Paul "T" stop. My feet hit the pavement and then energetically sprung forward, jubilant in their freedom away from the dull absorption of the treadmill which they had become accustomed to during the winter. It felt cleansing to my system to push myself on the open road, the cool fresh air filling my lungs, my heart pumping and muscles working. It felt like taking a car out on the highway and really flooring it after for months only driving it at slow speeds in the city.

The city seemed more alive with the change in the weather, as if it was awakening from hibernation. More people were out walking on the streets, many wearing sunglasses, and some shops even had their doors propped open. A few nut-jobs went so far as to wear shorts. It never failed to amaze me how Bostonians, when there was a slight spike in the temperature during the winter, acted as if it were a balmy summer day.

Sara was working at the real estate office, so I was on my own for the day. In the past she had infrequently worked on the weekends, but since last summer, she had begun to on a regular basis. Nothing had changed insofar as the dynamics of her office were concerned, meaning that her boss didn't require her to come in on weekends, and there wasn't more business than in the past. I knew she did it to create some space between us. It was her way of telling me that she was unhappy. It irritated me, and a few times I hinted to her that I knew the reason.

When I got home, I went into the bathroom to take a shower. I looked at myself in the mirror naked, observing the shape I was in. My stomach was relatively flat and there was a little definition to my abdominal muscles, though not to the point where I had a six-pack or anything. I had some muscles, but not too many. I didn't really do any strength training, except for an occasional set of pushups and sit-ups. My exercise regimen consisted almost exclusively of jogging. I failed to understand why guys devoted lots of time and energy to lifting weights in order to bulk up and get muscles. Doing calisthenics to stay fit, that was one thing, and that I could understand, it was what I did myself, but lifting weights to become a muscle guy, well, that I didn't understand. It seemed like a complete waste of time. It all turned to fat and flab when you got older, anyway. Standing in front of the mirror, I reflected on how at my old law firm I had been fifteen to twenty pounds heavier, most of it settling in at the mid-section and also filling out my face. Back then I didn't exercise as much, and I didn't eat as well, either.

After finishing up in the shower, I sat down on the couch with a tall glass of water and read *The Boston Globe*. Sara had told me she was going to head straight to the gym after she left the office for the day, and the plan was that I would meet her there at eight, and we would go to dinner and perhaps a movie afterwards. When eight o'clock arrived, I was standing outside of her gym waiting for her to come out. Five minutes passed, then ten minutes, and there was still no Sara, so I decided to call her cell phone.

"Where are you?" I asked. "I'm waiting outside."

"Outside where?"

"Outside at your gym."

"Why are you here?" she asked with surprise.

"Because we agreed that I'd meet you here at eight."

"No, we didn't. I was supposed to call you at eight."

"That's not true. Anyway, you didn't call me at eight."

"I'm exercising. I was going to call you in a couple minutes."

I sighed. "So you're not done?"

"No."

"All right, well, how long are you going to be?"

"I'm in the middle of exercising," she replied defensively.

"I'm just asking. Geez, you don't have to bark at me."

"Well, you're usually upset when I'm late."

"Which is most of the time."

"Yes, which is most of the time," she repeated with annoyance.

"Okay, so since you're going to take more time, I'm going to go get a drink. Can you meet me at the Kinsale when you're done?"

"You're going to a bar?"

She absolutely hated my going to bars, which was partly why I had decided to go to one. She didn't drink much and had rarely gone to bars, whether in college or afterwards. In her mind they were all pickup joints. I also believed that her mother's alcoholism contributed to her dislike of them. The Kinsale was an Irish bar with a polished, corporate feel to it that was not at all a pickup joint, but as far as Sara was concerned, I might as well have told her that I was going cruising at the most notorious singles bar in the city.

"Yeah, why?"

"Why don't you go to Starbucks?"

"I don't feel like coffee."

"I know you're going a bar to try to make me upset."

"It's not plausible that I genuinely want a beer rather than coffee on a Saturday night?"

"This is so embarrassing," she said in a lower voice. "There are people all around me."

"You have to get over this bar thing. After all the time we've been together, if you're still jealous in this way…" There was silence on the line. "Fine, I'll go to Starbucks. Can you please just hurry up?"

A half hour later she met me at Starbucks. She was wearing her long black winter coat and her hair was wet. I was drinking a coffee and reading *The New York Times*.

"So you resisted the urge to go out and drink?" she said.

"It was difficult, but I did. Anyway, it's a pleasure to see you."

"Yeah, you too. I'm *thrilled*."

We went to Antonio's, a small neighborhood Italian restaurant in Beacon Hill with excellent food and reasonable prices. After I ordered a glass of wine and Sara a diet coke, we looked across the table at one another in a way that acknowledged that we were putting our spat behind us and wanted to start fresh. I listened as she told me about her colleague, Cheryl, who had gotten upset when the office had lost a set of keys for a very nice two-bedroom apartment on Pinckney Street. Because the landlord was out of town, they were unable to show it and a competing agency with its own set of keys rented it.

"It's too bad, but she didn't have to make a big deal of it to the entire office like we were all involved or something. I never had the keys and Joe never had the keys." Sara took a sip of her drink. "She was literally storming around the office. It was unprofessional of her."

I nodded my head without saying anything.

"So you're not going to be nice tonight because you ended up having to wait fifteen minutes?" she said.

"I didn't think I wasn't being nice."

"Well, you're acting coolly towards me."

"I get this way when I'm hungry and need to eat. You know how I get. All I had was yogurt and a granola bar and I went jogging today."

"Yeah, you do. You do get that way."

"I agree. That's why I said it."

"That's good you went jogging. How was it?"

"Okay. I went to Brookline and back."

"That's pretty far."

"I was surprised that I ran that far after not having jogged outside for so long. Being the dynamic person I am, I sometimes surprise myself."

"Oh God," Sara said, rolling her eyes.

"See how lucky you are to have a funny boyfriend," I said, piling it on a little more.

"Yeah, I'm so lucky. Look at you, just feeding yourself compliments."

After our food arrived and I started eating, my mood improved and our conversation picked up too. We got into a lengthy discussion about reality dating shows on TV—whether or not they served a good purpose for their participants, or were exploitative, or commoditized women with their unrelenting focus on youth and beauty, or were a combination of all those things. Sara watched the program "The Bachelor," a guilty pleasure, and I sometimes watched it with her, and it was a reference to that show which had gotten us started on the topic.

For dessert we split an order of tiramisu. Our forks alternately dipped into its spongy body from opposite sides until a sliver was left that Sara let me finish. After paying the check, we went out into the night and held hands on our walk home. The dark night sky and chilly air seemed to put me in a contemplative mood. I got to thinking about our relationship, where it was and where it was heading. We had spent the past seven years together, and I was thirty-two years old. We were at the stage where couples typically thought about getting married and having kids, but that was something that we never really talked about. Sara had joked on a couple of occasions about not having a ring on her finger, but that was pretty much it. For my part, I figured that we needed to work through our problems before moving ahead to marriage and kids. I believed Sara wanted both in her life within the next few years, but I didn't know that for certain. It was something that we never sat down and talked about seriously.

14

Why was I always nervous when I entered the housing court on a day when I had to argue a motion or conduct a trial? Would the feeling ever go away? Did other lawyers have the same experience? My insides felt like a wet washrag that had been wrung out. Many times in the past I had performed just fine in these situations, yet in the run-up to it I was a bundle of nerves, worrying that my voice would shake, or that I'd forget what to say or jumble my argument. This particular Monday morning was no different for me. My throat felt dry and my heart raced a little. Reaching into my briefcase for my ever-present bottle of spring water, I told myself, relax. Be calm.

Now was the prime time for the settlement of Anna's case; a lot was at stake for both sides in the argument that would occur in just a few minutes. I had filed a motion to dismiss on the grounds that the 14-day notice to quit was improper. If I lost, Anna would face almost certain defeat at trial; but if I won, the case would be dismissed, and the housing authority would have to start it all over again. With this in mind, I arrived at court a little early in the event the housing authority was open to negotiations. I took a seat on one of the wooden benches, noticing that not many people were in the lobby, and reviewed the major points of my argument. I tried to bullet point them in my mind one after the other, but it was difficult, since my brain tended to function in a non-linear manner. When Kevin Merola entered the lobby along with the housing manager,

Jeannie, he and I greeted one another with nods; there was no acknowledgement between me and Jeannie.

"Kevin, could I speak to you when you have a chance?" I asked him.

He held up a finger to indicate he'd be one minute, said a few words to Jeannie, and then came over to me. "What can I do for you?"

I stood up so we would be at the same level. "We have this motion—"

"Yes, that's why I'm here," he interrupted with a grin.

"Very good. Very funny."

"So what can I do for you?"

"First, thank you for getting the repairs made to my client's apartment." After visiting Anna's apartment, I had faxed a letter to him requesting that repairs be made to her unit, and three days later, she excitedly reported to me that the window and the heat were fixed and there had been a visit from an exterminator. The other bad conditions had been repaired, too, with the exception of the mold in the bathroom which had not yet been treated. Supposedly the housing authority would remedy that in the near future. "I was also wondering if there's any chance we can settle this case?"

Kevin folded his arms across his chest and stroked his beard with his right hand.

"We both know that there's a risk for each of us here," I continued, "and I think there is a strong legal argument that point-three miles, which is the distance between the Rite-Mart and Washington, is not on or near the premises."

"I disagree with that."

"Even putting that aside, I think the housing authority should consider that my client didn't do anything wrong. She's a single mother who works part-time at Wal-Mart. The son, Miguel, doesn't live there."

"Yes, but he's on the lease."

"But he doesn't live there. There's one other thing you should know. My client, Anna, has another son, a high school senior, who has a scholarship to go to U. Mass. If you evict them, they'll have to move to Puerto Rico—because that's where Anna is from—and he'll lose the scholarship. It requires him to be a Massachusetts resident and graduate from a Massachusetts high school. That won't happen if the family is evicted."

"Hold on. Let's go back a second. The son has a scholarship?"

"Yes. It's a scholarship based on his grades and MCAS performance. But if he gets evicted, he won't be graduating this year because the family will be upended and will have to go to Puerto Rico, which is where they have family. They can't afford private housing here. It'd set him back and he'd miss this year's scholarship, and he wouldn't be attending a Massachusetts high school. As I understand it, there are a certain number of scholarships that are given out each year and he'd lose it."

Kevin nodded thoughtfully.

"I know you have a job to do and the housing authority has its policies, but this is an important human element. What I propose is that we enter into a probationary agreement. Ban the son, Miguel, from the apartment and let Anna and David stay."

Kevin winced as if he had just downed a shot of whiskey. "I don't know if I can do it. The housing authority has adopted a zero-tolerance policy with drugs. If the person arrested is on the lease, then everyone has to go."

"Will you check with Jeannie?" I knew I was beginning to sound desperate, which I always tried to avoid at all costs with my adversaries. But I felt this was my last chance to settle the case, and I really wanted to make it happen.

"Okay, let me go check. But the zero-tolerance policy comes from higher up than Jeannie."

It only took a minute for Kevin to come back and tell me that the best he could offer was one month for a move-out date. One month wouldn't get Anna and David to the end of the school year. I told him we'd have to argue the motion.

Watching Judge McCarthy ascend to the bench, I reflected on how this one man would soon make a decision that would have very serious ramifications for Anna and David. Just this one man had that much power. A dark and lugubrious feeling came over me, as if I were lost miles out to sea underneath a gray sky with no land in sight. Judge McCarthy sat down behind the bench and appraised us with a neutral expression. "Mr. Langley," he said. "What an exciting way for me to start off my week. Your motion?"

Ignoring his barb, I replied, "Yes, Your Honor."

Raising his hand in my direction, as if he was holding an object in his palm, he instructed, "Begin."

Immediately I defined the issue that was before the court: whether the Rite-Mart was on or near the premises so as to justify the service of a 14-day notice rather than a 30-day notice. Then I established that the store was 0.3 miles away and dove into my legal analysis. I placed a lot of emphasis on a provision in the Massachusetts school zone anti-drug law which stated that the sale of controlled substances within 1000 feet of a school was considered to be "near" the school. Consequently, a greater distance than 1000 feet did not qualify as "near" under the law. Because there was at least the same, if not a greater public policy interest in protecting schools than public housing projects from the sale of drugs, the school zone drug law could most certainly be analogized to the present case. Therefore, the term "on or near" on Anna's lease could not be construed to indicate a distance greater than 1000 feet. Finally, I also cited the Connecticut decision and told Judge McCarthy that it should be followed.

"Do you have legal authority that says I should consider the school law in this drug case?" he inquired.

"No, Your Honor, I don't. But again, one can certainly analogize. It's just inconceivable that 'near' means one thousand feet or less in the context of a school, but that same term means a greater distance in the context of public housing. That would essentially mean that it's okay to have drugs closer to a school than a public housing project. It wouldn't make sense."

I also talked about David's scholarship to U. Mass. and emphasized that he would lose it if evicted. To my surprise, Judge McCarthy seemed interested in that, his eyes narrowing but staying focused on me while I discussed it. In fact, when Merola objected to my bringing it up, Judge McCarthy gave him an outstretched hand and said, "No, I'm going to hear it. You can sit down."

When it was Merola's turn to speak, he said, "Your Honor, the only case cited by Mr. Langley is not from Massachusetts and is not binding on this court. The only statute cited by Mr. Langley does not even apply to this situation, that of drugs in public housing. I suggest that Mr. Langley cannot just pick out authorities with no relevance here and say they apply just to help his case. Besides, Your Honor, he is simply making a number-crunching argument. A fourteen-day notice as opposed to a thirty-day notice, tenths of miles—"

"Well, Mr. Merola," Judge McCarthy interrupted, "isn't the housing authority number-crunching itself, in a sense, by setting forth different notice requirements in the lease? Your client is the one who made the fourteen and thirty day notice distinctions in the first place." He appeared to take pride in making that point.

"The only reason that the length of the notice to quit is shortened when drug activity occurs on or near the premises is to dispossess those tenants more quickly, since they pose a threat to the health and safety of other tenants. What I am suggesting is that we should look beyond mere numbers and measurements because the point-three miles only gives one aspect of the distance. For instance, if you stand in the parking lot of the Rite-Mart convenience store, you can see the Washington towers very clearly. In addition, much of the population of George Washington goes to the Rite-Mart, too, so it is not a place that is removed from the housing complex. It's more of an adjunct to it. These are things that Mr. Langley doesn't consider in his argument, but should be taken into account in determining how near the Rite-Mart is to the project. There is no other store or business that is nearer to it than the Rite-Mart. And one more thing, Your Honor, is that the tenant got a fourteen-day notice. There hasn't been an ambush here. Fourteen days has been given." Merola raised his arms up in front of himself with palms upturned. "And what we have here at the end of the day is someone named on a lease who was dealing heroin right near the public housing project where he lives."

I tried to speak, wanting to reply to the powerful point Merola had just made, but Judge McCarthy shut me down.

"Given what we have here," he declared, "I'm not convinced that the Rite-Mart isn't on or near the premises. Therefore, I'm not going to dismiss this case because of three-tenths of a mile. The motion is denied."

When I returned to the office, I called Anna and told her the news. I was a little worried that she would take it badly, but she took it in stride. Or at least she seemed to, not betraying any emotion after I delivered the news. I then explained that the trial would come next.

"Does that mean I'll have to testify in court in front of the judge?" she asked.

"Yes."

"I don't want to do that," she said. I sensed fear in her voice.

"Let's go one step at a time, okay? It'll be all right," I said, trying to comfort and reassure her.

She paused for a moment. "Okay." But there wasn't much conviction in her voice.

"Now what I need to do is talk to Miguel and talk to his lawyer, too. Can you help me out with that?"

"I'll try. You know, I haven't seen him for a while."

"Okay, but when you get in touch with him, find out when he can meet with me and then let me know. Actually, if you see him, call me while you're both together and we can set up a meeting right then. However it happens, we need to meet."

After hanging up with her I leaned back in my chair. My defense of Anna and David depended upon Miguel's cooperation, which was a bad position for me to be in. I might never get in contact with him, and even if I did, who knew how he would present as a witness or what he would say? He might come off as someone who very much seemed like a drug dealer. He was, in short, a huge wildcard. On top of that, his criminal lawyer would likely advise him not to testify because, if he did so, he would waive his Fifth Amendment right against self-incrimination and anything he said in housing court could be used against him in his criminal case.

All in all, the case was not looking good.

That evening during my drive home from work my cell phone began to ring, and I saw from the number on the screen that it was my mother calling. I debated whether or not to let her go to voice mail, but after a few rings I picked up, figuring that this was as good a time as any to talk to her. I was in the car and didn't have anything better to do.

"You left work late," she remarked. "It's past eight."

"Yeah."

"Were you busy at work?"

"I was."

"So what's going on?"

"Same old thing. A number of cases I have to do stuff on."

"They should pay you more considering how late you stay sometimes. By the time you get home it's going to be after nine."

"Uh huh." Already I could feel myself shutting down emotionally toward her.

"It was nice that you came over recently to stay the night."

"Yeah."

"I know you like to go home after work, but it was nice that you came over."

"Okay, I understand."

"You should keep some extra clothes here so that when you felt like it you could just stay over rather than go all the way back to Boston."

"Okay, Mom," I said, feeling a little exasperated.

"So, have you eaten dinner yet?"

"Nope."

"What will you do?"

"I guess I'll see if there's anything in my apartment or else order out from somewhere."

"Well, is anything else new with you?"

"No, not really."

"I'm just trying to make conversation, Mark."

"I know. I'm sorry. I guess I'm just tired. And on top of that, you're asking me like twenty questions." Suddenly feeling bad for being brusque with her, I tried to rehabilitate the conversation. "Oh, actually, I almost forgot to tell you that I was in the newspaper for the Father Kelly thing. I emailed the article to you."

"I saw that and meant to mention it. Congratulations."

"Thanks. It was pretty neat for that to happen."

"What are you going to do next?"

"I'm not really sure."

"Can you actually sue the city over this?"

"Sure."

"Well, be careful."

I was now entering Framingham which meant that I had another half hour until I arrived home.

"Be careful of what?"

"The city and John Miller both have a lot of power."

"Not over me, they don't. I only work in Worcester. I don't live there."

"Well, just be careful."

"Okay, I will."

"I worry about you."

"Yeah, I know you do."

15

I t was the last place I wanted to be—at housing court defending Maria Roman against an eviction. When I learned that the housing authority was dragging her back into court, I instantly suspected that she would have a weak defense and that she would be as difficult to deal with as ever. I thought back to our last visit to the housing court, when she had abruptly walked out. That should have tipped me off right then that we would soon be back; she had left with an attitude that said, I'm going to do what I want and nothing is going to stop me.

I also knew that this time there would be no deal that I could finagle with the housing authority. This time it would want her out for good. This time we would have to go to trial before Judge McCarthy.

As if her case wasn't pressure enough, it was scheduled on the same day that I was defending another difficult client: a guy living in a rooming house who was being evicted based on allegations of drunk and disorderly conduct. I was fairly certain it was not going to be a good morning. In my judgment, the guy had much less at stake than Maria did, since she had children and her public housing was at risk. So I decided to focus my attention on her first. She had missed an appointment the day before, when I had planned to prepare her for the hearing. We'd have to make do with a short prep session in the lobby.

She and Jose approached me in the hallway. "Where were you yesterday?" I asked her gently, not wanting to set her off, though I was a little irritated.

"My son was sick."

"Sorry to hear that," I responded, "but you really should've called."

"I couldn't call," she answered defensively. "I had to bring him to the emergency room. He had a 103 degree fever."

I doubted that she really wasn't able to give me a quick call, but left open the possibility that she was telling the truth. "Is he all right?"

"He's sick, but he's better than yesterday."

"Well, we're going to have to do this very fast. We're going to get called into court soon and there's going to be a hearing."

I had approached Merola when I first arrived at court to get more information about the allegations against Maria. His motion contained only broad, general allegations that Jose was still residing with Maria as an unauthorized occupant. It otherwise lacked specifics, such as the dates and times he was observed at her apartment or the identity of witnesses. Unfortunately for tenants, these details were not required when a landlord brought a tenant into court for violation of a settlement agreement. But Merola told me earlier that morning that the two neighbors who were in court last time, Crystal and Amara, had seen Jose leaving the apartment on several occasions, and that security had seen his car parked outside the apartment overnight.

"When did this happen?" I asked Merola.

"You'll have to ask the witnesses that on cross-examination," he replied smugly.

I shook my head and then walked away, thinking, what an asshole. I scanned the lobby for Crystal and Amara and spotted them standing against the wall talking to one another.

When I told Maria what I had learned from Merola, she insisted that Jose had not visited her apartment. She admitted that his car had been there, but said that was only because she needed to borrow it sometimes to do errands and take the kids places.

I sighed. "Maria, having his car there makes you look guilty."

"But I need a car. What am I supposed to do? Walk with my young kids everywhere?"

"You don't use it. Or if you have to use it, you report to the housing authority that you have the car parked there."

"You never told me to do that," she said in an accusatory fashion.

"How was I supposed to know you would use it? And I seem to recall that you walked out of court two seconds after I handed you the settlement agreement last time." I stopped myself from going any further, realizing it wouldn't help matters if I started arguing with her. "All right, you'll just explain it on the witness stand. I'll ask why his car was there and you'll tell the judge what you told me."

There ended up not being much to review together. Maria and Jose denied that they had violated the agreement, so essentially it would come down to their word against the other witnesses. I impressed upon Maria that it was important for her not to get upset or emotional on the witness stand and that it would really help her case if she came off as nice and likeable.

"I'm gonna tell the judge that they're lying," she declared.

"No, don't do that. Trust me, that won't work with this judge. Just answer my questions and stay calm."

She didn't say anything.

"Will you follow my advice?" I pressed her.

"Yeah, sure," she agreed reluctantly.

I looked at my watch and saw that I had a little time left to talk to my rooming house client who was seated on one of the benches lined up against the wall. He was a thin, gaunt white guy in his early-forties, about five-feet-nine and one hundred forty pounds. His rooming house was located on Oread Street, probably the worst part of the South Main area.

"Think it's going to be soon?" he asked. He had a tense, jumpy manner of speaking, as though he was being pursued by someone who was hot on his tail.

"Yeah, it'll be soon."

He looked straight ahead, nervously stroking his chin. It was evident that he suffered from mental illness from the way he spoke, the vacant yet electric look in his eyes, his long greasy brown hair and facial growth, and his outfit of a ratty green army jacket and an old pair of work boots. All of my rooming house clients had been mentally ill.

Jeff's main problems were his alcoholism and a reluctance to take his psychiatric medications. He didn't like how the medications made him feel, so he didn't take them regularly. When he did take them, they didn't mix well with his alcohol consumption. According to Jeff's landlord, he made a lot of noise at night when he drank and sometimes acted belligerent. The crown jewel of the eviction case against him was that on one occasion, he was observed walking in the hallway with his pants down.

"So what now?" he asked anxiously.

"We wait for your case to be called into mediation."

"What happens then?"

I had previously explained the process to him, and I did so again, but this time in a more truncated fashion.

"I didn't do anything they said. It's all just made up," he said, looking up at me with sad, pleading eyes. I felt bad for him right then. I could tell he had a good core but was just really messed up.

"Let's see if we can get a good outcome for you in mediation."

"What do you mean?"

"We're going to get called into mediation. Let's see what type of deal we can work out. If it's better than taking the risk of going to trial, perhaps we can settle."

"But what they're saying isn't true. You see, I don't want to give in to that."

"I know, but let's just see what happens. There's no harm in going into mediation. If you settle the case with a good result, then great. If not, then you're still in the same position and we can try the case. There's no harm in it."

"Okay. I can agree with that," he said, slowly nodding his head. "I just don't want to give up my right to a trial."

In the motion session Judge McCarthy appeared to be in good spirits. He gave a single mother with two young kids an additional month to move out of their apartment, even though she was scheduled under a settlement agreement to have moved out two weeks earlier. That was more time than he normally would have allowed. Later, when a young boy in the arms of a Latino woman started crying, he summoned the court officer over to the bench and handed him a lollipop, and the officer then delivered it to the boy, whose eyes widened as he took it with an outstretched hand and began sucking on it happily.

I tensed a little when Merola argued a motion to evict a middle-aged woman from George Washington. She had a craggy face, some missing teeth, and was dressed in a shabby pair of jeans and an old Red Sox t-shirt. The galling part of the motion was that she was delinquent by just fifty dollars under a repayment plan. Merola justified his motion by explaining that this was the third repayment plan that the housing authority had extended to the woman and it couldn't give her any more breaks.

Judge McCarthy asked the woman, "Ma'am, can you pay the fifty dollars?"

"I ... I, try," she responded in broken English, "but it's hard when I lose my job." Her voice halted and she took a deep breath. She could have used help from my office, I thought to myself, but like many tenants in dire straits, she never contacted us.

"Why did you lose your job?" Judge McCarthy asked her.

In my view it was an inappropriate question. That she lost her job was relevant to the fact that she missed her payments, but that was all McCarthy needed to know. The reason why she lost it wasn't important.

"My car died. I couldn't get to the job anymore."

"Can you pay the fifty dollars?"

"I'll try to."

"Can you do more than try? Can you pay it in the future?"

The woman stood there searching for an answer to give. Meanwhile, I kept saying to myself, almost like a mantra, just say yes. All you have to do is tell the judge that you'll be able to pay. That's all you have to do, and you won't be evicted today.

"I'm getting a check in a week," she finally said.

"Okay, that's a start," said Judge McCarthy. "Now I'm going to give you ten days to pay the money back. Do you understand?"

"Yes, yes, I do."

"That's ten days," the judge repeated. "If you do that, you get to stay. Okay?"

"Thank you," the woman said gratefully.

Merola stepped in. "Your Honor, normally I wouldn't bring forth a case like this for only fifty dollars, but the issue here is that the tenant habitually pays late and we've been here several times in the past."

"Don't worry, Mr. Merola. The housing authority won't go bankrupt over fifty dollars."

There was a smattering of laughter in the gallery. It pleased me immensely to see the judge give a dig like that to Merola in open court.

The landlord in the next case was a tall, athletic black guy who looked to be in his mid-thirties, probably 6'2" and 200 pounds. The tenant was not present. The clerk turned around to face Judge McCarthy and whispered something to him.

Judge McCarthy said to the landlord, "I understand your tenant is a little late and will be here in about fifteen minutes. You don't mind waiting until he comes, do you, sir?"

Although rather physically imposing, the landlord seemed to have a rather gentle and refined manner. He looked off to the side, as if he were a little put-out but was nevertheless trying to be polite. You could tell that he saw this as just one more in a series of inconveniences caused by his tenant. "Well, you see, I'm the one who's always waiting."

"I'm waiting right now," Judge McCarthy responded.

"Excuse me?" the landlord said.

Judge McCarthy leaned forward wearing a slight grin. "I'm waiting for you to answer my question."

There was laughter in the courtroom.

Judge McCarthy handed the file to the clerk. "Put it on for next call."

When Maria's case was called, there were ten to fifteen people remaining in the courtroom. Suddenly I felt my body tighten up. In just moments I would be questioning witnesses in open court, everyone's eyes upon me, and Maria's tenancy would be on the block. Jose started in the direction of the counsel table, but I quickly directed him to sit in the gallery, hoping that Judge McCarthy hadn't noticed. Jose heading straight to the counsel table was a sign that he and Maria were close with one another, something that didn't exactly need to be highlighted.

The witnesses were sworn in as a group and we were underway. As his first witness, Merola called the security officer, a lean Latino guy in his late-twenties with a trimmed moustache and a tight buzz haircut. He had the look of a guy who wanted to be a cop and was using this job as a stepping stone. After eliciting his name and position, Merola asked him, "Mr. Gomez, what shift do you work at Washington?"

"Midnight to eight in the morning," he answered.

"Five days a week?"

"Yes."

"What are your job duties?"

"I respond to any calls or complaints about things happening at the George Washington housing project. We are summoned to the scene if a crime has occurred. I also drive around the project on patrol to monitor activities and try to ensure a safe environment."

Merola stroked his beard as if he found the description to be thought-provoking. "Officer Gomez, have you had occasion to see Jose Diaz' car at George Washington?"

"Yes, I have."

"Well, first, do you know who Mr. Diaz is?"

"Yes, he's back there." Gomez pointed at Jose in the gallery.

"Okay. And what type of car does he have?"

"It's a grey Toyota Celica, an older year, from the early-Nineties." He looked down at his file. "License plate number 2319 YU."

He was using his notes, but for the moment I decided to let it go. I could object, but Merola would be able to get the information into evidence if he took the appropriate steps under the rules of evidence. It would just eat up time to make Merola and the witness jump through hoops and, more importantly, it would likely annoy Judge McCarthy.

"How do you know that's his car?" Merola inquired.

"I've seen it at Washington and I've seen him in it. Plus we were made aware of it from prior proceedings involving Ms. Roman."

"When have you seen it at George Washington?"

He looked down at his notes. "The night of February 13, I went by and saw it at 2:00 A.M. and again at 7:00 A.M.—"

Now that the use of the notes was inflicting damage I decided to object.

"The witness can't remember all dates and times by memory," Merola argued to Judge McCarthy.

"Mr. Langley?" asked the judge.

"Well, if he's going to use them, I ask that I be able see the notes."

Judge McCarthy directed John the court officer to bring me the notes. I sat there at counsel table and reviewed them for a minute, conscious that all eyes were focused on me. The notes consisted simply of a list of dates and times that the car was seen outside of the apartment—four different occasions in total on two different dates. I handed them back to John who returned them to Gomez.

"So Mr. Gomez, when did you see Mr. Diaz' car at the project?"

"On February 16, I saw it at about 1:00 A.M. and again at 5:00 A.M. And on February 19, I saw it at 1:00 A.M. and 6:00 A.M"

"Where on George Washington property did you see the car?"

"Each time right in front of 79 Constitution Avenue."

"Where does Ms. Roman live, if you know?"

"At that address."

"Officer Gomez, how often do you go by Constitution Ave. on your shift?"

"Usually twice. Once earlier in my shift and once later in my shift."

"No further questions," said Merola taking his seat.

I stood up with my notepad positioned in front of me on the counsel table. I had Officer Gomez framed in the center of my vision, like an object in the lens of a telescope, and everyone else in the courtroom seemed to fade from my awareness.

"Officer Gomez, you say you saw the Toyota Celica outside of the tenant Maria Roman's apartment on those two dates, right?"

He nodded. "Yes."

"Were you told to look out for that car in recent months?"

"Yes."

"And I see your notes only refer to that particular car, right?"

"I'm sorry?"

"Your notes only pertain to that car and to no other cars."

"Well, I noted other things going on in the project."

"Let me say it another way, you weren't keeping tabs on other cars?"

"No, because Ms. Roman is the one suspected of having an unauthorized person living with her."

"Well, Washington has hundreds of apartments, right?"

"Yeah."

"And so Ms. Roman would be the only one suspected out of hundreds of public housing tenants of having someone not on her lease living with her? Is that your testimony?"

"I don't know. She was suspected. I can tell you that."

I paused to collect myself. "Now, on those two dates, you didn't actually see Mr. Diaz on the Washington property, did you?"

"No."

"You just saw his car, correct?"

"Yes."

"Nor have you seen him there at any other times since this case was last in court?"

"No."

"You didn't investigate to find out if my client was borrowing his car, did you?"

Gomez shook his head. "No."

"You just assumed that Mr. Diaz was at her place since his car was there?"

"It's his car. Yeah."

"You didn't knock on her door at any point to see if he was there, did you?"

He answered that he hadn't. I paused and looked down at my notes. "You received training for your job, prior to becoming an officer, right?"

"Yes."

"That would include training on how to conduct investigations?"

"Yes."

"In that training you learned how to gather evidence in investigations, right?"

"Yes."

"One way to gather evidence in an investigation is to take pictures, right?"

"Yeah."

"You've been taught that at some point along the line?"

"Yes, that's right."

"In this case, you never once took a picture of the Toyota Celica outside of the tenant's apartment, did you?"

"I didn't have a camera with me."

"My question wasn't about your access to a camera. My question was, you didn't take any pictures of the car, did you?"

"No."

"You just have these notes, right?"

"Yes."

"Since you raised it, does the security department at Washington have a camera in its offices?"

"Yes, but it's back at the office, and I'm out driving in my patrol car."

"Okay, well, you could go back to the office and get it, couldn't you?"

"I guess."

"In fact, you say you saw the Toyota twice on your shift, so after the first time you could've gotten the camera in case you saw it again, right?"

Gomez shrugged. "I suppose."

"No further questions."

Gomez' testimony had been damaging. I had done a little damage myself, but I doubted it was enough to save Maria.

Merola called Crystal, the neighbor, as his next witness. She didn't even glance at Maria as she walked to the witness stand. Merola was quick and to the point with her, establishing that she lived two doors down from Maria and saw Jose leaving her apartment at around ten or eleven in the morning on a couple of occasions. She wasn't sure about the dates.

During cross-examination I asked her, "What dates did you observe Jose outside Maria Roman's apartment?"

"The dates? I don't know."

"What's your boyfriend's name?"

"Luis."

"And Luis, he used to go out with Maria Roman, right?" I asked just a little tauntingly, trying to get under her skin.

"Yes," she answered, a hostile glint appearing in her eyes.

"And you live a couple doors down from Maria Roman, right?"

Crystal nodded.

"You have to give a verbal answer," Judge McCarthy instructed her.

"Yes," she said.

"And does your boyfriend, Luis, come and visit you at your apartment?"

"He doesn't come overnight like they do," she answered, pointing at Maria, who glared at her with eyes as hard as stone.

"Wouldn't you like to see Maria Roman evicted so your boyfriend won't see her at Washington?"

Merola rose from his seat. "Objection."

"Sustained," Judge McCarthy said.

"Don't you dislike Maria Roman for dating your boyfriend, and that's why you reported on her to the housing authority?" I asked in a prosecutorial tone.

Crystal gathered herself together like a loaded spring and then she let me have it. "No, I reported her because her boyfriend's there all the time. Why should he get to stay there all the time when my boyfriend can't? It's completely unfair. She breaks the rule and everyone knows it."

Her answer was the courtroom equivalent of a boxer getting hit square on the jaw by an uppercut. I was too knocked off balance to figure out how to rehabilitate my cross-examination and fix the damage. Afraid of taking her head on and making the situation worse for myself, I announced that I had no further questions and sat down, stewing in the juices of my poor performance. I couldn't bring myself to look over at Maria. I had blown it for her.

Merola next called the other neighbor, Amara, to the stand. She testified that on one occasion she had observed Jose leaving Maria's apartment and driving off in his car. When I rose from my seat to question her, I told myself, keep it simple, don't overextend and put yourself in a vulnerable position. Don't make the same mistake you made last time. In the end, all I accomplished was establishing that she was friends with Crystal, thereby raising the inference that she was biased to testify similarly. There was nothing else I could really do. Her story had been simple and straight-forward.

It was now my turn to put forth Maria's defense and I called her as my first witness. As she took the stand I hoped she'd keep her anger in check.

After some introductory questions, I asked, "Who do you live with?"

"Me and my two kids."

"How old are they?"

"Four and seven."

I reviewed the probationary agreement with her to establish that she understood its terms. She verified that she complied with them by not having Jose visit her apartment.

"You heard testimony that Jose Diaz was seen leaving your apartment in the morning and that his car was seen outside of your apartment?"

"Yes." Maria nodded.

"What's his relationship with you?"

"He's my boyfriend."

"Has he visited your apartment since you signed the probationary agreement?"

"No."

"You heard testimony by the security officer that his car was seen outside of your apartment. Is that true? Was his car there then?"

"Yes." She looked over at Judge McCarthy who suddenly seemed to perk up a little. "But you see, I have to use his car because I don't have a car of my own. Jose lets me use his car. I got to drive my kids places." Her tone was almost pleading, to the point where it made me cringe a little, because it seemed a bit too much, like she was pouring it on too thick, and I wondered if Judge McCarthy thought the same.

"Is his car an early-Nineties Toyota Celica?" I asked.

"Yes."

"Just so we have this straight, when his car was at your apartment since the probationary agreement, was Jose ever at your apartment?"

"No, he wasn't."

"How did his car get there? Did he bring it to you or did you get it somewhere?"

"I got it from him."

"Where? On or off George Washington property?"

"Off."

"Where was that?"

"I met him at my mother's place."

"No further questions."

Merola stood up and folded his arms across his chest. Then he just stood there silently for about ten seconds, perhaps in an effort to intimidate Maria a little and establish control. Maria had a determined look on her face, knowing a battle was coming that she couldn't afford to lose.

"Ms. Roman, you say that you got Mr. Diaz' car outside of George Washington, right?"

"Yes," she answered a bit nervously.

"At your mother's house?"

"Yes."

"How did you get there?" he asked in a skeptical tone.

"My mother drove me."

"It would've been easier for Mr. Diaz to drive the car to you at Washington, right?"

"I suppose. I don't know."

"That way you wouldn't have had to drive anywhere after getting the car, right? You'd be at your home?"

"I mean, yeah, I'd be at home."

"And Mr. Diaz would be able to visit with just you and not your mother?"

"Well, my kids are there."

Merola paused. "So you met Mr. Diaz at your mother's house which is where?"

"It's on Piedmont Street."

"Where does Mr. Diaz live?"

"At his brother's place."

"You never reported to the housing authority that you were just borrowing Mr. Diaz' car, did you?"

"No."

Merola announced that he had no further questions, which kind of surprised me, but then again, there wasn't all that much he could do. Maria had her story and the other witnesses had theirs, and the judge would have to decide who he believed. I was just glad that she hadn't lost her cool.

I had one more witness to call which was Jose.

"Where do you live, Mr. Diaz?" I asked him.

"With my brother."

"Where is that?"

"On Maywood Street."

"How far is that from Ms. Roman's mother's house on Piedmont Street?"

"Just a few minutes."

"How long have you been living there?"

"About a year."

"Do you have any bills in your name with that address?"

"No, I don't."

"Why not?" I asked him. It was a topic that I had to have him explain on direct examination in order to take the steam away from Merola when he raised it on cross.

"Because I don't get bills. I don't have a credit card or a bank account or that sort of thing."

"Is your name on the lease?"

"No. I just never thought to do that. The landlord knows, but he don't care."

I asked Jose if he visited Maria at her apartment after she signed the probationary agreement, and he replied that he hadn't. Had he loaned his car to Maria? Yes, because she needed it for the kids, but he didn't drive the car to Washington to give it to her. My examination of him lasted five or ten minutes.

"Mr. Diaz, you say you live with your brother on Maywood Street?" Merola asked him.

"Right."

"For one year, is that right?"

"Yeah."

"Where do you sleep?"

"I have a room."

"You testified that you have no bills in your name at that address, right?"

"No, I don't."

"And your name is not on the lease, right?"

"No."

"No receipts for rent payments?"

"No, I paid in cash to my brother."

"I see. For an entire year you didn't want to put your name on the lease and you don't have a receipt for a rental payment?"

"No."

"How about your driver's license? Does it have that address?"

"No."

Merola asked a few more questions about how Jose got around without his car that didn't really go anywhere and then he ended his examination. To my mind, it had been damaging.

Judge McCarthy looked down at the parties from the bench. I wasn't sure if he was going to take the matter under advisement and issue a written decision or make his ruling from the bench. I looked at him trying to discern which way he was leaning in the case, but he maintained a poker face. Finally he said, "Mr. Merola, having heard the testimony and having considered your motion, the court rules that it is allowed. Execution granted."

John the court officer commanded, "All rise." Judge McCarthy walked off the bench.

I looked over at Maria and saw a vacant expression on her face, as if she had just seen a ghost. Even though the result had not been unexpected, a feeling of shock coursed through my body. I felt anger towards Judge McCarthy and I also silently cursed myself for messing up my cross of Crystal. Outside the courtroom, Maria buried her face in her hands and cried. Jose gently rubbed her back in an effort to comfort her. When she finally looked up, her face was red and tears were running down her cheeks. "How could I lose my apartment?" she whimpered.

I felt uncomfortable standing there watching the two of them, as I was intruding on a personal situation. But I felt that I couldn't just walk away. (Hey, sorry you lost and that it was my fault, but I gotta run. Good luck.) If Maria was in the hallway mourning, then I was there doing my penance. When Merola and Jeannie walked through the glass doors into the lobby, they hurriedly walked past us, pretending they didn't notice Maria crying. After Maria and Jose finally left the courthouse, I wearily went over to Jeff.

"What happened over there?" he asked me.

"She just lost her housing," I said.

"Oh. That's too bad."

"Yes, it is."

"I've been looking around," Jeff told me. "The only person here is the rooming house manager. They don't have no other witnesses. You see, it's all a concoction. They don't have a case. The judge will laugh it out of the courtroom."

"Jeff, this judge will evict people. In fact, he just did. I don't know what the manager observed that he can testify to, and I don't know if a witness will come walking in at the last minute. Be that as it may, I have to tell you, you've come to my office drunk." I said this as delicately as possible, so that he wouldn't feel that I was judging him or that he was under attack from his own attorney. I believed that it was something that had to be said. "They're claiming that you've been drunk and caused a disturbance, so that's just something that ..." I paused. "Well, in any event, let's go to mediation and see what happens."

"But you see—"

"I know your side, Jeff. I'm not discounting that. Let's just see what happens in mediation."

Frank Green was representing the rooming house. One of the mediators, Mike, an even-tempered, middle-aged guy who was fair to both landlords and tenants alike, called us into his office and directed us to explain the case to him.

Frank said, "This eviction case has been brought because the tenant consistently gets intoxicated on the premises and causes a ruckus. And the other people in the rooming house are all complaining. He's reportedly a nice guy while sober, but when he's been drinking it's a completely different story. He says suggestive things to women, he acts combative. Once he was seen kicking a refrigerator in a common area. The big thing is that, well, he was naked in the hallway while intoxicated."

Mike raised his eyebrows as if to say, that's one I haven't come across yet. I grimaced.

"My client has given him many warnings," Frank continued, "but it hasn't stopped. The problem is that he doesn't remember what happens. My client will talk to him the next day about what he did the night before and he doesn't remember." Frank turned to Jeff. "No offense."

The rooming house manager, a short middle-Eastern guy of about forty, sat there patiently while Frank was speaking.

"People tell him things about me and he just believes them," Jeff said, a little agitated. "No one else from the rooming house is even here."

I extended my hand toward him to quiet him down. In response he folded his arms across his chest like a pouting child.

The manager reached into a bag and pulled out a small video camera. "We have this," he said in accented English with barely restrained anger. "This speaks for everyone at the rooming house."

"There are video cameras in some of the common areas for security reasons," Frank explained. "We have a video of the tenant intoxicated. Why don't we just play it?"

Oh shit, I thought, this can't be good. Whatever was on the video, I was surprised that Frank hadn't told me about it beforehand. I was sure I had requested photos and videos beforehand during discovery, and besides, Frank was usually pretty open and straight-forward with me.

Mike leaned forward with curiosity, as did Jeff and I, and the manager held up the camera so that the screen was facing us. He pressed play. At first there was an image of an empty hallway with white walls from the perspective of a corner of the ceiling at one end. A thin man who was unmistakably Jeff entered the frame, dressed in the same green army jacket he was wearing today, with his pants lowered to his knees and his pale white ass showing. Jeff walked straight ahead for a few steps and then his legs buckled underneath him like a boxer rocked by a hard punch, causing him to veer into the wall. He leaned against it for support in a hunched over position. After a few moments passed, he managed to right himself and take a few wobbly steps down the hallway. Then suddenly he careened into the opposite wall, bracing himself against it for support with open palms.

A couple of times I looked over at Jeff during the viewing and observed him watching the film without expression. When it was over he exclaimed, "It's illegal to have cameras in a place of residence. He could be arrested for this!"

The manager raised his hand in the air and pointed dramatically at Jeff. "Having your naked ass in my hallway, that's what's illegal!"

Frank Green was grinning as he told his client to calm down. The guy reluctantly crossed his arms and looked straight ahead.

"Do you mind if my client and I go outside for a moment?" I asked.

"No, not at all," said Mike who was also grinning.

I brought Jeff into an empty office and shut the door behind us.

"I don't know what to say about that. I mean..." I stood there shaking my head. "I don't know quite what to say."

"He can't do that," Jeff said indignantly.

"Yes, he can."

"He can?" Jeff asked in the tone of a curious child.

I nodded. "Yes."

Jeff paused, a troubled expression suddenly appearing on his face. "Well, what happens now?"

"First, we try to see if we can get you a probationary agreement that will let you stay so long as you don't cause any trouble. Otherwise, we try to get a move out date giving you enough time."

"I didn't hurt nobody in the tape. People do worse things at that place."

"What matters is that what you did will get you evicted. You know, given how you and the landlord seem to get along, maybe going somewhere else isn't a bad thing. Are you particularly attached to the rooming house?"

"But how can that get me evicted if no one saw me?"

Exasperated, I said, "You were showing ass. It doesn't matter whether anyone saw. You can't show ass!"

"Well, what do I do?"

"What I just advised."

"But I didn't hurt nobody."

"Jeff, you don't have to hurt someone to get evicted. Are you willing to let me try my approach?"

He turned away and mumbled something that I was unable to hear.

"Jeff?"

He turned to me. "Yeah, sure."

When we returned to Mike's office, I floated the six month's probationary term. The manager immediately folded his arms across his chest and shook his head. Mike asked Jeff and me to leave the office, which was a good thing. It meant that he was going to work on the landlord to try to reach an agreement. Five minutes later he met us in the hallway and told us that a probationary agreement was off the table, but that the landlord was willing to give Jeff three months to move out on the condition that he would not drink or be intoxicated on the premises. Mike left us alone to discuss the offer. I knew from experience that Frank Green was not someone who liked to negotiate, and three months was all that I was going to get out of him. I also knew that if I were to try the case I would lose. In accordance with my advice, Jeff decided to take the deal. And considering the facts, it was a very good deal.

Before leaving court, I handed him a copy of the signed agreement approved by the judge. I detected a hint of sadness in his eyes. "Jeff, you might want to consider going to a place like AA or a therapist to get some help," I suggested gently.

"Yeah, I've tried that," he replied, "but it never helps much."

I nodded, feeling sorry for him. "Well, take care of yourself."

PART TWO

16

Apparently Miguel wasn't going to come to my office. Anna and I had set up an appointment, and he had said that he would attend, but on the appointed day he was a no show. Right then I accepted the fact that the chances were slim to non-existent that he was going to meet with me before the trial date. Then Anna came up with an idea. She invited me to come to her apartment on the following Monday night for dinner, saying that she would arrange for Miguel to be there. He was less likely to be running around with his friends on a Monday night, she explained, and he might want a home-cooked meal. I was skeptical that he'd show up but decided to go along with it. I believed that she had another motive for suggesting this arrangement—she wanted me to come over and spend more time with David, and it was hard for me to say no to that. The thought of going to Washington after dark, however, did not exactly appeal to me.

Sara worked most of that weekend and our only time together, really, was on Saturday night when we went to the movies. We arrived twenty minutes before show time and got seats exactly halfway up at the end of the aisle. It was important to me to arrive early in order to secure an aisle seat. I had two reasons for doing this. First, I usually had to go to the bathroom during the movie and disliked having to get up and walk past people in their seats. Second, I disliked being surrounded by people. It increased the chances that I could end up seated near someone who had a loud or annoying laugh, or who munched popcorn loudly, which could ruin a movie for me. Sara, on the other hand, was perfectly fine with sitting smack in the middle of a crowded theater. She didn't mind it one bit.

I was in a goofy mood that night, and after we sat down, I put my arm around her in a slow, deliberate manner and suggested, "What do you say we make out during the movie?"

"Are we in high school or something?" she answered with a laugh.

The movie was a romantic comedy that she had wanted to see. We discussed it during our walk home—she thought it was good, and I thought it was just okay. I remembered one of our first dates. It was wintertime and we were walking together on the sidewalk and she picked up a big chunk of ice, raised it to shoulder height, and pretended that she was going to clock me in the head with it. Instinctively, I put my hands up, and she began to laugh. I laughed, too.

I reminded her of the incident. "Oh yeah, I remember that," she said with a laugh. I reflected with a little sadness that she no longer did that kind of thing when we were together. Some of her playfulness had left her, at least so far as our relationship was concerned. I looked around aimlessly as we walked, taking in the surroundings. I never failed to appreciate the beauty and old world charm of the Boston Common and the Public Garden; the old brownstones of Beacon Hill that lined the northern side, the elegance of the Back Bay to the west, and the winding paths lit by the pale light from the top of black lampposts. We walked up Newbury Street, a one-way street lined with brownstones that was the most fashionable shopping strip in the city. It was a place to see and be seen, especially in the summer, when the sidewalks were packed with people and flashy high end cars passed by.

"I'm sort of hungry," I mentioned.

"You want to go somewhere?"

"Yeah, but where should we go?"

Just as we reached the intersection with Clarendon Street, I heard a voice call out, "Hey, Sara!" Jeremy, a former co-worker of Sara's at the real estate office, was walking toward us, accompanied by two other guys. When they reached us, the first thing I observed was that all three of them were lean and in shape. They were dressed in fitted clothing, had well-coiffed hair and were clean-shaven. Jeremy was gay, and I assumed his friends were too. I felt like an unkempt shlub in their presence.

"Jeremy! It's good to see you!" Sara gave him a hug and a kiss on the cheek.

"Hey, sweetie, how are you?" he asked.

"I'm okay. You know." She shrugged. "Still at the real estate office."

"How's that going? You haven't committed yourself to a mental institution yet, have you?"

"Not yet, but I'm close." They both shared a laugh. "Seriously, it's tough. People aren't renting, and when they do they're very picky. And Jeff and Cheryl are as crazy as ever. Cheryl was acting terribly about these apartment keys that we couldn't find—it cost us a rental, because another agency had the keys and rented it out. Jeff is on this crusade to put a Republican on the city council. I argue with him and, anyway, why am I talking about him?"

"Yes, why would you do that? Let's not spoil the night." He laughed.

She tapped him affectionately on the arm. "How are you?"

"Good." He pointed to his friends. "We're just out and about."

We all exchanged polite nods. Jeremy introduced everyone—the guys were named Brad and Ryan—and we shook hands.

"How's your job at the airline going?" Sara asked him.

"The same. I get travel deals, so that's good; although schlepping out to Logan for work isn't always fun. I just got back from South Beach, actually."

"Oh, you're so lucky," Sara said. "I wish I could go there. Hey, you have a nice tan. I'm so pale in comparison."

"Thanks."

"Well, I miss you at the office."

"I miss you, too. You were always like a ray of sunshine there."

"Oh, thanks. That's sweet," she said, and I could tell that she was genuinely touched. "So what are you guys doing tonight?"

"We're going to go out for some drinks," Jeremy answered. "Want to come along?"

"That sounds like fun." Sara turned to me. "Do you want to?"

"Sure," I responded.

"Oh, you're hungry, aren't you?" she asked me.

"That's all right. I'm okay. If we go somewhere that serves food, maybe I'll get something. If we don't, I'll be okay."

"We can go to Benny's on Boylston Street," Jeremy suggested. "They have food."

We began walking up Boylston Street together. I found myself on the outside edge of our group, and when we encountered a group of people approaching us, I was the one who had to sometimes step off the curb in order to make room. It reminded me of times when, as a kid, I had felt left out when I was with a group of other kids. After we arrived at Benny's, we passed by a couple of huge bouncers stationed at the door, then were assaulted by loud, pulsating dance music that jarred my senses, making me feel as if I was entering a war zone. It was my first visit to the place. The lighting was dim and the place was crowded with people standing shoulder-to-shoulder. For the most part, they ranged in age from their early-twenties to mid-thirties. It was not my type of scene. I preferred laid-back bars where I could get a seat and people weren't in party mode. As I followed Sara through the crowd I felt a little irritated with her. She would never have come here if it had been just the two of us and I had suggested it; she only agreed to it because Jeremy had suggested it.

The first room we entered was small and rectangular in shape with an onyx top bar and barstools with cream-colored cushions. The floors had a polished black surface. The bar was manned by a tall, thin brunette with large breasts which were showcased in a low-cut black tank top. Two Guido-type guys brushed past me with two girls following dutifully behind. One was a short blonde with an artificial tan and the other had long brown hair and a narrow face. Both wore a lot of makeup.

The five of us passed through this room and entered a main room where a mass of bodies was gyrating on the dance floor. There were a number of pretty girls there and they were, for the most part, better-looking than the guys present. The bar was packed three-deep with people and was manned by three hot young ladies, who, like the first bartender, wore low-cut black tank tops that exposed ample cleavage. I stood there thinking, so this is where a lot of hot girls go at night. I see them during the day on Newbury Street with shopping bags on their arms, and this is where they go at night. I never knew that before.

Jeremy secured a half-moon-shaped booth for us. I took a seat on the outside and when a conversation developed, I found myself on its margins.

"How about ordering calamari and nachos," Jeremy suggested. "Is that copasetic?"

Everyone voiced their agreement and when the waitress came around we ordered the food and a round of drinks. I sat and listened as Jeremy told Sara more about his South Beach trip. He had gone with Brad and Ryan, and they had spent most of their time on the beach and at restaurants and clubs at night.

"We got the best facials there," Jeremy remarked.

"I'd love a facial." Sara turned to me. "It's been ages since I've had one." I felt she was trying to keep me involved in the conversation which I appreciated.

Jeremy turned to me. "Have you ever gotten one, Mark?" I could tell he was trying to include me as well.

"Him?" Sara laughed. "Are you kidding? You couldn't get him to use anything more than Dove soap."

"What's wrong with Dove?" I responded with pretend offense. "It's a fine soap. It has a quarter moisturizing cream or some shit like that."

When Jeremy and Sara began talking about the real estate office again, my attention drifted. Since I was seated at the edge of the booth, with Sara next to me and Jeremy next to her, and Brad and Ryan far away from me on the other side, there was no one for me to talk to. With nothing else to do, I watched the people in the club. A fair number of the guys were jacked up with muscles and wore a lot of hair gel. Some of them danced in a manic fashion, moving their feet quickly as if they were walking barefoot over hot coals.

The women danced in a more overtly sexual manner, some gyrating their hips while waving their arms in the air.

It wasn't long before the waitress delivered the nachos and calamari to our table along with a fresh round of drinks: two rum-and-cokes (Brad and Jeremy), a vodka tonic (Ryan), diet Coke (Sara), and Maker's Mark and ginger ale (me). Everyone began picking at the food with their fingers, which I really didn't care for. I only managed to get a couple pieces of calamari and a chunk of the nachos before too much finger action caused me to call it quits.

"Aren't you going to eat anything?" Sara asked me.

"I had a couple pieces of calamari."

"Is that enough?"

"I'm okay."

"But you were hungry."

"I'm okay," I replied, wishing she would cut off her line of questioning.

"Are you sure?" Jeremy asked.

"Yeah, I'm okay. Really."

By the time the food was gone, I had finished my third drink and was into my fourth; the sweet, syrupy taste of the bourbon went down easy, and I was feeling buzzed. Soon my thoughts grew a little sour. Looking out at the crowd, I decided that I disliked this scene and what it stood for—exclusion, elitism, and superficiality. I thought I had these people all figured out. They often rooted for the powerful instead of the underdog. They disliked spending time alone. They had never read Karl Marx and never would. At the same time, they made me feel inferior. I knew that I could never fit in with them. I knew that I made less money than most of them. I knew that if I was single probably none of the girls would be interested in me.

Then my focus shifted to how Sara wasn't including me in her conversation. If I ever put her in this situation, I thought, she'd be really upset. She might even walk out of the place without me. My mind began to roam at a fast pace through a tangle of disjointed and unconnected thoughts and images—the housing court, my last visit with my parents, a trip Sara and I took to Ogunquit, Maine. But then I went off the rails and, for no particular reason, I blurted out, "Isn't it kind of weird that they have directors for porn movies?"

Immediately everyone stopped talking and looked at me.

I sat there, thinking, I must have wanted to get involved in the conversation, but why did I say *that*? It had no relevance to anything.

"Wow, left field," Jeremy remarked.

"Well, it's true," I said, figuring I might as well back up the remark. "Aren't a cameraman and someone to do the lights and sound enough?" I shrugged, as if this was a self-evident truth, like that the earth is round and Jonas Salk developed the polio vaccine. "I mean, you just put the people in a room and roll the camera. The rest pretty much takes care of itself. Am I wrong?"

I looked over at Sara for some sign of acknowledgement, but instead she looked at me as if I had lost my mind.

"You know, he has a point," Brad said in a slightly sarcastic way that didn't offend me.

I decided to barrel ahead. "Say you're a porn director. Wouldn't you feel like you were a third wheel?"

"So you watch porno movies?" Sara asked in a slightly disturbed tone. "This is what you're thinking of when we go out? Porno?"

"No, of course not. I would never watch pornography. It's degrading to women."

The guys laughed.

"You're so full of it," Sara responded, shaking her head.

I continued to drink, knowing that I had put some space between me and the group that could not be bridged. While the early part of the night was a distinct, unbroken chronology of events, I could only remember isolated blocks of time from that point forward. At some point the five of us were out on the dance floor together. Sara moved her body in a sexy way, at times putting her hands over her head and gyrating her hips. Jeremy danced in a compact manner with quick movements that reminded me of Michael Stipe in concert. While I disliked dancing, fueled by the bourbon I was out there moving and shaking with them, and at one point I clapped my hands high above my head, Mick Jagger-style. I noticed that Sara, Jeremy, Brad, and Ryan had slowed down their dancing and were all looking at me with amused expressions. I pretended not to notice them, gave it another minute or so, and then stopped dancing. I waited until the guys were a little out of Sara's orbit, then sidled up to her and asked, "What's so funny?"

"You have a lot going on," she said affectionately.

"What do you mean?"

"Your body. You move around too much. You clap. It's ... a lot."

"What do you mean?" I asked again.

"I mean just that!"

"That I move too much?"

"You have to let yourself go with the music. You're doing too much. You know, the clapping, it's a lot."

She can have her opinion, I thought, but it doesn't mean that she's right. She's not the only judge. I thought I was moving really well. I was convinced that I was a talented, if not exceptional dancer, and that I could prove her wrong. I moved away from her and the guys to have my own space, and when a remix version of "Stayin' Alive" began to play, it sent a jolt through the crowd and the energy level went through the roof. People who had been standing around were suddenly dancing. I picked up the pace and decided to really go for it, at one point placing my right hand on my hip and shooting my left arm into the air Travolta-style. A guy and a girl near me began clapping their hands with broad smiles on their faces. They're cheering me on, I thought. I'm a great dancer and they recognize it. Sara and the guys don't recognize it, but they do. Wanting to give these people a good show, I switched to a style of dancing I had never tried before, moving my open palms in front of my body as if simulating a mime trying to get out of a box, while my torso flowed to the rhythm like an undulating snake. A couple of other people joined in to watch me which boosted my confidence. As the song entered its instrumental finish, I reached my hands over my head one at a time like a 1980's aerobics instructor.

Then, all of a sudden, I realized that some of the people watching me were no longer smiling, but instead they were laughing at me.

One girl even covered her mouth and bended over at the midsection, she thought I was so funny. In my buzzed state, I failed to understand how I could be dancing poorly. It didn't seem possible. I decided that these people were assholes to laugh at me, and I was determined not to let them get the best of me. It suddenly became important to me that I finished up on my own terms. I began doing a vaudeville routine by shuffling my feet and twirling my fists over one another. The girl who had covered her mouth really went over the edge and started laughing even more uncontrollably. I exited the dance floor and went back to our table where I proceeded to order another drink, figuring I might as well get stinking drunk.

Sara joined me shortly afterwards and I told her, "People were laughing at me when I danced."

She put her arm around me. "It's all right. You were cute."

"Let's get out of here. Okay?"

"Okay." She patted me affectionately on the head. "My little dancing boy. By the way, you've drank a lot."

"I'm okay."

"You're slurring your words."

"Really?"

"Yeah."

It was strange to hear. I thought I sounded fine.

17

After work on Monday I kept my commitment to have dinner at Anna's place. Although my last trip to Washington, when I picked up David and measured the distance to the Rite-Mart, had gone without incident, driving there I felt a little nervous about my personal safety, especially since this time it was dark outside.

I wondered if Miguel would show up, and if so, what he would be like—how he would look, what his demeanor would be, if he'd be cooperative.

Anna greeted me at the front door, more dressed up than usual, in black pants and a light purple sweater. Entering her apartment with a seven-dollar bottle of cabernet in my hand, I saw David standing near the dining table next to a woman in her late-thirties with a chunky and compact frame. Behind them in the living room was a well-built young guy watching TV who I figured was Miguel.

"Let me introduce you around," said Anna.

The woman was her cousin, Ernestina, and the guy in the living room was indeed Miguel. He had dark eyes and a strong, square jaw, and when he stood up to shake my hand, I estimated that he was about 5'9" and 170 pounds. He looked tough, like someone who could handle himself, but it was a quiet toughness.

I placed the wine bottle on the kitchen table. "It's not as cold in here."

"They fixed the window," Anna informed me. "They fixed a lot of things. Let me show you." She brought me over to the window, which now closed properly and had no gaps. Then she led me to the bathroom to show me that the tub no longer dripped. There was still mold, though.

"You should follow up to make sure the mold is fixed," I advised her. "It can cause people to get sick."

When we went into the kitchen the first thing I noticed was that she had left a number of cooking ingredients out on the counter, including yellow rice and raw chicken in a bowl. There were two pots and a skillet on the stove top. The brown linoleum tiles had been repaired with new black tiles that made the floor look like an off-color chess board.

"I can walk around in here barefoot," Anna said. "They fixed the cabinet door, too. It don't hang any more. And the oven works. They had two guys in here who made the repairs."

"That's good," I said.

"It was so cold this winter. We was always wearing sweaters and coats in here. Now I'm just in a regular shirt sometimes. It's great."

"That's good," I said once again.

"And the mices, already we don't see them anymore. I mean, we caught one in the trap they put down, but we ain't seen no more of them. I think they plugged up the holes."

I instantly had a vision of a mouse jumping into the bowl of chicken which I tried to vanquish from my mind.

Anna motioned to me to leave the kitchen. "I'm going to finish the cooking. You go out there and talk," she directed.

I chuckled at her bossy manner as I exited the kitchen. Ernestina was standing next to the dining table, smiling, with her hands resting on the back of a chair.

"So do you live here?" I asked her.

"In another building," she replied in accented English.

There was silence between us, and I felt a little awkward just standing there. David was in the living area and I walked over to him and asked how school was going.

"Good," he replied.

I figured that now was a good time to talk to Miguel, so I said to him, "As your mother probably told you, I wanted to talk to you about what happened that day at the Rite-Mart. Could we have a few minutes?"

He stood up and pointed in the direction of the hallway. "Sure. Let's go down here."

I followed him into David's bedroom and closed the door so that it was only open a couple inches in order to give us some privacy. Miguel sat down on the bed, and I sat on a small wooden chair. I extracted a pen and legal pad from my bag. "The reason I need to speak with you is because the trial is going to focus on what happened the day of your arrest, so I need to hear what happened from you."

I began scribbling notes as Miguel related the events of his arrest. It was basically the same story Anna had told me: his friend, Joe Sanchez, picked him up at his girlfriend's apartment to take him to the mall. Joe said he wanted to buy a baseball cap and Miguel decided to go along for the ride. The Rite-Mart was on the route, and as they approached it, Sanchez pulled into the parking lot without saying anything. In what seemed like just a couple seconds, and completely to Miguel's surprise, a guy appeared at the driver's side window, and Sanchez made a deal with him right in broad daylight. Then the cops were all over them.

"That's it?" I asked.

"Yeah man, that's it."

"A deal right there in the daylight?"

"Yeah."

"Where were you parked in the parking lot?"

"In the front near the store, but off to the side."

"Your friend, Sanchez, who is he? How do you know him?"

"We hung around together."

I noticed that Miguel was wearing a couple of gold chains and a gold pinky ring, and I wondered where he had gotten the money for them. "Where's Sanchez now? In jail?"

"I don't know," Miguel answered with a shrug. "I haven't talked to him since. He got me in a whole lot of trouble, I'll tell you that."

"Are you still friends with him?"

"After what happened, no. I don't want nothin' to do with him."

"How long have you known him?"

He shrugged. "I don't know."

"You were friends?"

"Yeah."

"Did you know that he was involved with drugs?"

"Did I know? Yeah, a little. I mean, I'm not going to lie. But I didn't know he was involved with heroin, and I didn't know he was dealing. I just knew he used sometimes. That's it. A lot of people do, you know? I wasn't involved with it, if that's what you're asking. I didn't know a deal was going down." Miguel shook his head wearily. "I was in the wrong place at the wrong time, man, and now we're all paying for it. Me, my Mom, my brother."

I shifted in my seat. "Before this happened, did you see him once a week, once a day, once a month?"

"I'd see him, but it wasn't like anything consistent. We were friends. Sometimes we saw each other, or I might be with people and we might run into him, you know what I'm sayin'? It was different all the time. I could see him two days in a row or I might not see him for three weeks."

"But you knew him well enough that he'd call you up to go to the mall?"

"Yeah, I guess so."

He spoke with a level of sincerity that made me want to believe him, but my better judgment told me not to. I was sure that Miguel knew which of his friends or acquaintances were drug dealers. I also suspected that most drug dealers didn't bring unknowing guests along with them when transacting business. The story about the two of them going to the mall to shop for hats sounded a little bizarre, although when I thought about it, as a kid I had gone to the mall for reasons that were not exactly compelling. In any event, it didn't really matter what I believed. My job was to put forth the best defense I could for Anna.

"Where did the drugs come from?" I asked.

"What do you mean?"

"Well, Sanchez pulled out the drugs from somewhere, right?"

"Yeah, from the center armrest between the front seats."

"And you hadn't seen them before?"

"No."

"Was it heroin?"

"I didn't get to see it. All I saw was the folded up plastic bag. The police, they said it was heroin."

"How long was the guy at the window who was going to buy the drugs?"

"I don't know. Maybe five seconds."

"Did you see him pull out any money and exchange it with Sanchez?"

"The guy had already handed the money over and Sanchez was handing him the stuff when the cops came on us. It was fast."

I delicately asked him about the times in the past that he had been in trouble with the law. I explained that if he was going to testify, I had to know, because past convictions could be used to impeach him. He told me that the marijuana charge during his youth was just for possession, not distribution, and it resulted in a guilty plea.

"Your mother mentioned something about a motorbike theft?"

"That wasn't anything. The cops questioned me but I was never arrested or anything."

I nodded. "Well, I'd like you to testify at the eviction trial." I didn't think he was going to make a great witness; he came off as too disinterested and his toughness seemed to indicate a criminal propensity.

He looked down at the floor, contemplating my request, and then peered up at me. "I got them into it. I'll do it."

"The police are going to testify about the arrest, and if you don't testify, I'll have no rebuttal case, so you're necessary. However, you should know that if you do testify, you waive your Fifth Amendment rights in your criminal trial. That's coming up, right?"

"Yeah."

"What that means is that if you testify in housing court, you won't be able to refuse to testify in criminal court by asserting the

Fifth Amendment. The second thing is that the prosecutor can use anything you say in housing court against you in your criminal trial. You should talk to your criminal lawyer about it. I can't advise you on that since I'm not your lawyer."

"My little brother has a lot riding on this. My criminal attorney, I can't even get in touch with him hardly, so I'll say yes now. I mean, they can use anything I say against me if they want, but what I'm saying is the truth. I was at the wrong place at the wrong time and that's all there is to it."

"Okay. Since you'll be testifying, we need to prepare together before the trial, okay? When your mother comes in to do that, you should come with her. We'll essentially go over things again, and I'll give you some rules for testifying. Is that okay?"

"Okay."

"Let me ask you another thing. How often do you stay overnight here?"

He clasped his hands together and let them dangle between his legs. "About once every couple weeks maybe. Something like that."

"Is there a phone number you can give me if I need to contact you?"

"You can call me here."

"But you don't really stay here, right? Do you have a cell phone or another number?"

"You can just call me here. I'll get the message," he said in a way that made it clear he wasn't open to any other options.

When we returned to the living area I could hear Anna and Ernestina preparing dinner in the kitchen. David was seated on the couch watching TV. I was a little surprised when Miguel put his coat on, as I had assumed that he would be staying for dinner.

"I'll see you later," he told me, and then he waved to David. "See you, bro."

David gave him a lazy wave without turning away from the television. On his way to the door, Miguel stopped at the kitchen and gruffly told Anna, "I'm leaving." I didn't hear any response from her, and without another word Miguel walked out the door. There was silence in the kitchen for the next few minutes, and I had the feeling that Anna was pissed. When she emerged from the kitchen carrying a serving dish and announced in a cheery tone that it was time to eat, it sounded forced, as if she was doing her best to cover up her anger but was barely able to manage it.

She had made a traditional dish of arroz con pollo, and its rich smell wafted through the apartment.

"I brought wine," I said in an effort to shift the focus away from Miguel and his absence.

"Thank you, Mark, that's nice," said Anna.

We sat down to eat. I savored the tender and juicy chicken and rice, so light and fluffy it practically melted in my mouth.

"This is great," I remarked.

"Thanks," Anna said. "It's David's favorite."

I glanced at David who didn't even seem to register the comment.

"He's always been shy," Anna told me, as if David wasn't sitting at the same table as us. "That's why he does good in school. He can be quiet and stay in his room and study. Not like me, I always have to be doing something or talking to somebody. And not like Miguel. Miguel is like his father."

"His father?" I said in a tone intended to elicit information about him.

"He passed on."

"I'm sorry."

"It's been over ten years now."

It seemed like something Anna wasn't uncomfortable talking about, so I asked, "How did it happen? That is, if you don't mind my asking."

She put her fork down. "Pedro was out on the street here in Washington." She pointed in the direction of the street. "It was a hot summer night and lots of people were out. A few days before he had gotten into an argument with a guy, and he didn't know it but the guy was in a gang, and so the guy came back in a car with his friends. I was there and I saw it happen. I saw the car going slow, and the guy leaned out of the window with a gun and he shot him right there in the street. Pedro died just like that, on the street right outside here."

"I'm so sorry," I said softly. "That's awful."

David continued to eat without reacting to what his mother had just said.

"God took him and He has his reasons," Anna said soberly. "Let me show you a picture of him."

She went into her bedroom and came back a few moments later with a slightly creased photo and placed it on the table in front of me. The photo, taken at the beach, was of a Latino guy in his twenties, of medium-build with a moustache and an extremely wide smile. He was wearing a Celtics tank top and had his arms around two young kids.

"That's David's and Miguel's father with them at Hampton Beach," Anna told me.

David looked to be six or seven years old, a thin string bean of a kid with thick, longish hair. His head was at a slightly downcast angle, like he was shy about having his picture taken. Miguel was physically larger than David and had a big mop of hair and a gregarious smile that jumped off the photo. His smile surprised me, given how impassive he now seemed as an adult.

"Let me show you another picture of David," said Anna.

"No, Ma, don't," David protested wearily.

"Oh, it's so adorable," Anna said, rising from the table. In a moment she was back with a picture of David from the fourth grade dressed as Peter Pan, wearing green tights over pencil-thin legs.

"You were Peter Pan?" I asked him.

"He was," Anna answered for him. "You should've seen him. He was so cute."

David rolled his eyes. "I was nine or something. This is embarrassing, Mom."

"You should've seen him, Mark. He's shy, but when he was on the stage he was outgoing. I have more pictures."

"No, Ma, please," he said this time more forcefully.

"Was this in school or something?" I inquired.

"It was a summer program I got David into. His schools wouldn't have been able to afford this. They couldn't even afford the tights," she added sarcastically.

"What were your schools like?" I asked David.

"His school now?" Anna shook her head disapprovingly. "One kid was stabbed last year and he died. Imagine someone dying in your school. How do you learn when that happens? There are fights and the kids cause trouble in class so the teachers can't teach."

As a teenager I had heard stories about how rough his high school was. As unpleasant as I considered my own high school experience to have been, it was the top public high school in the city and I wouldn't have transferred to his school in a million years.

"Yeah, there's violence," David confirmed. "There's not enough money for things, too. Like my teachers have to photocopy readings because there aren't enough books. A lot of kids drop out or they just don't go to class, and some of the ones who do go to class are really bad with the teachers, so you can't get much done."

After we finished dinner I offered to help clear the table, but Anna wouldn't hear of it. Feeling a bit tired from the food and two glasses of wine, I got up from the table to stretch. I wandered over to the stereo where I began to look through the collection of CD's.

"Are some of these, salsa?" I called out.

"Some are," Anna answered from the kitchen. "What have you got there?"

"Willie Colon."

"That's a good one." She came out of the kitchen drying her hands with a towel. "You like salsa?"

"I don't know it."

"You don't?" she asked with surprise.

"No."

"What kind of music do you like?"

"Bob Dylan, The Rolling Stones, that sort of stuff."

"You have a girlfriend? I never asked you that."

"Ma, you're always in everyone's business," David said.

"Yes, I do," I responded with a chuckle.

"Do you ever take her dancing?"

"Dancing? No, I wouldn't want to embarrass her," I said, thinking back to my shameful performance at Benny's.

"Oh, come on. All you have to do is be out there and feel the rhythm and dance to the music. You won't embarrass her."

"Trust me, it's happened before."

"Oh, come on."

"That's the problem, my being out there. I shouldn't be out there. I should be anywhere but out there."

"You can dance. You're a thin guy. You're young. You just move with the music."

Ernestina emerged from the kitchen and stood off to the side. I liked how she played it cool, just watching and listening without saying much.

"I'm going to show you how to dance to salsa," Anna declared. She came over to me and took my hands in hers. I instinctively jerked my body backwards a little.

"Don't worry," she said. "You're too uptight."

"That's true," I admitted.

I wasn't much for physical contact with people other than Sara, but I reluctantly went along with Anna, not wanting to seem like a stick in the mud. We danced to the music with her leading me. I tried to follow her as best I could, but kept messing up the rhythm, and she patiently but firmly corrected me every now and again. I felt awkward and out of place dancing with her, like a guy plucked from a barbershop quartet and placed onstage to sing with a rock band.

"The salsa spices up things," Anna told me as we danced. "You have to let yourself feel it, feel the joy of it, and then you'll get it."

I quickly moved my feet to keep up with Anna as she spun us around. When the song ended, Anna and I separated from one another and everyone clapped their hands, while I stood there with a slightly embarrassed smile on my face.

It was ten o'clock by the time I left Anna's apartment. The combination of wine, food, and dancing made me a little tired, and sleeping at my parents' house seemed like the best course of action. While driving out of Washington I called my mother to let her know

I was coming. She sounded happy to hear the news, but was also curious about what I was still doing in Worcester and why I wasn't going back to Boston. I told her that I'd fill her in when I saw her. Next I called Sara to let her know my plans. At first she seemed suspicious of me, like she thought I was out carousing. I wondered, will she ever really trust me? We ended the conversation on a fairly good note, though, and I regretted a little that I wasn't going home to her and she'd be sleeping all alone in the apartment.

I walked up the front steps of my parents' house and put my key in the door. I was surprised that my balance was a little off. I was by no means drunk, but I had a buzz going, having consumed most of the bottle of wine at Anna's place. I told myself that I should be more careful in the future when it came to drinking and driving. My mother rose from her seat at the kitchen table and hugged me somewhat dramatically, as if she hadn't seen me for months. My father was asleep. He'd be up early in the morning, not long after sunrise, drinking coffee and reading the paper while talk radio played in the background. Like me, my mother was something of a night owl, though less so now that she was approaching sixty.

"Do you want something to eat?" she asked.

"No thanks. I'm stuffed." I explained that I had been at Anna's house for dinner.

"I didn't know you went to clients' houses for dinner," she remarked.

"I did it so that I could meet a witness I needed to talk to. He wasn't going to come to my office and this was a way to meet him."

"Are you sure you don't want something to eat? I have some pecan pie I got from the bakery that's really good."

"I'm fine."

"It's really good. Are you sure? How about just a piece?"

"I'm sure, really." I added, "You shouldn't keep asking me things repeatedly. It makes me feel like you don't hear me."

"If you don't eat it, I'm just going to end up throwing it away."

I didn't say anything.

"Geez, Mark, you're very touchy tonight."

"I don't think I'm acting touchy. Okay, maybe I am. But like I said, it's like you don't hear me."

"Well, let's just talk about something else. It's late. As a matter of fact, it's good you came here. It's so far for you to go back to Boston late at night."

I sighed. "We've gone over this a million times before."

"What did I say wrong?"

"We've been over it a million times before, that I live in Boston and work here in Worcester and that it's a long commute."

"I didn't say that."

"You were getting to it," I said with a sigh.

"No, I wasn't, Mark. You seem to really want to pick a fight with me."

Maybe I was trying to pick a fight. I felt raw and irritated in response to her nagging and criticizing me over the years, like it was a pebble in my shoe that over time had changed from being annoying to downright painful. Before I knew it, her remark about my commute to Boston somehow triggered me to tell her for the first time the real reason why I ended up working as a legal services lawyer in Worcester. "I didn't quit my firm job to pursue an idealistic career with legal services. I was fired." I looked at my mother and saw that those last three words seemed to hit her with the force of a blow.

"I don't understand," she said. "What happened?"

Suddenly I regretted bringing up the subject and wished that I could turn back the clock and take it all back. Suddenly the thought of telling that story seemed exhausting, as if the only point of it would be to hurt her, something I didn't want to happen. But I knew it was too late. I had to tell her.

I explained everything from the beginning—how piggish the manager had been, that I had purposely lost the summary judgment motion, that I had been unable to get another job in Boston, and that Sara had largely supported me until I started working at legal services. The words came out of my mouth one after another, like air trapped in a balloon and suddenly let out. While it was liberating to finally tell the truth to my mother, I also felt shame for hiding such a secret from her and my father, and for my failure to be able to hack it at the firm, despite my belief that what I did was morally right, at least on a personal level.

"You were unemployed?" my mother asked.

I nodded.

"How long?"

"I think about four months."

"And you didn't even tell us?" A look of hurt filled her eyes.

"I didn't want you to know."

"You could've told us."

"I felt like you would've judged me, like you would've criticized me for doing what I did."

"We wouldn't have judged you. We would've tried to help you. Your father and I have always been there for you. We've always tried to help you whenever we could."

"If I had told you that I had been fired, I don't know," I said, my voice trailing off. "I felt like you wouldn't have been able to just listen to me and say something supportive. Instead you would've criticized me for what I had done, or given me your advice on how to fix the situation."

"I don't think that's true. You're just assuming that."

"Maybe you're right." I shrugged. "And if so, I'm sorry. But see, even when I tell you that I thought you would've judged me, you don't ask me why I feel that way. You just deny it."

I could see that my mother was still surprised at my revelation. She looked off to the side every once in a while, as if taking time to process this new information. There was an expression of pain on her face, too, that made me guilty.

"I don't know how many times we helped you and your sister move into new houses and apartments. I cook for you when you come home. We do a lot of things for you."

"You do. I don't dispute that. But that's doing things for someone. It's different from being supportive. You know how it is, Mom. You put a lot of pressure on me to succeed all of my life." I crossed my arms and leaned forward in my chair. "Look, I want us to have a good relationship. That's why I'm telling you these things."

"I just want what's best for you. I want to know if major things happen in your life."

I nodded. "I know."

We sat there for a little while in silence. I didn't look over at my mother, but I could sense that she was looking at me. I felt we had taken a journey together and reached a destination where things would be all right between us. I couldn't expect perfection from her or instant change—and God knows I wasn't a perfect son—but I had cleared the air with her, and that was significant and felt good. Tonight there was nothing more to be said. We had said enough. I had wounded her a little and felt bad about that, but on the other hand, I felt confident things would improve between us. For a while I had been carrying anger towards her, and that night I felt some of it slip away from me.

My mother placed her hand on my forearm and said good night in a soft, melancholy voice. After she went upstairs to bed, I sat alone in the dimly-lit kitchen and aimlessly looked around. I had lived in what seemed like countless houses and apartments during college and law school, but this kitchen was the one place that remained an anchor in my life. Under the soft glow of the overhead light, the stove, the refrigerator, the white coffee maker, and even the red oven mitts that my mother had used for years, all filled me with a sense of place. The floodgates of memory suddenly lifted. I remembered grabbing drinks from the refrigerator after playing outside with my friends, reading the sports section over a bowl of Total cereal in the morning before going to school, doing my homework at the kitchen table in the evenings. I never really interacted with my parents or my sister in the other rooms of the house. We watched TV together in the living room, but when we talked to each other it happened in the kitchen. We were much like the Keatons in "Family Ties" in that way.

I went upstairs to my room and lay in bed, staring at the ceiling through the darkness. My conversation with my mother still weighed on me, and I worried that she might still be awake because of it. I didn't want her to feel hurt. I wondered if maybe she was right. Maybe she wouldn't have criticized me if I had told her the truth about getting fired immediately after it had happened. After all, she hadn't criticized me for it tonight. Then again, the surprise of it might have thrown her off, and the fact that it had happened two years ago sort of made criticism beside the point. Tonight, I hoped, will make things better between us and bring us closer together as mother and son.

18

When I received the police report for Miguel's arrest, I braced myself for the worst, expecting that he had made an incriminating statement or that the police had found drugs on him. It didn't end up being that bad, but it wasn't very good, either.

Merola provided the report to me as part of the discovery process. Discovery is the part of litigation that occurs between when a lawsuit is filed and when it goes to trial. The rationale for discovery is that the parties should have a free exchange of information, so that when the case gets to trial there are no surprises for either side. Discovery is much more truncated in the context of eviction cases, because they move quickly through the system and are generally not complicated affairs.

All of the police reports I had read during my two years at legal services related to drug eviction cases. The vast majority of those were written in a stream-of-consciousness style, and I had the sense that the cops wrote them in a hurry just to get them done, not caring too much about meeting the expectations of their old high school English teachers. The report for Miguel's arrest, authored by a Sergeant DelVecchio, was no different, and it read in its entirety:

At 14:28 Officer Sullivan and I had Joe Sanchez under surveillance while in an unmarked vehicle in front of his apartment at 15 Queen Street. Officers had received tip from confidential informant that Sanchez was heroin dealer. CI placed a call to Sanchez to make a heroin buy and it was to occur at the Rite-Mart convenience store on Worcester Center Boulevard.

Officers trailed Sanchez in his black Lexus to 17 Williams Street where he picked up young Latino male, and they proceeded to the Rite-Mart arriving at 14:43. In the parking lot the CI approached the driver's side of the car to make the transaction and the CI exchanged $100 in marked bills to Sanchez for heroin. Officer Sullivan and I apprehended the two suspects in the car, identified as Joe Sanchez and Miguel Rivera, with Rivera having $200 on his person and Sanchez the $100 in marked bills and $50 regular bills. A search of the vehicle revealed seven packets of heroin in the center arm rest and paraphernalia on the passenger side floor of 3 plastic baggies. We proceeded back to the station with Sanchez and Rivera under arrest. Later testing found the seized substances to be heroin.

I put the report down on my desk. I didn't know that paraphernalia had been found on Miguel's side of the car, and it raised the inference that he was involved in the drug activity. What about Sanchez driving a Lexus? Obviously, that was a significant detail, unless it was an old junker, since drug dealers are known to drive around in nice cars. I thought to myself, that's something I'd like to have already known. I also chided myself for failing to discover during my interview of Miguel that he had been carrying two hundred dollars. I realized that I had been too perfunctory with him and had not gotten enough information. These additional facts all raised the inference that Miguel had been involved in the drug deal. I would definitely need to meet with him again before the trial.

Merola had also sent me a *motion in limine* which he had scheduled for oral argument the following week. A *motion in limine* is a request that the court prohibit the introduction of certain testimony or evidence at trial. Merola was seeking to prevent me from making any reference at trial to the fact that if Anna was evicted, David would lose his college scholarship. His arguments were two-fold: first, the scholarship was not relevant to the underlying eviction action, and second, its admission into evidence would be prejudicial to the housing authority's case. Even without conducting any legal research, I knew he had strong arguments and would most likely prevail. I was hard-pressed to think of reasons why the collateral consequences of an eviction were relevant to whether or not a tenant should be evicted in the first place.

I received one other piece of mail that related to the case—a notice from the court scheduling the trial in just two weeks, on March 11. I picked up the phone and called Anna to tell her about the trial date. I also wanted to set up another meeting with Miguel to go over the information contained in the police report. Predictably, she had not seen or heard from him since dinner last night and didn't know how to contact him.

"Thanks for inviting me over," I told her before getting off the phone. "It was fun."

"It was," she agreed. "Did you like salsa dancing?"

"Yeah, it was good. It was interesting."

"Good. When you got home did you tell your girlfriend that you're going to take her out dancing?"

I chuckled. "Give me a little time."

"Mark, one other thing."

"Yes?"

"Does David need to come to court?"

"No, he won't be testifying. But we do need Miguel."

She paused. "You know, I've been thinking, and the truth is, I'm scared to testify. I don't like courtrooms."

"I don't think there's much that can be done about that, unfortunately. It really looks like the housing authority wants to go ahead."

"Okay," she replied weakly.

I considered tracking down Joe Sanchez to ask him about what had happened and determine if I should call him as a witness. But the more I thought about it, the more it seemed like a bad idea. Miguel claimed to be ignorant of the deal that had gone down between Sanchez and the informant. To be helpful, Sanchez would have to admit both that Miguel's story was true and that he himself was dealing drugs. Not only was that unlikely, but on the off chance that Sanchez agreed to it, it would cause his criminal lawyer to read him the riot act.

Feeling a little restless and wanting to talk to someone, I went over to Alec's office and asked if he wanted to go to lunch. He said yes, and we decided to go to the deli next to the office. I sat down across from him in a small booth. I specifically wanted to discuss the recent developments in Anna's case and hear what he had to say.

"Merola's going to win the *motion in limine*," he told me.

"I agree. I was thinking that if that happens, I'm probably going to withdraw my jury request. I only requested one for the sympathy factor, because David would lose the scholarship. If I lose the motion, that aspect of the case will be gone. I'd actually rather have Judge McCarthy than a jury in a straight drug eviction trial. He knows what's at stake for the family—that they'll lose public housing. A jury wouldn't know that."

"You can't unilaterally withdraw it. You and Merola both have to agree."

"I don't think he'll fight that."

"Judge McCarthy would rip his nuts off if he did."

I laughed.

"He'd perform an *in camera* castration," Alec said.

Our discussion shifted to the police report, which he didn't consider to be as harmful as I did. "The paraphernalia stuff isn't fatal," he said, taking a bite of his sandwich. "It's sandwich bags. If there had been any drugs in them, it would've said so in the report. Is it illegal to have sandwich bags in your car?"

"No, but it doesn't help to have them in the car. I don't have sandwich bags in my car. Do you? Plus they were on my client's son's side."

"But it wasn't his car," Alec pointed out. "Don't get me wrong, you're still up shit's creek with this case, but I don't think that detail is such a killer. I think you're in worse shape with the brother just being in the car while drugs were being sold, forget about plastic bags. I say you just try to get the best deal you can out of Merola. Whatever you get will be better than what will happen at trial. Meaning, even if all you could get is three weeks or a month, I'd take it. I don't believe the brother was an innocent bystander."

"Yeah, I have strong doubts myself. As for Merola, he won't give me enough time to get the son through the school year. I can't agree to anything less. There's really no point."

"The kid has nowhere else to stay to get him through the school year?"

"No. They'd have to move back to Puerto Rico."

Alec shrugged, as if to say, tough break.

"They don't put these scholarships on layaway, either," I said. "It'll go to some other student." I paused. "Actually, I went over to the clients' apartment for dinner the other night."

"Whose apartment?"

"Anna's. You know, my client."

"You went to a client's apartment at Washington for dinner?" he asked incredulously, a smile appearing on his face.

"Why? What's so funny?"

"I can't picture you doing that."

"Why? You can picture yourself going there and not me?"

"I didn't say that, but you're right. I can't picture you going there."

I chuckled. "Okay, whatever. Will you tell me why, though, or do I have to keep asking?"

"Because you're a Boston Back Bay type. You're too refined."

"Oh, fuck off. I'm from Worcester."

"Yeah, but you don't live here anymore. Seriously, why did you go?"

"Because it was an opportunity for me to meet Miguel, the son."

Alec leaned backward. "You've been putting a lot of time into that case."

"Yeah, I have."

"What does the colonel think?"

"He thinks it's a bad case. He doesn't know to what extent I've worked on it, but I know he'd think that I'm devoting more time to them because I think they're so-called good poor people. In his mind we shouldn't differentiate between so-called good poor people and bad poor people. I agree with that in principle, and maybe he's right about me, but it's a more complex case and that interests me. It's compelling because it's not just someone's apartment at stake here, but an opportunity for a college education too." I shrugged. "I don't know. It makes me feel a little guilty, like I'm doing something good but also something not so good at the same time, if that makes sense."

"In my opinion, if you're doing all of your work and giving all your clients a fair shake, then at the end of the day you can't fault yourself for anything. We make forty grand a year. We don't deserve too hard of a time when we don't need it."

After lunch I got a cup of coffee from the Dunkin Donuts across the street and then drove to St. Anne's for a meeting. We needed to discuss our next step, now that the article had been published. A strange sort of lethargy had come over our group, as if we had crashed from the collective high we felt at having our issue profiled in the newspaper. Although some people in the community had talked to us about it, there wasn't a big outcry, and there had been no change in the city's plans. In short, nothing had really happened as a result of the article.

As usual, Father Kelly was the first to speak. "I know you all saw the article. I've had parishioners talk to me about it and they've been supportive. I think now we have to decide where exactly we're going with this." He paused. "As you all know, the city still hasn't done anything and it doesn't look like anything is going to happen. My own opinion is that we should consider litigation. As I've stated before, there are drawbacks to doing this, but quite simply, if we

166

don't do it the money could end up being spent." He looked directly at me. "I'm curious as to what you think, Mark."

Everyone looked at me, making me feel like a deer caught in headlights. I was surprised that he had introduced this idea without first talking to me in private. His asking me in front of everyone put me on the spot.

"I'd have to discuss it with my litigation director," I responded. "He's the ultimate decision-maker. If we go that way, though, I can say that it'll be a battle. It's a tough case. Courts don't like to get involved in political matters, which is likely how they will view this. The case would also require money for expenses such as depositions."

"How much would that be?" asked Nancy Brightman.

I shrugged. "I don't know. It's hard to say at this stage. It could be five thousand, but it could conceivably be ten or twenty if there is expert testimony or a lot of depositions."

We discussed the issue for the next twenty minutes. There was talk of scrounging up some funds from the groups and agencies represented at the meeting to cover litigation costs. In the end, everyone agreed that we should go forward with the case. We had come this far, the reasoning went, and we shouldn't quit now. I told everyone that I would have to check with the colonel and get back to them.

I lingered after the meeting was over and asked Father Kelly if I could talk to him. I felt that his springing the idea of litigation on me without warning merited a conversation. An uncomfortable feeling was swelling inside me, since if the colonel said no to the idea of a lawsuit, I'd feel really crappy. I would have attended all of the meetings only to jump ship at the last moment.

Father Kelly invited me to his living quarters in the back of the rectory. I followed him down a long hallway with rusty pipes suspended from the ceiling, then up a set of creaky wooden stairs that led to his residence.

Fifteen years had passed since I had last been there; fifteen years since I had sat with him in his living room and opened up about personal matters: family issues, college plans, my high school struggles. He used to listen to me with understanding, never passing judgment. This was one of the few places I had been able to go where I felt truly safe and secure. Taking a seat on the couch in his living area, while he sat in a stately brown leather chair, I felt like a teenager again, as if I had regressed and was no longer a thirty-two year old lawyer.

With the passage of so many years, I had forgotten what his quarters looked like. The thick burgundy carpet covering the living room floor looked new; I couldn't remember if it had been there years ago. Framed pictures filled two middle levels of a tall bookshelf in the corner. Among the many volumes on the other shelves were Aquinas, Lonergan's *Insight*, and a biography of Lincoln. His windows looked out over the parking lot, and he kept the blinds pulled down to prevent people from looking in.

"I'm sorry for springing the issue of litigation on you at the meeting."

"I was going to ask you about that."

"I thought so." He crossed his legs. "I was going to talk to you about it first, but then I thought about it and figured that if I did, it might look like you and I were a little cabal. I wanted everyone involved in this together, so I brought it up at the meeting." He lifted his hands a few inches from the arms of his chair and then let them drop back down. "It may have been the wrong decision, and I'm sorry if it was. But I did think about it carefully before deciding."

I nodded, understanding his rationale. "I appreciate that, Father. Well, as I said before, I'll check with James, my litigation director. It's his decision in the end." I looked over at the bookcase. "You have some interesting books. I remember that you used to read the ancient Greeks and the Romans."

"Yes, you can't go wrong with them. I remember your being a reader when you were younger. Are you still?"

"I try to, but work and my commute chip away at my free time."

"I recall you always liked history." He rose from his seat and went over to his bookcase where he removed a thick hardcover and handed it to me. "This is a great book. It's a biography of Alexander Hamilton by Ron Chernow that I just finished."

"I've heard good things about that. I've been meaning to get around to it."

"Take it."

I looked down at the cover and then looked up at him. "Thanks a lot."

He returned to his chair. "So how are things going with you?"

"Okay, I guess."

"Just okay?"

I could tell that he wanted me to open up to him, and I was tempted to. I hadn't shared my feelings about my relationship with Sara with anyone, and I felt a need to. Then there was the conversation with my mother last night. It'd feel good to talk to someone about that, too, and in fact Father Kelly would be the perfect person for that since he knew my mother. But I was hesitant to broach those subjects with him, thinking too much time had passed since I used to confide to him as a teenager.

"Yeah, I'm okay," I replied.

"Your mother told me you've been in a relationship for a while."

I was surprised that Father Kelly brought Sara up, almost like he had read my mind. "Yes, her name is Sara."

"How long have you and she been a couple?"

"Seven years."

"That's quite a while. I'm sure she's very special."

"Yeah, she is."

"What's she like?"

"Umm, she's a really lovely person. She's kind to people and looks for the best in them. She has an innocence about her and a good sense of humor. And she has a good heart. Like if she sees someone on the street who looks hurt or in some kind of jeopardy, she'll try to help them."

"I'd like to meet her sometime."

"Yeah, that'd be nice. She doesn't come out here much, but yeah, that'd be nice."

"You must be pretty serious if you've been together for seven years?"

"Yeah, we are." All of a sudden I decided to open up to him, in spite of my earlier reluctance to do so. "But we have problems."

Father Kelly looked at me in a way that invited me to elaborate.

"The seven years, well, it's kind of like we're at a standstill and not moving forward. We don't communicate well. It's like we both assume the worst about the other and are on the defensive. She resents me for past wrongs. We had some nasty fights where we each said hurtful things to one another and, well, that hasn't gone away. It lingers. Our relationship is different now."

"People get into arguments," Father Kelly said. "They sometimes say things they shouldn't. None of us is perfect."

"Yeah, well, there's been a lot of imperfection with us. I know there has been on my part."

"Do you want to stay together?"

"I know things aren't good with us, but I can't picture being without her. I'd miss her too much."

He mentioned that when he counseled couples whose relationships were foundering, he often found that the most effective thing they could do, above all else, was listen to each other and try to understand each other's feelings. A common problem was that each person thought his or her feelings weren't being respected. It all sounded true, it all sounded reasonable. In fact, I recognized that it was the same message that Eileen used to give to me and Sara during our therapy sessions.

"If you need to talk again, you know where to find me." Father Kelly smiled warmly, then he moved the conversation forward by saying, "I also wanted to mention to you that I hear you're representing Anna Rivera in her eviction case."

"I am. Do you know her? How'd you find that out?" I asked with surprise.

"She's one of my parishioners."

"She is?"

Father Kelly nodded. "She told me about the case. She's very worried about going to trial."

"It's a tough situation. A tough case."

Father Kelly kind of raised an eyebrow, as if inviting me to continue. I gave him an overview of the case, making sure not to disclose any privileged information, and explained the effect of the *Rucker* decision issued by the Supreme Court.

"Sounds like she's up against tough odds. That's too bad. You know, Miguel used to come here with his mother when he was younger. He stopped some time ago. I hear he's involved with drugs, but please don't tell Anna I told you that."

"How do you know this?"

"A lot of information passes through this church."

"Is it well-known? Does Anna know?"

"I don't know if it's well-known. As for Anna, I think she knows but she doesn't know, if you get my meaning. She doesn't want to know."

"How do you mean?"

"She's had a tough life. She's on SSI for psychiatric reasons. She's poor and has lived in Washington for years. The drugs and crime, the bad conditions, seeing Miguel's and David's father gunned down. She has a lot of spunk to her and personality, but she's also a troubled person."

"I see."

"Never really feeling safe, either," Father Kelly added. "It does something to a person. I think all these factors contribute to her condition and keep it from improving. She probably doesn't want to tack on other problems, meaning getting involved with Miguel and his problems."

I had never before really considered Anna's emotional problems in a meaningful way, even though I knew she was on SSI for depression and anxiety. I had accepted those two diagnoses as mere labels without considering their implications. I felt bad for her. I sat there for a little while longer with Father Kelly, our discussion shifting once again, this time to the changes that had occurred in Worcester over the years. People who worked in Boston and its outskirts were moving farther and farther out of the city in search of affordable housing, and in recent years had migrated beyond I-495 and into Worcester. Reportedly, the train carried a much larger number of commuters into Boston each morning than it had just a few years earlier. Even a small development like the skywalk was important to city leaders, Father Kelly theorized, because it contributed to their overall goal of making the city more modern and more desirable. As I thought of all the changes that had occurred in Worcester in the years since I had left for college, I wondered if maybe the skywalk was a part of that change. Until that point, I had only thought of it as an isolated, impermissible use of federal funds. But perhaps the skywalk was something that was going to be built one way or another, almost inevitably, much like the slow spread of Boston commuters past I-495 and into Worcester County.

19

When I entered the colonel's office, I saw that he was dressed in a maroon cardigan sweater with a white button-down shirt underneath. This was unusual for him, since he wore a shirt and tie every day, and I wondered what the cardigan was all about. His outfit was nicer than mine, certainly, as I was wearing jeans and a sweater. I simply wasn't accustomed to sartorial variations on his part.

Anyway, I was there to ask his permission to file a lawsuit against the city.

We began by reviewing the federal regulations, and we shared the opinion that they were somewhat vague and ambiguous and might not support our cause of action. But we also agreed that the underlying policy behind the use of CDBG funds—that they were intended to provide assistance to low and moderate-income residents—gave us a leg to stand on.

"Filing suit is the next logical step," I suggested, "since nothing else has worked. And I've already invested so much time in this and have gone to meetings on it. If we back out now, it won't look good."

The colonel leaned back in his chair. "You know what this means. We'd have to depose the city manager and city council members. That's serious stuff."

"I know, but I think it's a worthwhile case. A lot of money is at stake—money that was wrongfully allocated and could really help people and make a difference in their lives."

"It'll be a lot of work, and it'll cost money to take depositions."

"I know. I brought that up and that's something that can be worked on. We'll figure it out. The community groups may be able to put up the money."

"Community groups don't have money," the colonel responded.

I feared that his conservative nature would lead him to say no. I imagined myself reluctantly having to deliver that message to Father Kelly and the rest of the group.

"Okay. Go ahead with it if you want to," he said.

I was surprised at both his decision and the speed at which he had reached it.

"I don't think it's a terribly strong case," he observed, "but I think you have legal footing and, importantly, the moral high ground. You'll have to get an injunction to freeze the funds."

"Yeah."

I left the colonel's office feeling almost jubilant. I had a romantic vision of myself going up against enormous odds and emerging as a champion for the underserved. Of course, I wasn't considering the tremendous amount of work that would be involved or the possibility that I could be biting off more than I could chew. It'd be a much bigger case than I had ever handled on my own, and I'd certainly be outgunned by the other side.

20

I was certain that I was going to lose the *motion in limine*. Merola had drafted a good legal memorandum and my opposition wasn't as strong, basically because there was no case law backing my position.

Judge McCarthy heard a few motions ahead of ours, and I watched him carefully to discern his mood, which appeared to be fairly good. One case involved a Latina single mother with two young kids who had missed a rent payment under a settlement agreement; he gave her the chance to remain in her apartment if she could pay the arrearage within ten days. When Judge McCarthy was in a bad mood, tenants sometimes felt the brunt of it and didn't get that kind of chance.

When it was time for me and Merola to argue his motion, we took our places at the counsel tables. Judge McCarthy peered down at us from the bench, almost as though he was wondering what we were doing in his courtroom. "You two again," he muttered. He thumbed through the court file for a few seconds. "So I see this is a *motion in limine* brought by Mr. Merola. I also see Mr. Langley has requested a jury on this case." He seemed visibly annoyed by that fact.

"Your Honor," Merola said. "I know you have some background knowledge of this case from the motion to dismiss, so let me get right to the point. This is a *motion in limine* to exclude evidence from the jury of the fact that the tenant's son was awarded a scholarship to U. Mass. at Amherst, and that if the tenant loses at trial, the son could lose the scholarship. The reason for the motion is that the housing authority has reason to believe that the tenants will try to bring this up at trial. It was, in fact, brought up by counsel at the motion to dismiss hearing. But this information should clearly be excluded because it is totally irrelevant to the underlying eviction case and would unfairly prejudice the housing authority. It would make an emotional appeal to the jury by trying to tug at their heart strings, but that is all that it would accomplish. It has no relevance. Now, I have set forth in my supporting memorandum some cases which I think are controlling on this issue. No one disputes that it would be unfortunate for the son to lose the scholarship. However, if the family is evicted, the housing authority isn't forcing them to leave the area. They could stay here and the son could keep it. It's just not something that is part of this case."

"Your Honor," I said. "The facts about the son are relevant. This is his chance to get out of Washington and go to college. He's lived there all of his life, and he has struggled against immense odds to do well in school. He ignored other outside pressures that kids growing up in the projects face and stayed on a straight path."

While addressing the court, I felt almost as if I had floated outside of my body and was objectively observing what was going on. Typically, I was so immersed in argument that I had no real perspective on what was transpiring. But I noticed that Judge McCarthy had his lips pursed together in a thoughtful manner and was listening intently, and it was then that a light flicked on inside my head. I could see the path that my defense of Anna and David would take, and it was as clear to me as a long flat stretch of highway running ahead for miles. I had to do more than just make a legal argument, because my legal argument was a loser. I had to fully impress upon Judge McCarthy, right here and now, what was at stake for David. I had to educate him in this hearing about the injustice that would occur if he and Anna got evicted. Then I could try to withdraw my jury request.

I continued, "I believe the scholarship is relevant because the whole story needs to come out in this case, not just a fifteen-second episode involving a drug deal in a convenience store parking lot.

The person accused of being involved in the drug deal is my client's other son, Miguel, and he doesn't even live in the apartment with them. Unfortunately, his name is on the lease because my client neglected to take it off. That's why we're here, because she neglected to take his name off—a woman who has depression and anxiety and is on SSI. She forgot to take him off, so a good kid might lose his shot at college because of that simple oversight. He has an actual college scholarship and he'll lose it if evicted. He and his mother will have to move to Puerto Rico because she can't afford a market-rate apartment. He won't graduate from high school here and that will be the end of it. If ever there were innocent tenants, Your Honor, it is these people, because they weren't involved in the deal at all. They had no knowledge of it."

"Your Honor, I object," Merola interrupted. "We're going off point here. Mr. Langley is making an argument that's not part of this motion. In fact, what he is saying is the very reason I filed this motion. If we go in front of the jury, he's going to argue that the eviction is unfair and that the scholarship will be lost, but none of that is relevant. The question is quite simple: Was the son on the lease and was he involved in a drug deal? That's it. Not whether the other son will be able to go to college."

"The eviction is unfair," I responded. "Mr. Merola just wants to hide that and pretend it doesn't exist."

Judge McCarthy put his hand up in the air to stop us. "Mr. Langley, the potential for prejudice greatly outweighs the relevance, of which there is practically none here."

"But Your Honor, at trial I should be able to introduce who the players are, meaning both of the sons and what their stories are."

"Enough," Judge McCarthy said firmly. "I've made my ruling. The motion is granted."

I exited the courtroom, the wind suddenly out of my sails, frustrated that I hadn't been able to further tell David's story. I felt angry at how Judge McCarthy had cut me off, and I couldn't help but wonder if it was retribution for having requested a jury. On the other hand, at least I had managed to communicate the sympathetic aspects of the case. I had at least done that. But the problem was that

Judge McCarthy didn't seemed fazed at all by them, save his initial thoughtful reaction. Now, if I could convince Merola to consent to the withdrawal of the jury request, the case would be in Judge McCarthy's hands. I hoped I was doing the right thing. I hoped that Judge McCarthy would be moved by David's situation. I was painfully aware that so far he didn't seemed moved at all.

I waited two days to call Merola because I wanted to put a little time between the hearing and my call to him. I began the conversation on a cordial note by talking about the weather. "I'm surprised the snow is already starting to melt. Maybe we've seen the last of winter."

"You never know in New England," he replied.

"I'm actually going to Vermont this weekend." I had decided that a trip out of town might help my relationship with Sara and had suggested to her that we go to Vermont. She eagerly agreed, as she loved to travel.

"Where? I love Vermont."

"I'm not sure yet. Maybe Stowe."

"Stowe's great. The snow won't melt up there. I wouldn't worry about that. At least I'm sure the skiing will be fine." He paused and then almost dreamily said, "I look forward to going hiking with my wife and children when the winter's over."

"I didn't know that you hike." An image entered my head of him and his family climbing up the side of a mountain like the Von Trapps at the end of *The Sound of Music*. It brought a smile to my face to think about it.

"I love the outdoors. That's why I live in Princeton."

Princeton was a small, rural town in central Massachusetts that was the home of Mt. Wachusett, a local ski area.

"I look forward to sitting in front of a warm fire this weekend with my family and reading a book," Merola said, continuing his reverie. "That's one of my favorite things to do in the winter."

"Okay, well, anyway, I was just calling about our case. I want to withdraw my jury request, so I'm calling to see if you'll agree."

"Hmm … what brings this on?"

"Just a decision I made. No one ever requests juries and it obviously irked Judge McCarthy that I did. Plus I lost the *motion in limine*. What's the point of a jury now?"

Merola paused. "The interesting thing from my perspective is that you requested it in the first place and now you're withdrawing it. That type of vacillation raises a whole host of questions."

"What does Vaseline have to do with it?"

"No, I said vacillate. It means to change."

"I know what it means. I was making a joke."

"Well, you have a very dry delivery."

"See, dry, all the more reason for Vaseline. That's a joke, too. Anyway, what's your position?"

"I'm not sure. I'm thinking that if a jury is something that you don't want, then maybe it's something that I do want."

"Okay," I replied indifferently. "What I'll do is file a motion with the court to withdraw the jury request, and when we go before Judge McCarthy, you can explain to him why you insist on having a jury in his courtroom. I'm sure he'll be very interested in hearing your reasons. By the way, you didn't request a jury in your complaint."

Merola chuckled. "Very clever." He paused. "You have my consent."

After getting off the phone with him, I drafted a withdrawal form for us to sign and submit to the court. Holding it in front of me, I thought, I'm choosing to put all of my faith in Judge McCarthy, and that's a very scary thing to do.

21

That Friday evening Sara wasn't in the apartment when I arrived home from work. We were leaving for Vermont the next morning. I immediately headed out to buy her a gift to give her on the trip, another part of my plan to rehabilitate our relationship. I hardly ever bought her gifts outside of her birthday and holidays.

I reached Newbury Street and headed to The Gap with the intent of purchasing a replacement for Sara's red pants and seashell shirt. The seashell shirt was starting to look shabby; it had a small hole on the left shoulder and the seashell pattern was fading away. The red pants had also seen better days. At The Gap I purchased a light blue shirt with some thin zigzag lines on the front. There were no good lounging pants to be found, so I headed to Victoria's Secret in the Copley Place Mall. I felt awkward shopping there, as if I was some type of pervert, but I couldn't think of anywhere else to go. It wasn't long before I was approached by a salesgirl in her early-twenties. She had long brown hair with dark red highlights and a slim, fit body.

"Hi, can I help you?" she asked with a cheerful smile.

"Sure," I responded. I did my best to explain what I was looking for and she led me to a sleepwear rack.

"What size?" she asked.

"Small."

She began thumbing through the rack and then picked out a pair of pants that were a shiny purple. "How about these?"

I rubbed the material between my fingers. "What's this made of? Silk?"

She looked at the tag. "Yeah. They're silk." Then she looked at me as if my question was amusing.

"I'd rather have cotton. I'm not that crazy about silk. I'm not that crazy about the waistband, either. It's too thin. They're like pants a genie would wear."

She giggled. "You're very discerning."

"You better believe I am."

I followed her to another rack where she showed me light-weight cotton pants in light purple and light pink colors. I pinched the fabric between my thumb and forefinger; it seemed comfortable and like it breathed well. This was what I was looking for. "Are these the only colors you have? Do you have anything in red?"

"No, this is it."

I stood there debating what color to get. "Purple seems a little classier. What do you think?"

"You know, it's all a matter of taste. I like the purple. It's probably what I'd get."

Light purple pants and blue shirt. It wasn't as catchy as red pants and seashell shirt, and the colors didn't match particularly well, but I figured that sometimes you just can't recreate the past and have to go with what you've got. I was all set to purchase them, but I wanted to make sure the cut of the pants was okay, so I held them in front of my lower half to examine them. They touched the top of my shoes and then broke an inch or two.

"Do they seem long to you?" I asked.

"They look all right to me."

"Are they supposed to be that long?"

"Women's bodies are a little different than men's," the girl replied with amusement.

Still holding the pants in front of my lower body, I took a few strides to see how they behaved while walking, thinking this might tell me if they were too long. When I happened to look up, I couldn't believe what I saw. Standing in front of me was Chris Bloom, a junior partner I had worked directly under at my old law firm. He was dressed in a dark suit, white shirt and maroon tie, and with him was a tall, attractive blonde dressed in a low-cut, black-sequin dress revealing ample cleavage. She appeared to be in her late-twenties, but mature for her age, like she was the type who only dated guys who were wealthy and at least ten years older than her. She seemed to be looking at me with a mixture of disdain and odd fascination.

I guessed that they were walking through the mall on their way to the Westin Hotel for a function. That was the only reason I could think of for their being so dressed up at the mall.

"Shopping for a new pair of pants, Langley?" Chris remarked with a self-satisfied smile. "They look very becoming on you."

"Very funny," I replied.

I suddenly remembered how much I disliked his sense of humor, which wasn't nearly as sophisticated as he thought it was and usually involved putting other people down. The surprise of running into him knocked me off my game, so to speak, and I wasn't able to think of a good comeback.

Chris and I had been like oil and water together when I was at the firm. He had been a football player at Bucknell and approached our work relationship in a sports-minded way, as if he was the team captain and I was a freshman player. He acted tough with me when it came to our actual work environment, but then expected that we would have a fraternity-like camaraderie after the work day was done, tossing back beers and slapping each other on the back or something. Implicit in this compact, it seemed to me, was that over time we would rise through the ranks together until we were both full-fledged partners, with him, of course, always being a little senior to me.

In a subtle yet clear manner, I let him know that I would be having none of that and was not on his "team." I displayed no interest in the two of us having a mentor-mentee relationship. When he was tough on me at work, I would either talk back to him or coolly and indifferently take it, and I politely rebuffed his invitations to go out for a drink after work by claiming that I had other obligations. I didn't really care much about what he thought of me, even though he was my superior, since the senior partners—who held the real power—liked me and thought I did good work. I knew my life at the firm would have been easier if I had been willing to suck up to him, but I just couldn't bring myself to do it.

Chris introduced me to his date and she warily said hello.

"So Langley, how are things going?" Chris asked.

"Fine."

"So it's been a couple of years."

I nodded. "Yeah, it has."

"Where did you land after leaving the firm?"

"I work at legal services."

"Oh yeah? Where?"

"Worcester."

"All the way out there, huh?"

"Yup," I said coolly.

"So you're representing poor people in what, civil cases? Social security benefits, uncontested divorces, that kind of thing?"

"Evictions."

"Evictions. Defending tenants who don't pay their rent."

"From your point of view, yes."

Chris looked down at the pants I was still holding in my hand. "All these changes, Langley. It's a lot to take in."

"I guess we all find ourselves in different ways."

Chris chuckled. "Well, we have to run. We're late as it is. You take care of yourself." He gave me a pat on the shoulder and walked away with his date holding onto his arm.

I watched the two of them walk away from me. As much as I hated to admit it to myself, in a way I felt envious of him. He had managed to stay with the firm and his future was assured. He was climbing up the legal ladder whereas I had moved down a number of rungs.

I purchased the pants and then hit the street, replaying my interaction with Chris over and over again in my mind. I was so caught up in analyzing what he said and what I said that I was oblivious to my surroundings and navigated home on what seemed like autopilot. I scolded myself for not thinking up better comebacks, for not being quick-witted enough.

I thought back to my days at the firm. My office there was about six feet wide, my desk spanning almost its entire width. Behind me on two rows of shelves were my case files and various law-related books. I pictured the faces of some of the partners I had worked for, as clearly as if they were still frame images right in front of me. Angry expressions often ruled their faces. They were unhappy people who frequently took out their frustrations on associates. I remembered how they would have me sit across from them at their desks and quiz me about minutia contained in voluminous records and transcripts from cases that no one person could possibly remember. If I failed to answer a question correctly, their faces would suddenly flood with rage and they'd lash out at me. They were always on top of me, waiting to pounce at the slightest error, and it used to rattle me. I managed to perform well, but I was still a nervous wreck most of the time. I couldn't understand why they were so angry. They were wealthy and had little work to do, seeing that they delegated nearly everything to the associates. If I was in their shoes, I used to think, I'd be as happy as a pig in shit.

Walking home I did manage to comfort myself with the knowledge that despite the loss of prestige and a good salary, it was a good thing that I wasn't at the firm anymore. I didn't fit in with Chris and the other lawyers there and never would have, no matter how hard I tried. Maybe, I thought, this particular rung of the legal ladder was where I should be. Maybe I shouldn't expect to be a big shot Boston lawyer. Maybe being a legal services lawyer in Worcester was just right for me.

22

The next morning Sara woke up earlier than usual and seemed to be walking on air as she packed her things. It was a little after ten when we left for Vermont. I had stowed the Victoria's Secret pants and the Gap shirt in a brown paper bag in the trunk of my car so that she wouldn't discover them. We cruised north on Route 93 through the indifferent gray morning, past the Massachusetts border and into New Hampshire, and when we reached Concord we branched off to Route 89. A number of cars on the road had skis on their roofs. I used to ski when I was a kid but no longer cared for it. I had come to view skiing as a joyless exercise of going downhill with wooden sticks on your feet for about ten minutes, risking injury to life and limb, and then freezing for the next thirty minutes while standing in line to take the ski lift back up to the top of the mountain, only to do it all over again.

The further north we traveled the more rural the surroundings became. Barns appeared along the highway and the gray silhouette of mountains framed the horizon. It was difficult for me to imagine living in such an area; it seemed that life would be interminably boring. For many young professionals without children, like myself, the nation essentially consisted of a network of large cities and the remainder of the country could be divided into two categories: popular vacation spots and everywhere else. Sara and I listened to one of her 1980's mix CD's and talked about myriad things such as friends and our families and our jobs. We were getting along well, and I felt glad that we were making this trip. I felt connected to her.

At one point she turned up the volume up on the radio, and we were mostly silent as the songs went by one after the other: "Holiday," "Invisible Touch," "Billie Jean," "Unconditional Love," and "The Way It is." When "The Power of Love," the hit 1985 power ballad by Huey Lewis and the News, came on we both sang along playfully, pointing at each other during the chorus. Then things slowed down with Eric Carmen's "Hungry Eyes" and "After All," the syrupy duet performed by Peter Cetera and Cher that I knew Sara secretly loved, though she wouldn't admit it. After that song, I needed a breather and inserted *Exile on Main Street* in the CD player.

The village of Stowe was a postcard replica of a small Vermont town. The architecture was old New England, very quaint and pretty. The main street was lined with a number of shops and restaurants, and people strolled on the sidewalks dressed in ski jackets and winter boots. Sara and I decided to check out the rates at a hotel that was expensive-looking, hoping there was an off-chance it would offer a reasonable rate. We parked in the lot behind it, and after getting out of the car, I breathed in the cold, crisp air, noticing that it seemed more pure than the air in Boston. Suddenly I felt the thump of a snowball against my right hip and turned to see Sara in the after-extension of a throw, a devilish expression on her face like a kid caught with her hand in the cookie jar.

"What are you doing?" I asked.

Instead of responding to me, she quickly formed a new snowball and hurled it at me. It landed short at my feet.

"You're declaring war, aren't you?" I said.

I made a snowball and threw it at her with half-velocity—it wasn't cool for a guy to throw a snowball with full force at his girlfriend—landing it a little wide off the mark. She threw one back at me that was dead-on accurate, but I dodged out of the way. We stood across from one another, our arms down at our sides like cowboys facing off in a showdown, each waiting for the other to make the next move.

"Can we call a truce?" I offered.

"Okay."

As I approached her she quickly made a snowball and threw it at me, striking me in the leg.

"No fair!" I exclaimed.

She ran up to me, wrapped her arms around my waist, and tried to wrestle me down to the snow. She didn't have the strength to do it, though.

"I'm invincible!" I declared, laughing.

All of a sudden she managed to get my legs out from under me and we both went tumbling down into the snow. An older couple walked by us holding hands and looked down at us as if they thought we were deranged. We lay there tangled up in one another, laughing.

The hotel lobby had a maroon carpet, two fireplaces with large mantles, and several deep brown leather chairs positioned next to reading lamps. A curved, lacquered wooden staircase led upstairs. The front desk clerk, who was in his early-twenties with bushy, curly light brown hair and a goatee, appeared to be a stoner-skiier type. He was good enough to shave $50 off the $350 rate because it was later in the day, and although it was more than I wanted to spend, I was willing to take it because I didn't feel like hunting for a more affordable hotel.

My initial reaction upon entering the room was amusement at the prospect of sleeping in a canopy bed for the first time in my life. "I'm going to be a real princess tonight," I joked to Sara. But what surprised me most about the room was the amount of technology it had in it. There was a large flat-screen TV and DVD player, a computer with a flat-screen monitor, and a fancy single cup coffee maker. None of this meshed with my idea of Vermont. I walked into the bathroom to check it out. There was a marble bathtub with a whirlpool feature, a glass-enclosed stand-up shower, and the toilet was made of glistening white porcelain and was set far apart from the other fixtures. It seemed like a grand place to take care of one's business.

"Wow, this is really nice," Sara remarked.

"It sure is," I agreed, lying down on the bed.

"I saw in the lobby that there are sleigh rides. They're going to start in twenty minutes. Let's go," she urged.

"I just got finished driving four hours to get up here. I want to rest."

"But we'll miss the sleigh ride."

"Who cares? It's just sitting behind a bunch of smelly horses. I hear that they sometimes take dumps when they're going along. Who wants to get involved in that?"

Sara took hold of my arm and tried to pull me up off the bed. "C'mon, let's go."

"Seriously, I don't want to. I'm tired."

She stepped away from me. "You never want to do anything."

"That's unfair," I replied with irritation. She looked at me with upset eyes. "Oh God," I muttered. "Here we go."

"You never want to do anything," Sara repeated.

"I just drove four hours and now you're laying that on me? That I never want to do anything?"

"So you're not going to go?"

"No, I'm not," I said resolutely.

"Fine, I'll go by myself."

She put on her winter coat and collected her hat and gloves. She didn't say another word to me before going out the door.

When Sara returned she didn't say anything to me, and I made a point of not asking how the sleigh ride was. We ate dinner at the hotel restaurant mostly in silence. I looked across the table at her, and her face was like glass. This argument seemed more significant than others since we were away on a trip. Somehow there was more at stake. We slept together that night without touching, and more than ever before, I felt Sara closing herself off and slipping away from me. How could this all be the result of not going on a sleigh ride? It didn't make sense to me. But then again, looking back at all of our issues, maybe it did make sense. Maybe it was the culmination of them, all piled up on top of each other, their collective weight crushing us. The trip had been a failure.

In the morning over breakfast a subtle change seemed to come over Sara. I couldn't quite put my finger on it. It was like something broke inside her.

"What is it?" I asked.

"This just isn't working," she said softly.

"What isn't?"

"You and me. It's not working."

"What are you saying?"

"You heard me, Mark."

"Are you saying what I think you're saying?" I couldn't believe that she was breaking up with me.

She nodded. "Yes." She looked down at the table. I could see a tear roll down her cheek.

I looked away through the window we were seated next to, out onto the main street. I felt numb all over, and at the same time as if my stomach had just fallen to the floor. When I looked back at Sara she was wiping away more tears with the back of her hand.

"I want to go home," she said. "Can you take me home?"

"I'm sorry." I felt exhausted inside. I wanted to stop what was happening, but it seemed like there was no way I could.

"I want to go."

Tears began to flood my eyes. "Okay," I said.

On the drive home I tried to talk to Sara, wanting to get to the root of her reason for breaking up with me, wanting to understand it. Even though we had fought for essentially the entire trip, what happened seemed so sudden. But she didn't want to talk about it. All she would say was that for years now our relationship hadn't been working and she needed to be apart from me. She said we both needed that if we wanted to be happy.

Our problems had been like a giant tidal wave looming over us, and it had finally come crashing down. Our bitterness toward one another had accumulated for too long and had metastasized into a cancer on our relationship. Although I knew that was all true, I still didn't want our relationship to end. I couldn't picture living without her, or her going through life without me. And it sent a shiver through me to picture her experiencing life on her own—or worse, with someone else.

"Sara, will you change your mind, please?" I asked with desperation in my voice.

"No," she said, shaking her head. "I can't."

"Please?"

"Stop, Mark. Just please stop."

After we arrived in Boston, I found a parking spot a block from our apartment. We walked in silence carrying our bags, and after entering the apartment, I put them down in the bedroom. I turned around to see Sara standing in the doorway.

"I want you to leave," she said in a soft, sad tone.

Hearing her say that felt like having the wind knocked out of me. On a certain level what had been said so far that day was just words, but this made it real. I had a strange sensation all of a sudden that if I reached out to her just then she'd disappear from right in front of me. I feared that maybe I'd never see her again. I went into the bedroom and mechanically filled a suitcase with clothing and personal items. When I came out, Sara was gone. Just like that, she was gone.

I drove on the Mass Pike to my parents' house, and when I entered Framingham I called them to say that I would be arriving soon. My mother sounded pleased to hear the news that I was coming. "Are you staying over?" she inquired.

"Yeah."

"That's nice. What brings this on?"

"I'll tell you when I get there, okay?"

"Okay. But Mark, you don't sound very good."

"I'm okay. We'll talk when I get there."

I didn't want to tell her and my father what had happened until I arrived at their house. I kind of dreaded how they would react. I was certain that they'd feel bad for me and I didn't want their pity. I also suspected that they'd see this as an opportunity to affirm that they were never crazy about Sara to begin with, and I didn't want to hear that from them.

I pulled into their driveway and let myself into the house, leaving my belongings in the car. My parents were in the kitchen, and they got up and greeted me in the foyer with hugs.

"What happened?" my mother asked with a concerned expression. "You look upset."

"No, I'm not," I said reflexively. Then realizing that I probably did look upset, and that I had to eventually tell them about what happened between me and Sara, I said, "Sara and I broke up."

"Oh, wow," said my father, obviously taken aback. "I'm sorry."

"Oh, Mark, I'm sorry," said my mother. I wondered if she really meant it, since she had never been a big fan of Sara's. "What happened?"

"I don't really want to get into it, if you don't mind," I answered gently.

My mother reached out to touch my arm in a comforting gesture, but I edged slightly away from her.

"Mark..."

"I don't feel like it, Mom."

"Are you sure you don't want to tell us?"

"Yeah."

I made a couple trips to bring my belongings up to my room. I felt like I couldn't stay up there, as if it would be too confining, and also like it would signal weakness to my parents, like I was so emotionally distraught that I couldn't be around people, so I went downstairs. My father offered me a bottle of Miller Lite, his beer of choice. A drink was exactly what I needed. After taking a couple of long swallows, I put the bottle down on the coffee table in the living room, sat down on the couch, and turned on the television. I wasn't interested in watching anything in particular, and in fact, didn't feel like I could pay attention to the TV if I wanted to.

My father soon came over, lifted the bottle, and placed a coaster underneath it. "It'll ruin the finish on the coffee table," he said.

I didn't respond and felt pissed that he had said that. At that moment I didn't give two shits about the coffee table.

For the next half hour or so, my parents hovered around me, coming in and out of the living room for no apparent reason, while

I pretended to watch a basketball game. A little while later I went upstairs to my room in order to have some solitude. I still didn't really feel like being in that small space surrounded by stuff from my childhood, but it now seemed preferable to the living room. As I unpacked my things I began to feel depressed about losing Sara. I only saw bleakness ahead of me living with my parents in Worcester. I thought about how each night Sara and I sat on the couch eating and watching TV, and wished I could be beamed back in time to one of those moments. I wished we were lying in bed together with my arm draped around her and my cheek nuzzled against her hair. I didn't care that we had problems. I just wanted to be with her.

Meanwhile, my parents were downstairs, probably talking about me and feeling bad for me, their poor son who broke up with his girlfriend, their son who didn't tell them much about himself and quickly became irritated with them, who didn't tell them for two years that he had been fired from his job, who in many ways they didn't know or understand. I began to feel guilty that I had remained distant from them for so many years. I could've visited more, could've been kinder to them. Despite all of that, they were the ones I went to that day. I was acutely aware that there was nowhere else for me to go.

23

The following day I received a call from Father Kelly telling me that Susan DiMarco, a member of the city council, had called him about CDBG.

"She did?" I asked.

"Yes, she wants to meet with me this evening at seven."

"Where?"

"At a diner. It has me very curious. I'd like you to come with me."

I considered it for a moment. "I don't think I should. I think she'd be more open with you without me there."

"Hmm, now that I think about it, you may be right."

"I wonder what she wants. Did she say?"

"No, I asked but she said she couldn't get into it."

"Wow. Well, could you call me afterwards and let me know what happens?"

"Yes, of course."

"This is interesting."

"Yes, it most certainly is."

My office had a group membership at the YWCA downtown, and that evening I used it for the first time. I saw it as a way to kill two birds with one stone: exercising and spending less time at my parents' house. I still hadn't told them exactly what happened between Sara and me; all they knew was that we had broken up. While jogging on the treadmill, it came to me as a revelation that there was no reason to fear telling them the truth. Sara and I had been coming apart at the seams for a while and finally did on our trip to Vermont. It was something that happened in many relationships and it happened in ours. I could tell them in a general way why she and I were no longer together and that would be it.

I arrived home at about nine. My parents were both upstairs watching TV in bed. I ate dinner alone at the kitchen table while reading the newspaper. When I was nearly finished, my mother came downstairs to the kitchen to get a glass of water. "Were you working late?" she asked.

"No, I went to the gym."

"What gym?"

"My office has a membership at the Y downtown."

"I didn't know that. That's nice." She took a seat next to me at the kitchen table. "Are you okay?" she asked somewhat dramatically.

"I'm okay," I assured her.

"Your father and I don't really know what happened with you and Sara, but we're concerned about you. I just want you to know that."

"Thanks."

It was then that I told her about the break up. She asked me a couple of questions in response—who had initiated it and if I had seen it coming. The first was easy to answer, but the second caused me to think a little before answering.

"I did see it coming," I said, "but I didn't acknowledge it. I guess I didn't think either of us would actually do it."

"I feel bad seeing you unhappy like this. You've been moping around. I understand that, but I wish there was something I could do."

"I know. But this is how it goes. Sometimes people are sad."

My mother patted my hand and told me she was going back upstairs to bed. I felt relieved that the break up was no longer the elephant in the room. I also felt glad that I had said, "Sometimes people are sad." It was a fact of life that my family never really acknowledged with each other.

The next morning Father Kelly called me at work. "Councilwoman DiMarco told me that the head of the city council, Mike Flanagan, has a stranglehold over the rest of the council, and he's the one who's really behind this project. She said she thinks Miller paid off Flanagan. She doesn't know for sure, but she thinks he transferred property to him to get the skywalk deal. A quid pro quo. She also said that there was no bidding for the project, that Miller's company just got it."

I let the news wash over me. It was remarkable that a member of the city council would reveal that information. I had never even considered that we would get help from the inside like that. DiMarco must have been disgusted by what had happened, but without the power to take on Flanagan, figured this was her only way to do something about it. "I'll check the Registry of Deeds. I have eviction cases against him all the time, and he owns property under the name of a trust. I can search both his name and the trust name."

Immediately after getting off the phone I began searching the Registry of Deeds website. It took me all of about a minute to discover that Miller, alone or through a trust, owned ten buildings in Worcester. I widened my search to include recent transactions where he was the seller of the property and quickly found one on Grafton Street where his trust conveyed the property to Flanagan for one hundred dollars—a common value used when property was intended to be transferred for free, since some amount of consideration, no matter how minimal, had to be stated in order for the transaction to be valid.

We have them, I said to myself.

Near the end of the day I received a terse voice mail message from Chris Bloom asking me to call him. I wondered why he called me. Maybe he wanted to continue making fun of me for the pants episode at Victoria's Secret?

I dialed him up, and the first thing he said to me was, "Langley, this makes it twice that we cross paths."

"Huh?"

"The Worcester City Council has hired us to defend it in this action you brought for this CDBG matter. Personally, I don't think you have much of a case."

My mind spun in what seemed like fifty different directions. I was having difficulty connecting the case against the city to my old firm, surprised that the city would go all the way to Boston to retain a law firm. "Well, we'll see about that," I replied. I didn't want to tell him about my discovery of the property transfer just yet. I wanted to wait and size up the situation first. "You know I have a preliminary injunction scheduled."

"I know that. That's one of the reasons I'm calling."

"Well, we can go ahead with it or you can agree to freeze the funds for now, and then we meet to talk about this. I think it'd be a good idea to talk."

"What's to talk about?"

"I think it'd be good to meet. Trust me. It'll be worth your while."

Chris exhaled, a little annoyed. "It seems like a waste of time."

"It's just temporary so we can talk. We can argue the motion afterwards if you want."

"Let me call my client. I'll give you a call back."

We both hung up. I knew that before doing anything he would first pass this by one of the senior partners. He didn't have the authority to make this type of decision on his own. I wondered who he was working with on the case. An hour later he called me and agreed to send a letter confirming a freeze of the funds and that a meeting would be held. We arranged for it to occur at his office the following Wednesday at 3:00 p.m. I felt a little apprehensive about going there. I could picture people looking at me strangely and whispering behind my back, wondering what I was doing there. On the other hand, envisioning myself besting Chris with the property transfer was a delicious revenge fantasy. A little sadly, I wished that I could tell Sara about this. I had told her many times about my conflicts with Chris, and I could picture her reacting excitedly, grabbing onto my forearm and saying, "No way!"

I called Father Kelly to let him know about this development and also told him that I intended to show Bloom the deed at that time. He asked if he should come along, but I thought it'd be best if he didn't, since it would be a meeting of attorneys. I didn't say it, but I knew that bringing a priest with me would only look comical to Bloom and any other Morgan & Reilly lawyers who would be present. I believed, however, that I would need to bring along some extra legal manpower with me. I didn't want to go there alone.

The next day I placed a phone call to Sergeant DelVecchio, the officer who wrote the police report for Miguel's arrest. It was my fourth or fifth call to him, and each time I had left a message that he didn't return. This time I didn't bother leaving one and resigned myself to the fact that I wouldn't get to interview him before the trial. He'd be helping out the housing authority.

I called Anna to confirm our trial prep on Friday and see if she'd be able to get Miguel to accompany her. She told me that she had unsuccessfully tried to get in touch with him.

"Try to find him," I urged her.

"I will." She paused. "Mark, I'm nervous about court."

"I know. But don't worry, when you start testifying it'll be easier than you think. We'll practice and go over everything on Friday."

"Okay," she said, sounding uneasy.

I walked into Alec's office and took a seat across from his desk.

"Mark, it's a pleasure to see you. Welcome. Please make yourself at home."

"Thank you very much," I said in a courtly fashion. "Your hospitality and graciousness, as always, are appreciated. I've come because I need a favor from you."

"What's that?"

"I have a meeting at a law firm in Boston. My old firm, as a matter of fact."

"You do?"

I nodded. "For CDBG, and I'd like it if you came with me."

"What's it for? Why is it at your old firm?"

"The firm is representing the city. It's a meeting in which I hope I can settle the case."

"Sure, I'll go. But why do you want me there?"

"Because otherwise it'd be just me going, and the way they operate, I suspect they're going to have at least two lawyers there. I don't want them to think they're up against just me. They'll think I'm outmatched since I'm their former junior associate. Introducing another attorney makes it seem like it's a bigger operation on our end, and they don't know you. Don't worry, you won't have to do anything. All you have to do is just sit there."

Alec put his hands behind his head. "I like to take part in legal negotiations. It helps me develop professionally."

I chuckled. "Maybe you could make an exception this one time?" I explained that I had discovered the property transfer and planned to drop that bomb at the meeting.

"Wow, that's great," he said. "You don't usually get something like that in a case."

"Yeah, I know."

"So how are we working transportation considering that you live in Boston?"

"Actually, my situation has changed. Sara and I are apart. I'm living with my parents now until I figure things out." I felt a little awkward telling him that, since we generally didn't share many details about our personal lives.

"You are? Since when?"

"Since this past weekend."

"Sorry to hear that." He gave me a look of sympathy. "I don't mean to pry, but is it permanent?"

"Probably." My tone and body language were matter-of-fact, letting him know I really wasn't up to answering further questions. I felt afraid that if we stayed on the subject, my eyes might start to tear up, and I didn't want him to see me that way. I had been crying a lot since Sara and I broke up.

"Sorry," he said again.

"Thanks." I rose from my seat. "Umm, the meeting is next Wednesday. To answer your question, I'll drive us both ways."

24

I arrived at court at 8:30 A.M. on Monday feeling as nervous as ever. I only had a small cup of coffee that morning so I wouldn't have to go to the bathroom during the trial. For a change I ate a good breakfast of yogurt and cereal, forcing it down even though my stomach felt uneasy. There had been times when I had eaten an insubstantial breakfast and, late in the morning at court, felt light-headed and distracted. That was something I couldn't afford to have happen on this day.

I sat down on one of the benches in the nearly empty lobby and tried to clear my mind, figuring it would be counterproductive to review my file for the umpteenth time. I knew the case backwards and forwards, and, at this point, trying to cram in more information wasn't going to be helpful. I bounced my knee up and down and looked straight ahead, not focusing on anything in particular. Anna wasn't there yet, and I hoped that she'd show up soon and that Miguel would be with her. While she had showed up at my office on Friday for a prep session, Miguel had been a no-show.

At 8:45 a.m. Merola and Jeannie entered the lobby together. I grew more and more nervous that Anna wasn't going to come on time. Ten minutes later she arrived with Miguel trailing slightly behind, and I breathed a sigh of relief. She looked presentable dressed in black pants, a light purple blouse, and a leather jacket. Miguel wore baggy jeans and a black t-shirt underneath a heavy winter coat, an outfit I wouldn't have hand-picked for him.

"Sorry we're late," Anna said.

I gathered from the look she gave Miguel that he had been at fault. We huddled together to quickly prepare. Because I had already spent an hour with Anna preparing her testimony, my prep focused on Miguel. After all, he was the most important witness of the two of them.

"I'm going to call you first," I told him, "and then you," I said, gesturing to Anna. I looked directly at Miguel. "On direct examination, I ask open-ended questions and you do most of the talking. It'll be like, where were you? What did you do next? That type of thing. I ask basic questions, you do most of the talking. But listen to my questions carefully so you know where I'm heading with them. Cross-examination is different. You still listen carefully to the questions, but you answer them more simply and more to the point without volunteering any other information. Don't argue and don't get combative, even if you feel irritated at the attorney. And he can be irritating. Basically, on cross you don't have to score on any points, but rather just play it safe and try to avoid any damage being done. I can always ask you questions on re-direct if I need you to clarify anything."

Anna had her arms folded tightly across her chest, like a person standing outside in the cold.

"Are you all right?" I asked her.

She didn't respond.

"Anna?"

"I don't know if I can do it," she said, her voice quivering.

"What's the matter?"

"The last time I testified in court ..." Her voice choked up. "The last time was when their father was killed. I don't want to go in there."

Shit, I thought. It hit me that I should've seen this coming. She had expressed nervousness all along and I had dismissed it as a typical case of the jitters. I had *heard* her but I hadn't *listened* to her.

"You can do it, Anna," I reflexively told her, not knowing how else to approach the problem except to be positive and supportive. "I know it's hard, but it's important and you'll be able to do it."

Shaking her head, she muttered, "I can't. I can't."

John, the court officer, came into the lobby. "Time to enter the courtroom," he announced.

Out of the corner of my eye I saw Merola and Jeannie Roberts walk through the glass doors.

"Listen, Anna, I'll lead you with questions and you just answer them, okay?"

She nodded her head only slightly, and it was unclear to me if she would follow me into the courtroom.

"It'll be like when you taught me salsa. One person leads and the other follows. Okay?"

"Okay," she responded, this time nodding her head with a little more confidence.

I gestured towards the courtroom. "Let's go in there, okay?"

Just then I saw a police officer walk past us and through the glass doors. He appeared to be in his mid-forties and had a buzz cut. Sergeant DelVecchio, I assumed.

"It's time," John told me.

"Okay, we're coming," I responded.

I turned to Anna and gave her a look that communicated it was now or never. Tentatively, she turned in the direction of the glass doors and then walked towards them.

Seated at counsel table with Anna, waiting for Judge McCarthy to enter the courtroom, I felt calmer than I expected, which I attributed to the enormous amount of preparation I had put into the case. It took some of the pressure off to know the case backwards and forwards. Suddenly I remembered how a partner at my old firm used to say that a trial was the purest form of combat. He seemed to relish making that statement, as if trying a case was a mark of manliness. I never understood his perspective and never looked at it that way. I saw a trial as a place of danger where my client could get hurt, especially now that I was a tenant lawyer. All I wanted to do was to keep a roof over my client's head, and when I went into the courtroom to try a case a possible outcome was that my client could end up homeless.

Soon Judge McCarthy entered the courtroom and Merola got his case underway by calling Jeannie to the witness stand. Through her testimony Merola established that Anna lived at George Washington, and he introduced into evidence her lease, which indicated that Miguel was a household member. The lease was a few years old and was annually updated with recertification forms, all of which he had Jeannie identify.

"Is there a recertification process for the lease in this case?" Merola inquired.

"Yes."

"What is that?"

"The tenant comes to the housing authority and has to sign this form. Tenants are supposed to tell us about changes in income and also if there are changes in household composition."

"Did that happen in this case?"

"Yes, the tenant came to us last July."

"Were there any changes to the household composition?"

"No, there were not."

"Who were the tenants, then, at that time, according to the form?"

"Anna Rivera and her two sons, Miguel and David."

"And how long is the recertification form in effect for in this case?"

"One year. Until this coming July."

Merola then asked Jeannie to explain how she had learned about Miguel's arrest and how it had served as the basis for the eviction, having her read aloud the relevant section of the lease. Then he ended his examination.

When I stood up to begin my cross-examination, I noticed Jeannie curl her upper lip with disgust. Man, she really hated me. Good, I thought. If she is at all emotional during cross, it might detract from her poise and concentration. Then again, I realized, it hardly mattered; her testimony was pretty much inconsequential to the case. Judge McCarthy would accept that Miguel was a household member of Anna's apartment, based on the lease and recertification form. And the remaining question would be whether he had actually been engaged in illegal drug activity, something she wasn't a witness to.

I started off by having her admit that she wasn't present at the recertification and didn't have first-hand knowledge about what questions were asked, or if Anna had reviewed the form carefully before signing it. I next got her to admit that she had never personally observed Miguel engage in any drug activity, and, in fact, had never seen him at Washington. When I was finished, Merola didn't have any re-direct.

His next witness was Sergeant DelVecchio. He walked to the stand and took his seat in a casual manner, as if he had testified a hundred times in the past, which was probably the case. Merola ran through DelVecchio's education and experience: regular patrol officer duty, followed by an assignment in the gang unit, then duty in the vice squad, where he had been a sergeant for the past six years.

"Do you have experience in your job arresting people for illegal drug activity?" Merola asked him.

"Yes, plenty. I've arrested hundreds of people for drug offenses: possession, distribution, you name it."

"Now, you arrested Miguel Rivera at the Rite-Mart on January 5 of this year, right?"

"That's correct."

"Can you please tell the court what you were doing earlier that day before the arrest?"

DelVecchio put his hand to his mouth and cleared his throat. "Officer Sullivan and I had a guy named Joe Sanchez under surveillance. We had information from a confidential source that he was a drug dealer. This was in the afternoon that we had him under surveillance, and we were waiting outside his apartment in an unmarked car."

"Where was his apartment?"

"Queen Street," DelVecchio said.

"So then what happened?"

"Our confidential source made a phone call to the subject, Sanchez, that he wanted to buy drugs—"

I was on my feet. "Objection, Your Honor, and move to strike. That's hearsay."

Judge McCarthy sustained my objection.

"Let me ask it this way. Did you speak to the informant about his phone call to Sanchez?"

"Yes."

"What was said?"

Again I was on my feet with the same objection, and again it was sustained by the judge.

"Did you have any conversation with the informant where you told him to do something?" Merola asked.

"Yes, I told him to call Sanchez to set up a deal."

"Okay. What happened next?"

"Well, like I said, we were outside the apartment, and Sanchez eventually came out and got in his car and we followed him."

"What type of car was it?"

"A black Lexus. A recent model."

I looked at Judge McCarthy to see if he was reacting to this piece of information, but I was unable to tell.

"Where did the Lexus go?" Merola inquired.

"It went to Williams Street where it picked up one Miguel Rivera."

"Do you see Mr. Rivera in this courtroom today?"

"Yes, I do." DelVecchio pointed over my shoulder directly at Miguel who was seated in the gallery, leaning backward in a way that seemed too relaxed for my taste. "He's right over there." Suddenly Miguel straightened up a little.

"What happened when Mr. Sanchez got to Williams Street? Did he get out of his car?"

"No, he stayed in his car, and Mr. Rivera came out of his place and got into it."

"Then where did they go?"

"They drove directly to the Rite-Mart on Worcester Center Boulevard."

"When did they arrive at the Rite-Mart?"

DelVecchio asked if he could read the police report, and Merola had him authenticate it. DelVecchio looked at it for a moment, then raised his head and said, "Two-forty-three p.m."

Merola had been standing behind the counsel table and now he took a few steps to the side. "What happened at the Rite-Mart?"

"Sanchez pulled into the parking lot, then we pulled in right after him. The informant had instructions from me to buy heroin and we had given him one hundred dollars in marked bills. There was a drug deal between the informant and the occupants of the car."

I rose to my feet. "Objection, Your Honor. He can't say there was a drug deal involving people in the car, since there were two people, and he hasn't laid a proper foundation."

Judge McCarthy sustained the objection and told Merola to go through what happened step-by-step. I was surprised that Judge McCarthy was ruling in my favor with respect to my objections, since he usually was annoyed by them.

"What did the informant do after Sanchez and Rivera arrived in the parking lot, so far as you observed?"

"He approached the driver's side of the black Lexus."

"Did you have a full view of this?"

"Yes, I did. We were parked behind them in the lot close by."

"Okay. And Mr. Sanchez was on the driver's side?'

"Yes."

"How about Mr. Rivera?"

"He was sitting on the passenger side."

"What happened next?"

"I could see something switch between their hands, the informant and Sanchez, and it appeared to me to be packets that are the type used for heroin, and I saw money go from the informant to Sanchez. Officer Sullivan and I got out of our car and ran over and apprehended the suspects in the car. We found the one hundred dollars in marked bills on Mr. Sanchez, along with fifty dollars in regular bills, and the informant carried five packets of a substance later found to be heroin from the exchange."

"Did you see the substance at the time?"

"Yes, I did," answered the sergeant. "It was a white powder that I examined and recognized as heroin through my training and experience."

"You were able to recognize heroin?"

"Yes, I've seen heroin hundreds of times. I've seen fake stuff, too. This was real."

I objected to this but the judge overruled me. In drug cases he never required more proof than an officer's conclusion that the substance seized was a certain type of illegal drug.

"What else did you find?" Merola inquired.

"Mr. Rivera had two hundred dollars on himself. We performed a search of the car and found seven additional packets of heroin in the center arm rest of the car along with three plastic bags on the passenger side floor."

"Are plastic bags used in the drug trade, to your knowledge?"

"They are. They're used to package drugs."

I happened to notice Judge McCarthy pop a mint into his mouth. Shit, I thought, that's never a good sign. In a typical eviction case, it generally signaled that he had already reached a decision and was bored.

Merola finished up by having DelVecchio give a brief account of how he placed Sanchez and Miguel under arrest and transported them to the police station for booking.

When it was my turn to ask questions, I stood up with my legal pad in hand. It contained an outline of my cross and also some notes I had just scribbled down during the direct. I was suddenly a little nervous. Conducting a cross-examination of a police officer was not an easy task, and DelVecchio came off as a confident witness.

"Sergeant DelVecchio, this informant you've testified about is not in court today, correct?"

"No, he was scared to come."

"Objection, Your Honor," I said, "and move to strike. The witness can't testify to the informant's state of mind or to why he didn't come here."

"Sustained." Judge McCarthy turned in the direction of the witness stand. "Sergeant DelVecchio, you can only testify to matters within your own personal knowledge."

"You know the informant through the drug scene in Worcester, right?" I inquired.

"Yes."

"The informant, in fact, is a known drug user, right?"

"Yeah."

"He's been in trouble with the law before, right?"

"Yes, he has," DelVecchio admitted willingly.

"You didn't instruct him to call Mr. Rivera, right?"

"No."

"So far as you know, Mr. Rivera only came on the scene when Mr. Sanchez picked him up, correct?"

The sergeant nodded. "I suppose."

"Meaning, he was not an intended target of this operation, was he?"

"Not formally, no."

"Not formally?" I asked incredulously.

Sergeant DelVecchio shifted in his seat a little uncomfortably.

"The first time he came into the picture was when Sanchez went and picked him up, right?" I looked expectantly at him for an answer.

"Yes."

"And isn't it true that you had no indication that would happen beforehand?"

DelVecchio paused. "That's correct," he said.

My nervousness had disappeared a few questions back, and I was beginning to feel a surge of energy. "Now, Mr. Sanchez and Mr. Rivera arrived in the Rite-Mart parking lot at two-forty five, right?"

Merola was up on his feet. "I object, Your Honor. According to the police report, they arrived in the parking lot at two-forty-three."

I turned to him. "All right, Mr. Merola, I'll give you your two minutes."

"Well, it's not two-forty-five."

"You can have your *two minutes*, Mr. Merola. In fact, we can even call them the Merola minutes."

Judge McCarthy chuckled and so did John, the court officer, who was standing off to the side. Merola shook his head, knowing he'd been bested, and then took his seat, saying in a barely audible voice, "I made my point."

I turned back to DelVecchio. "Shortly after they arrived, you saw the exchange take place between the informant and Mr. Sanchez?"

"Yes."

"But you didn't see Mr. Rivera make any exchange with the informant, right?"

"Not that I observed."

"You didn't find any marked bills on Mr. Rivera, did you?"

"No."

"And you testified that the informant had packets of heroin on himself after the deal?"

"Yes."

"You didn't search him before the deal, did you?"

"No."

"Did you see anyone search him before the deal?"

"No."

"You don't know if he had any heroin on his person before he engaged in the deal, isn't that true?"

"No, I don't know that. But I don't know why he would if he's participating in a sting with us."

"Move to strike everything after the first sentence as non-responsive and argumentative," I said.

"Sustained," Judge McCarthy ruled.

I looked down at my notes again. I was just about to wrap up my cross.

"The other heroin packets, they were found in the armrest, right?"

"Yes."

"Not in plain view, right?"

"Not in plain view," DelVecchio confirmed.

"The plastic bags. What size were those?"

"Like sandwich bags."

"That's not the size used for drug deals involving heroin, right? What I mean is, small packets are used for heroin, correct?"

"That's correct, but plastic bags of this size are used for other drugs, like marijuana."

"Okay. Did you find marijuana in the car or on Sanchez or Mr. Rivera?"

"No, I did not."

"Do you have plastic bags at home?"

Merola sprang to his feet. I looked over at Judge McCarthy, and it was immediately apparent to me that he was not pleased with my question. "I'll withdraw the question, Your Honor. No further questions."

Merola announced that the presentation of the plaintiff's case was complete. Now it was my turn to put forth Anna's defense. I called Miguel as my first witness. My rationale was that if he turned out to be a poor witness, it was better to have him over and done with sooner rather than later. I also thought that because Anna was a sympathetic figure, she might make a more lasting impression on the judge if she testified last. I started off by leading Miguel through some introductory matters, and his demeanor was calm and cool, too much so for my liking.

"Now you've heard testimony that you're listed on your mother's lease," I said. "Where do you live?"

"I stay with my girlfriend a lot of the time, sometimes with friends. I only used to stay with my mother about one night every week or two weeks or something. Sometimes even longer. I was hardly ever there, you know. I don't go there no more, either, because of all this trouble."

"Was this true at or around the time of your arrest in January?"

"Yeah."

"You heard testimony that Joe Sanchez picked you up on the day of your arrest. Is that true that he did that?"

"Yeah."

"Where did he pick you up at?"

"It was at my girlfriend's place on Williams Street."

"How did he get in touch with you?"

"He called me on my cell phone."

"What was the substance of that conversation?"

"The substance?"

I nodded. "Yes, the substance. What did you say, what did he say?"

"He just said he was going to the mall to get a hat, and did I want to come with him? I had nothing else to do so I said yes."

"Was anything mentioned about drugs?"

Miguel shook his head. "No."

"Did you have any knowledge that Mr. Sanchez was involved in drug dealing?"

"No, I didn't."

"How did you know him?"

"We were just friends."

"How did you end up at the Rite-Mart?"

"On the way, he said he wanted to get a drink and that he had to meet someone, and I didn't ask nothing about it. We got to the parking lot, then all of a sudden the guy comes to his window and the cops, they were in plain clothes, they were all over us. It happened just like that. I didn't know what was happening."

"Did a drug deal happen?"

"I mean, the guy came to the window and he gave some money to Sanchez and then Sanchez slipped him something. I couldn't see what it was, since I didn't have a good view. Of course now I know." Miguel shook his head as if regretting what had happened.

"You were found with two hundred dollars. Is that true?"

"Something like that."

"Where did you get that money?"

"I work sometimes, not steady or anything, but I get jobs through a labor for a day type service. I'd been paid and I don't have a bank account, so I had cash."

Right before Merola began his cross he looked as if he was relishing what was about to come, and that worried me. I feared that he would outmatch Miguel and inflict damage. Watching the cross-examination of a witness like Miguel, whose testimony was vulnerable, sometimes felt like driving a little too fast on a snow-covered road in that you were at risk of suddenly losing control at any moment and going off the road.

"I have a few questions," Merola said in a cocksure manner. "Do you usually carry that much money on you? Two hundred dollars?"

"Not always, but sometimes."

"What was your job that you earned that money for?" Merola's voice was taunting, implying that he didn't believe Miguel's story for a second.

"I was doing some construction. I was a helper."

"Are you doing that now?"

"No."

"How long had you been doing it before the arrest?"

"I don't know. Not long."

"What company did you work for?"

"I don't remember. I've worked for so many different ones," he answered, not sounding very convincing.

"You don't remember?" Merola asked, raising his eyebrows.

"No," Miguel answered tersely.

"Mr. Rivera, what does your friend, Mr. Sanchez, do for a living?"

"He's not my friend any longer."

"My question is, what did he do for work at the time of the arrest?"

Miguel shrugged. "I don't know."

"You don't know what he did for work?" Merola asked, looking around the courtroom as if to emphasize his disbelief.

Miguel just shrugged.

"Well, how long did you know him for?"

"I don't know for sure."

"Well, you didn't meet him a week before the arrest, did you?"

"No, I didn't," Miguel replied with a little irritation.

"So you knew him for some time, that's fair to say?"

Miguel straightened up in his seat. "Yeah, you could say that."

"And you never asked if he worked? Or what he did?"

"I don't remember it coming up."

"Okay, now he was driving a newer model black Lexus, right?'

"Yeah."

"How did he afford it? Do you know?"

I stood up. "Objection. How is whether or not the witness knows if Mr. Sanchez could afford the car at all relevant?"

Judge McCarthy overruled me. "Please answer the question, sir," he instructed Miguel.

"I don't know," Miguel answered.

"So your friend Sanchez, you didn't know what he did for a job or how he was able to afford a Lexis?"

"That's right," Miguel replied in a steely voice. Meanwhile, I felt my insides tighten like they were in a vise.

"Mr. Sanchez picked you up in his new Lexus to go buy a hat at the mall, is that right?"

Miguel nodded.

"You have to verbalize your answer," Judge McCarthy instructed.

"Yes," Miguel said.

"But you didn't have any intention of buying anything at the mall when you got into his car, did you?"

"I might have bought something there, I might not have. I don't know."

"But you didn't have anything specific in mind, did you?"

"I don't remember."

"You pled guilty to possession of marijuana a few years back, correct?"

Instantly I was on my feet with an objection, though I knew I would lose this one.

"No, I'll allow it," Judge McCarthy said, waving me off. "The witness will answer the question."

"I did," Miguel admitted, his jaw tightening. He looked noticeably uncomfortable, like he wanted to get off the witness stand immediately.

"So you've used drugs in the past?"

Miguel hesitated.

"You have, haven't you?" Merola asked.

"Yes."

"But we are to believe that you weren't involved with them when you were arrested by the police with a drug deal going down?"

Again I was on my feet. "Objection, Your Honor. Argumentative. We've been down this road and this is purely argumentative."

"Sustained," Judge McCarthy ruled. "Mr. Merola, let's move on."

"You stay with your girlfriend and stay with friends, too, right? That's what you testified to?"

"Yeah."

"What proof of address do you have with you today that you live anywhere else but with your mother?"

"What proof?" Miguel asked.

"Yes, a license, credit card, a bill?" Merola gestured dramatically by raising his hands up in front of himself.

Merola was doing the same thing he had done to Maria Roman's boyfriend. He knew that a lot of these young Latino guys in Worcester, whose lives were based out of the slums and projects, who lived on the margins of society, didn't have any bills in their name or any proof of address.

"I don't have that stuff."

"You have a license?"

"Yeah, but I never changed the address on it."

"It's your mother's address, isn't it?"

"I don't even know."

With a self-satisfied air, Merola announced that he had no further questions and took his seat. And he had good reason to be satisfied.

When I called Anna as my next witness she sat there looking straight ahead and it appeared that she wasn't going to move. I felt myself start to panic, not knowing how to deal with the situation, my insides clenching up. I was filled with relief when she got up and walked slowly and tentatively to the witness stand. After taking a seat, she folded her hands in her lap and appeared nervous and uncomfortable. I elicited some basic information from her—her name and address, that she worked part-time as a clerk at Wal-Mart and received SSI for anxiety and depression, and how long she had lived at George Washington.

"Who do you live with?" I inquired.

"My son, David."

"Is David here today?"

"No, he's in school."

"How old is he?"

"He's seventeen. He's a senior in high school."

I maintained eye contact with her with the hope that it would make the examination seem like it was just the two of us having a conversation. Although she still seemed nervous, she was less so than when we started.

"Does David have plans for college?" I asked.

Merola shot up from his seat like a firecracker had been lit underneath him. "Objection. Your Honor's ruling for the *motion in limine* precludes any testimony about this. Counsel has stepped over the line."

Judge McCarthy looked like he was pissed off.

"Your Honor, the motion only precludes testimony that if the tenants are evicted, David will lose his scholarship for college. It doesn't preclude me from asking if he has plans to go to college. In any event, I'll withdraw the question."

"Don't go there again, Mr. Langley," Judge McCarthy warned, wagging his finger at me.

It may have been a miscalculation on my part to have raised the subject of David's college plans, given the result of the *motion in limine* and that I had obviously irritated Judge McCarthy, but I felt it was necessary to remind him about the scholarship. What if he forgot about it?

"Your son, Miguel, did he live with you at the time of his arrest?" I inquired.

"No. He used to stay with me maybe one night every other week or so, but that was it."

"Does he live with you now?"

"No."

"How about staying over the once every other week or so. Does he still do that?"

"Not since his arrest. No."

"Miguel is on your lease, correct?"

Anna nodded, then turned to the judge and said, "He is. I just never took him off. I should've, but I just never did it."

I approached the witness stand and showed her the same recertification form that was referred to during Jeannie's testimony. "On here it has your signature, right?"

"Yes."

"And it lists here that you, Miguel and David lived in the apartment, right?"

"Yes."

"Did anyone ask you at recertification about changes in household composition?"

"I don't remember. I just remember signing the form. It was a very short process."

"When you signed the form, did you think or understand that you were saying Miguel lived with you?"

"No."

"Do you remember who was present for the housing authority during your recertification?"

"No."

"Why didn't you correct the form with the housing authority at some point to eliminate Miguel?"

"I just didn't think to. I never thought about that form again. I'm just not good with paperwork, you know."

"Was it explained to you, the recertification process? That is, did someone walk you through it to make sure everything was correct and accurate?"

"No, it was fast."

"Okay, I want to ask you about the day of the arrest. Did you see Miguel that day?"

"No."

Anna and I were maintaining good eye contact which, combined with her directly addressing Judge McCarthy, made me feel good about her as a witness. She had gotten into sort of a groove.

"Did you know what he was doing that day?"

"No, I hadn't seen him for a while at that point."

"How long?"

Anna shrugged. "Probably a week or two. You know, I don't really know. Miguel never saw me regularly or nothin'. He does what he does."

"Had you ever observed Miguel with drugs before the arrest?" I asked.

"No. Not me."

"Do you have any knowledge of your son using drugs?"

"No."

"He was arrested for marijuana when he was younger, right? You heard that testimony?"

"That was in high school. It was like three years ago or something. Yeah, I knew about it when it happened. It was a small amount, they told me. But I never saw him with that stuff."

I told Judge McCarthy that I had no further questions and took a seat. I felt pretty good about Anna's testimony. Her personality didn't completely shine through, but she had done well, giving all the right answers, and that was what counted most. When Merola rose from his seat and took a moment to appraise Anna, I felt myself tense up. Just get through this, I silently prayed. We're almost done.

"Ms. Rivera, we've established that Miguel was on your lease at the time of his arrest. You have to get recertified for your lease every year, right?"

"Yes, I do," Anna replied curtly.

"When you recertify, you're supposed to tell of changes in household composition, too, right? Who lives with you?"

"I don't remember that being asked."

"But isn't that was you're supposed to do?"

"I mean, I guess. I don't know. I just do what I'm told there. I don't know what their rules are."

"Ms. Rivera, I want to show you your lease." Merola approached the witness stand and handed it to her. "That's your signature on the last page, isn't it?"

Anna examined it and then looked up. "Yes, it is," she replied in a business-like manner.

"Now when you signed that lease, you agreed to its terms, didn't you?"

Anna looked confused.

"Didn't you?" Merola repeated, this time more sharply.

"Yes," she agreed.

Merola flipped through the pages of the lease. "And here doesn't it say that tenants, household members and guests are not to engage in drug activity on or near the premises?"

Anna looked at the page that Merola was showing her. It took her a little while to read it. Finally she looked up and said, "Yes."

Merola paused for a moment to collect his thoughts. "Ms. Rivera, I want to ask you about your son's arrest. We established that he was arrested for marijuana when he was in high school, right?"

Anna nodded. "Yeah."

"Did you ever ask him afterwards if he used illegal drugs?"

"No."

"Do you have evidence that afterwards he stopped?"

I objected to the question.

"Withdrawn," Merola told the judge. "No further questions."

Judge McCarthy looked over at me and I announced that I had a brief re-direct. I showed Anna the recertification form and asked her if the parts filled out aside from her signature were in her handwriting. I had wanted to ask her that during direct but had forgotten. She said they weren't, and I concluded my examination. Although I knew Judge McCarthy would ultimately determine that Miguel was on her lease, it was nonetheless a point I wanted to make.

"You're excused, ma'am," Judge McCarthy told Anna.

She walked back to our table and I whispered to her, "You did a good job."

In a way I was surprised that Merola had conducted such a short cross-examination of Anna, but then again, there was not much he could accomplish with her. She couldn't testify about the arrest since she wasn't there, and she had been firm that Miguel didn't live in her apartment. He had no evidence to impeach her with on that issue.

Lawyers typically did not deliver closing arguments to Judge McCarthy in eviction cases. After the testimony was concluded, his customary practice was to announce, "Parties waive closings" in a tone that clearly and unmistakably indicated it was much more a command than a question; yet on the trial transcript it would come out as a question. He would then wait for the parties to say yes before ending the case, making it impossible for a party to claim on appeal that he had denied them the right to make a closing argument.

I rose from my seat and asked if I could make a brief statement to the court. I used the word "statement" instead of "closing" because Frank Green had advised me that Judge McCarthy had a negative reaction to the word "closing."

Merola followed suit by also expressing an interest in making a statement.

Judge McCarthy seemed put-out by the request, but with a weary nod decided to indulge us.

Because he represented the plaintiff, Merola went first. Watching him in the brief moment before he began to speak, I realized that I didn't feel inferior to him with regard to my legal ability as I had in the past. This particular trial had been a game-changer for me. It was kind of like being in a fight with someone you're scared of, but then after trading a few blows and realizing you can stand toe-to-toe with the guy, your fear suddenly evaporates.

Merola said, "Your Honor, the evidence clearly shows that Mr. Rivera was involved in the drug deal. His friend, Joe Sanchez, was under surveillance, and when called to make a deal, the first thing he did was pick up Mr. Rivera. It was the first thing he did. Then they drove straight to make the deal. Sanchez picked up Mr. Rivera because they were both involved with the deal. That's the only reasonable explanation for it. Otherwise, why else bring him? Why else go straight to make the deal? This excuse that they were going to the mall to buy a hat just strains credulity, as does Mr. Rivera's claim that he didn't know Sanchez was a drug dealer. The police knew Sanchez was a drug dealer, since they had him under surveillance. But are we to believe Mr. Rivera didn't know? And keep in mind that these two men were good enough friends, apparently, to go shopping at the mall together in the middle of the day, if we are to believe Mr. Rivera's testimony. Yet he didn't know? It's just not believable. He doesn't know how Sanchez, a known drug dealer, came to have a new Lexus, either? It's just not believable.

"At the Rite-Mart the heroin deal goes down, which there is no dispute about, and drugs are found in the car. Mr. Sanchez has the marked bills and Mr. Rivera has two hundred dollars on him. Two hundred. That's drug dealer money, plain and simple.

"All the housing authority has to show in this case, by a preponderance of the evidence, is that Mr. Rivera was engaged in illegal drug activity at the Rite-Mart. I submit that's been done. Furthermore, it doesn't matter if Ms. Rivera was ignorant of her son's activities, which Mr. Langley has been trying to show. She had him on her lease, and as a legal resident of George Washington, he engaged in drug activity. According to the lease, this warrants an eviction. It's that simple. It should also be noted—and this is significant—that while Mr. Langley has tried to show that Mr. Rivera didn't live with his mother, there has been no real evidence introduced that he has another address.

"Also, as has been established in the motion to dismiss hearing, the Rite-Mart is on or near the premises of George Washington. I won't go over those details again with the court, so as not to waste time, and I know the testimony of the witnesses didn't address it—"

Judge McCarthy interrupted, "You can move on Mr. Merola. I've already made my ruling on that particular issue."

Merola touched the tips of his fingers together. "The housing authority is in the business of trying to provide safe and decent housing for the low-income people in Worcester. Drugs tear public housing projects apart and destroy communities. It's a battle for the housing authority to keep drugs out of public housing projects. A battle. By having Mr. Rivera on her lease, the tenant here makes the public housing complex a more dangerous place. It makes for a tougher battle. If the housing authority doesn't bring eviction cases in these situations, it sends a message that it's okay to be involved with drugs. It says it's okay to have drug dealers in your apartment or on your lease as long as you turn a blind eye. The housing authority simply cannot permit people who engage in drug activity to live there. It simply can't."

Merola sat down and placed his folded hands in front of him on the table. In my opinion he gave a masterful performance. His analysis of the issues was very sharp, and he ended by highlighting the emotional appeal of his case which up until that point had largely been ignored. Now it seemed to suddenly cast a large shadow over the proceedings.

I rose to my feet knowing I would have to deliver a really good closing if I wanted to stay in the game with Merola. Like Merola I wasn't using any notes.

"The housing authority has not proven that Miguel Rivera was involved in the drug deal. He was just in the wrong place at the wrong time. Mr. Merola has to prove it—it's his burden of proof— but the facts are clear that Miguel was never seen with drugs in his possession, nor did he have the marked bills used in the deal on him. There's been no witness testimony that he was part of the deal or otherwise had advance knowledge of it. Even Sergeant DelVecchio said that Miguel was not a target of his operation. He was in the wrong place at the wrong time, and Mr. Merola has not met his burden of proof of showing otherwise.

"Mr. Merola claims that it's not credible that Miguel was going to the mall with Sanchez who was going to buy a hat. But people go to the mall just to hang out, to shop, to do whatever. People go to the mall with a lot less purpose than Miguel Rivera did that day. If we think about it, if the story about going to the mall is a fiction, wouldn't it sound better if Miguel at least testified that he had plans to buy something, especially given that he had money on him? If it's a manufactured story, it wasn't manufactured very well. Miguel could have said he was going to shop for something, but he didn't say that because it wasn't the truth. And he is telling the truth—that a friend asked him to go to the mall and he said yes. Again, he was in the wrong place at the wrong time.

"The two hundred dollars that he had—he testified that it was from work. It's not like he was carrying a thousand dollars. He had been paid and he doesn't have a bank account, so he had the money on his person. Carrying two hundred dollars doesn't make someone a drug dealer. If we infer that someone committed a crime because he has two hundred dollars in his pocket, well, then, we'll have a lot of criminals out there.

"Another important fact here is that the drugs were concealed in the center console of the car. They weren't out in the open, so there's no evidence that Miguel saw the drugs at any point before the deal happened. Again, Mr. Merola hasn't met his burden of proof here. Rather, guilt by association is the theory he's proceeding under. I would also like to point out that one thing we know for sure is this: whether or not Miguel was a participant in the drug deal, Anna Rivera—" I pointed directly at her—"and her son, David, did nothing wrong. They did absolutely nothing wrong. There is no evidence that Anna even knew where Miguel was that day. Yet they will be evicted here, and public housing is very important to them. It's the difference between having a roof over their heads and being out on the street.

"Mr. Merola calls this a battle against drugs. I ask, if there is a battle, why target innocent people in that battle? This one-strike law is so very harmful when used without discretion. It leads to collateral damage that irrevocably harms the lives of innocent people. Anna Rivera and her son, David, are real people who will face severe consequences if they are evicted. Evicting them won't hurt Miguel, since he doesn't live in the apartment, and it won't make George Washington a safer place. Mr. Merola talks about sending a message. What kind of message is an eviction here? An eviction is just collateral damage. If this is a battle, then why do Anna and David have to be the casualties?"

I took my seat and gazed downward at the grainy pattern in the wood table top. It swirled around in my vision, coming in and out of focus. A moment later I was back on my feet when John commanded us to rise when Judge McCarthy left the bench. I watched him lumber out of the courtroom with the court file in his hand. It felt strange to realize that the case was over, and it was now up to the judge to decide the result. It also made me feel uneasy that one man could have that kind of power over others. But I had created the situation by withdrawing the jury request.

"So what do you think?" Miguel asked when we were out in the lobby.

"You both did well," I said.

"Now we just see what the judge does?" Anna asked.

"I'll get the decision in the mail, probably in a few days. When I do I'll call you right away."

Miguel reached out to shake my hand. "Thanks for helping my mom and brother."

"You're welcome." I felt discombobulated, as if my mind was running in a hundred different directions.

Anna looked up at me with solemn eyes. "Thanks, Mark. I know you worked really hard. You did a good job in there, too. I can't thank you enough."

"You're welcome," I said again.

We stood across from one another for an awkward moment, and then she stepped forward and hugged me. I stood in her grasp not knowing exactly how to react, and after a moment passed, I put my arms around her and hugged her back.

That evening it actually felt good to go home to my parents' house, especially since a home-cooked meal was waiting for me on the table. During dinner I had two glasses of red wine which took the edge off. Because we had the trial to talk about our dinner conversation was much more fluid than usual, though I did get a little impatient with my mother when she asked if a tenant could really get evicted because someone else named on the lease had gotten arrested in a drug deal off the premises. I specifically remembered talking to her about that topic in the past.

After dinner my father went into the living room to watch TV, and I helped my mother load the dishwasher. She seemed pleased to have help and to have someone to talk to. She talked to me about my sister's children and remarked that my sister might bring them to the house that coming weekend. I realized that I hadn't seen them for a few months. I should see them more often, I thought.

After we finished, I went up to my bedroom and shut the door in order to block out the noise from the TV. I missed Sara just then, and wished I was with her back in our apartment. I wished that I could tell her about the trial, too. I could picture myself giving her a blow-by-blow account of the testimony and her following along with interest. She was the only person I confided in about the nervousness and anxiety I felt when I went to court. And she was the only person in my personal life who would truly understand the significance of the trial to both me and Anna and David.

25

I pulled into the driveway of a two-story Cape located only about a mile away from where my parents lived. It was the first time I had ever been to Alec's house. He's living fairly well as a legal services attorney, I thought, no doubt due to the fact that his wife has a good job as an accountant.

There were hardwood floors throughout the house and a good-sized living room with a large flat-screen television. I pictured Alec lounging on the couch watching his beloved Patriots on Sunday afternoons in the fall. Standing in the foyer waiting for him while he got ready for our trip to Boston, it seemed strange that after two years of chumming around at work, this was my first visit to his house. Now that I was living near him, I imagined that he could be a friend I visited often, like how sitcom friends always dropped by to visit for no apparent reason. At the same time, I knew that wasn't going to happen. His wife and kids kept him busy, he saw his parents frequently, and when it came to a social life, he had friends from childhood he was still close with. There wasn't enough room in his life to add me as a friend outside of work, even if he wanted to. In any case, I think he was just fine with the status quo.

He appeared at the top of the stairs dressed in a dark gray suit and a tie that instantly drew my attention; it had pink and blue streaks that brought to mind a Hawaiian sunset.

"C'mon Alec, you need to change your tie," I said somewhat desperately.

"Why? What's the matter?"

"You need a more conservative tie. Do you have a maroon one or something?"

"This tie is perfect."

"Alec, please," I beseeched him. "Can you change it."

He smiled broadly. "I'm just fucking with you."

"Bastard," I said.

"Wow, you were really nervous."

"Yeah," I said. "This is a big deal."

The weather was in the mid-fifties and the sun shone brightly on the drive to Boston. We talked during the ride, mostly about work, until before I knew it up ahead of us was the famous Citgo sign marking the location of Fenway Park. Since I had been away for a while, entering the city felt electrifying, almost like a new experience. Thinking about how Sara was somewhere in it, perhaps at the real estate office or out showing apartments or in our apartment, I began to feel sad. Keep her out of your mind, I told myself. You have important work to do.

We took the Copley Square exit, went through the Back Bay and then around the Boston Common. My old firm was located in a high rise just past the State House. I began to feel anxious about how I would perform at the meeting. Just the thought of walking into the firm and seeing secretaries and paralegals and lawyers I used to work with made me feel uneasy. They all knew the circumstances surrounding my leaving the firm, and I was sure they'd all whisper about me to one another when they saw me.

We parked in a garage on Cambridge Street and began walking in the direction of the firm. The Starbucks at Government Center, where I used to go regularly, was up ahead, and I told Alec that I wanted to stop in to get a cup of coffee. I remembered the countless times I had gone there at 6 or 7 p.m. to get a caffeine boost to power me for the next two or three hours of work.

"Jesus Christ, you and that yuppie coffee," he remarked.

"It's good stuff. Plus I never get to drink it living in Worcester. There's only one Starbucks and it's on Park Ave. I have to take advantage."

I entered the Starbucks wondering if I would see any of the employees I used to know from the old days, but they were all unfamiliar faces. I ordered a vente bold drip coffee and we continued our walk to the firm. We checked in at the security desk and passed through the ornate marble lobby which had a granite fountain that propelled a single stream of water high into the air immediately followed by multiple lower-positioned sprinklers that shot with less force in different directions. As we were whisked up to the thirty-second floor in the elevator, which had gold-plated doors and a TV screen, Alec raised his eyebrows as if to say, fancy place.

The elevator doors opened and ahead of me was the familiar sight of the full-length glass doors of the firm's entrance. I could see the large waiting room just beyond filled with black leather furniture set apart in a contemporary fashion. I entered ahead of Alec and checked in with the receptionist, who hadn't worked there during my tenure. The view of Boston Harbor seemed more magnificent than I remembered. Man, I thought, it's so weird to be back. Alec and I stepped forward past the receptionist and both took a seat. Magazines, mostly financial in subject matter, and *The Wall Street Journal*, *The New York Times*, and *The Boston Globe* were laid out on black marble coffee tables. We sat down on adjacent black leather chairs. Alec massaged the arms of his chair and looked over at me. "Is this real Corinthian leather?" he said.

"Why don't you ask Ricardo Montalban?" I replied.

"Maybe I will." He reached into his bag and pulled out a worn copy of Gibbons' *The Decline and Fall of the Roman Empire*. "Nice view," he remarked while cracking open the book.

"Some light reading?"

"It's a classic."

"Yes, I know. I've heard of it."

He lowered the book. "We can learn much from the fall of the Roman Empire, considering that America has entered a similarly decadent period in its history and faces the threat of decline."

"People draw comparisons between the Roman Empire and every civilization that—" I cut myself short when out of the corner of my eye I saw Mary Mitchell, a long-time associate at the firm. She noticed me, too, and stopped walking to do a double-take. Her eyes widened when she recognized that it was me. Mary was a lesbian in her late-thirties or early-forties who lived in Cambridge with her partner. I always liked her because she was one of the few associates who didn't drink the kool-aid at the firm. For her, working there was simply a job that paid the bills.

"Mark, what are you doing here?"

I rose from my seat. "It's good to see you."

I was about to make a move to her hug her, but then decided not to. I didn't want to put her in an awkward position, caught in an embrace with me, the guy who got fired for sabotaging an important firm case.

"I never thought I'd see you here again. What's going on?"

"It's for a case. I have a case against Chris Bloom."

"You do? Wow, the two of you. I can't imagine that. What for?"

I gave her the thirty-second version of the case.

"That's interesting. Well, I wish you luck, although I probably shouldn't." She rolled her eyes.

We talked for another minute and then she said, "I'd better get back to work. You know how it is here."

"All too well."

We both chuckled.

"Well, it was good seeing you," she said.

"You too."

My pulse quickened a few minutes later when the receptionist led us to conference room C-1, located just past the reception area. It was one of the larger conference rooms. Seated at the far end of a long black marble conference table were Chris Bloom and Arnold Landers, a senior partner at the firm and chair of the litigation department. Chris had his head tilted towards Arnold and was saying something to him in a soft voice. When they noticed me and Alec, they ended their conversation and stood up to greet us.

I'm in over my head, I thought.

Arnold was one of the firm's leaders and was known for being one of the top litigators in the city. With his pleasant baritone and distinguished silver-haired appearance, he seemed custom-made for the courtroom. I had heard stories of his conducting three-week trials in federal court without the aid of notes. Attorneys often settled cases against him instead of trying them, fearing they could not match up against him in the courtroom. When I was at the firm I was a mere peon and he was like a God.

After we all sat down, Chris remarked to me, "Funny how we ran into each other just recently at Victoria's Secret in the Copley Place Mall. Did you end up buying those women's pants for yourself?"

Alec chuckled. During our ride together I had told him the story about running into Chris. Arnold also smiled which signaled to me that he was in on the joke.

"I'm still trying to make up my mind. It's a very difficult decision," I said with utmost gravity. "But I'll be sure to let you know."

Arnold clasped his hands together and placed them on the table. "The skywalk is an important project for the city of Worcester. My clients have an interest in trying to reignite the downtown area and the skywalk is part of their plan. Another thing it will do is bring jobs to the city which will benefit low and middle-income residents, since those are the people that will find employment. We're talking about jobs in the construction process and jobs afterwards with the hotel and the arena. Chris and I—" he gestured with his hand to Chris, who was looking at me intently—"have met with the city council and we've looked at some of the documents, and we think we have a strong case. The city council has always used the CDBG money appropriately in the past, and we think they are doing so now. Still, we'd like to avoid litigation so the city can go ahead with this, and we realize your clients have concerns, hence we're here and willing to talk."

"I'd like to see those documents," I said.

"Well, let's just talk now, which is what we're here for," Arnold replied.

"I have something—"

Putting his hand up in the air, Arnold interrupted me. "Let me cut to the chase. The city is prepared to offer some money to resolve this."

It surprised me that he was already putting money on the table, though I didn't expect it to be much.

"Ten thousand," he said. "You can pick the cause the money will go to. I imagine it could help some people."

"Or you can lose and get nothing," Chris predicted.

I was about to reject the offer but before I could do so Alec leaned forward and said, "Gentlemen." This surprised me, since I thought it had been clear that he was only present at the meeting to support me. I had a foreboding that what was going to come out of his mouth wasn't going to be good.

"In World War Two, before America became involved," he said, and suddenly I felt my stomach drop, "Mussolini presented Greece with the humiliating demand that it allow Italian troops to occupy strategic points within the country. This outraged the Greeks and they rejected Mussolini's demand. Against Hitler's advice, Mussolini decided to invade Greece, but the Greeks were energized to defend themselves, and in the end, they soundly defeated the Italians. Today a major holiday in Greece celebrates this event."

In the past I had heard Alec make references to Mussolini's actions toward Greece—it was one of the aspects of World War Two that he talked about most, along with the abject failure of the Maginot Line on the French-German border—but I had strong doubts about whether this was the proper setting for it.

"And what may I ask is your point?" Chris said.

"What I mean to say is, you can make an offer of ten thousand," Alec said, "but such an approach sometimes in the end only makes a situation worse."

"Well, that is all very entertaining." Arnold looked over at Chris. "But we've made our offer. If you're not willing to engage on reasonable terms, then there's nothing we can do but each go forward."

He was about to get up when I held up one finger and said, "There's one more thing you'll be interested in." I reached into my briefcase, pulled out a manila folder, and placed it on the table in front of me. "In fact, it's very interesting. Mr. Flanagan is the president of the city council and the construction company that is going to do the work is owned by John Miller, who happens to be a major landlord in the city. I went to the Registry of Deeds website and found something that you might want to see." I slid the folder across the table to them. "Miller transferred real estate to Flanagan for one hundred dollars. It's a recent transaction."

Chris examined the copy of the deed and, maintaining a poker face, gently pushed it over to Arnold who, after reviewing it, pursed his lips together, obviously troubled by it. Breaking the silence that seemed to dominate the room, Chris said, "This doesn't change the merits of the suit."

"This changes everything," I replied. "Arnold knows that. We want more than ten thousand. If you want to speak to your client, please do."

"Obviously this is new information," Arnold said in a measured tone. "We have to evaluate it."

I placed my hands on the arm rests of my chair and then stood up. "I'll wait to hear from you if you want to talk more. Just don't take too long."

I left the conference room with Alec trailing behind me, adrenaline pumping through my body. I could hardly believe that I had bested Arnold Landers and Chris Bloom in a negotiation.

"It went well, right?" I asked Alec on the elevator ride down. Of course I knew it had, but out of lingering insecurity I asked anyway.

"Yeah, it sure did," Alec confirmed.

"Arnold seemed to get it, right?"

"Oh yeah. Loud and clear."

The elevator doors opened and we walked into the lobby. "Mussolini and Greece?" I remarked, shaking my head. "Jesus Christ, you're like Pat Buchanan or something with your World War Two references."

"It was a horrible blunder by Mussolini, making such a humiliating demand. Greece actually gained a large area of southern Albania where Italian operations were based as a result."

"Jesus Christ," I muttered.

We walked back to the car. Still on a high from the meeting, I didn't want the day to end with a long drive back to Worcester and settling in for the night at my parents' house. I wanted to go out for a drink at a bar where there were young people, where I could hear music playing and look at attractive women and feel I was in the mix of things. I didn't want to try to pick up a girl or anything like that, not that I had any skills in that department, anyway. I was too emotionally raw and sensitive for that. I just wanted to be in a happening environment.

"Interested in having a drink?" I asked Alec.

"No, I should get back home. The wife is expecting me."

"Okay," I responded, as if it was no big deal. But I felt let down. Soon we were in my car on Storrow Drive, heading out of the city. I wondered when I would next return, and when I would go back to my apartment.

26

Three days later I was in the conference room doing an intake with a new client when Lucelia buzzed me on the intercom and told me in her clipped and unfriendly tone that Chris Bloom was on the line. Normally I had her put my calls into voice mail when I was meeting with a client, but this time I excused myself and took the call in my office.

"We're willing to offer two hundred thousand," Chris told me. "You can use that for whatever you want so long as it meshes with CDBG."

"Two hundred thousand isn't going to cut it."

"It's a risk for you to go up against this firm head-to-head. Two hundred is an awful lot of money, especially for community groups in Worcester."

"Look, we both know what the risks are. I'm really not interested in the two of us posturing."

"I don't know your position," Chris said with frustration. "You haven't made a demand, and I've offered two hundred thousand. That's a lot of money. You can't just tell me to keep offering you more money. Give me a demand."

I thought he made a fair point. Since he had put up a real number, it was indeed now incumbent upon me to give him one of my own, and it would have to be less than the full amount at stake. My only bargaining chip was the property transfer, and otherwise my case was pretty weak on the merits. If I demanded the full amount, our negotiations would end right there. Yesterday evening I had met with Father Kelly and the rest of the group in the church basement, and we had agreed to accept a bottom line of six hundred thousand. While the property transfer could get Miller and Flanagan into trouble criminally, the issue of whether or not it was a violation of CDBG rules to apply the funds to the skywalk was an altogether different matter.

"Nine hundred thousand," I told Chris.

He exhaled loudly. "I'll have to get back to you."

That evening when I was about halfway home to my parents' house, I muttered, "Oh, shit," out loud in my car, realizing that I had forgotten to inform the colonel about the recent CDBG developments. Since he was the litigation director in the office, not to mention my direct supervisor, it was a fairly significant oversight on my part. I wondered if he'd be upset about it or, for that matter, if he'd think that I should have demanded a higher amount or forced the city to come up with a higher figure before giving one of my own. And he might be pissed that we were negotiating a settlement, considering the corruption going on. He might think we should go straight to the authorities.

"What's up?" he said when I went into his office the next morning.

I took a seat in a chair across from his desk and explained what had happened so far with CDBG. He didn't seem bothered that I had begun negotiating and wasn't critical of my demand of nine hundred thousand, which was a relief. However, he did say, "We should probably report this to the U.S. Attorney."

"Yeah, but who knows what would happen at that point? The whole thing could unravel and we might never see the money. It's a slush fund, so HUD might want it back for all we know. Criminal investigations take a long time, so this could be hung up for a while, and then an indictment might not even be sought. Or if a criminal case was brought and was ultimately successful, the money could just end up going in some other direction. The U.S. Attorney won't care if the money is used properly. They'll only care about getting a conviction." I paused. "All I'm saying is that we have control now, but we might lose control."

The colonel leaned back in his chair. "I think we have to tell the authorities, though."

"We're in settlement talks so we're close to wrapping this up. There's no obligation in a civil suit when there is possible criminal wrongdoing that you have to put the civil suit on hold. And we both know you can't use a threat of criminal action to obtain a settlement in a civil action."

"Which we've come very close to doing."

"Correct, which I pretty much did do." I paused. "How about if we send a letter to the U.S. Attorney and at the same time just see if I can wrap this up?"

"I've never been in this situation before."

"And what if they demand we keep quiet with a confidentiality clause?" I said, thinking out loud.

"We'd never sign it. It might be unenforceable, anyway, given the subject matter. We're talking about federal funds. Besides, if we send out the letter now, that would be something of a moot point."

We both sat there without speaking, mulling over the complexity of the situation.

"So, anyway, what do you think about a settlement figure? We all came up with a bottom line of six hundred."

"Six sounds fine. You do know that there would have to be court approval of all of this, and it would have to oversee use of the funds. You can't just take that much money and use it for what you want."

"Yeah, I know," I said, even though I hadn't thought that far ahead. I left the colonel's office with the understanding that I could proceed with settlement talks, even though he didn't explicitly grant me permission to.

The following afternoon I received a call from Chris Bloom. He made an offer of $400,000 and I flatly told him that I couldn't accept that amount. After going back-and-forth with him a bit, I told him that I could probably settle the matter for $750,000—thinking that by giving him that number I could ultimately get something over $600,000 out of him. He said he'd check with his client and get back to me. The next day he called me and we resolved the case for $700,000. He tried to push a confidentiality agreement, but I said it wasn't an option, given that government money was at issue. Although it was apparent that he desperately wanted the agreement, he backed off when I resisted. He knew that a court would never accept such an agreement when government funds were involved. I also told him that a confidentiality agreement could make both me and his firm liable for obstruction of justice if it was ever determined that the city council should be prosecuted. I had no idea if that was true or not, seeing that I wasn't a criminal lawyer, but then again, neither was he. In any event, what I said worked its intended purpose since it helped to get him to back off.

I didn't tell him that I had sent a letter to the U.S Attorney.

After putting the phone back in its cradle, I sat there thinking, wow, I can't believe this is over. It was the largest settlement I had ever obtained on my own. I thought about how the money could be used for the benefit of the population that I represented. After so many eviction cases where I just tried to keep my clients' heads above water, I had accomplished something that would affirmatively make a difference in their lives. Jubilantly rising from my chair, I went to see the colonel to tell him the news.

"That's good," he said, his voice rising only slightly. "That's good. Is that as high as they would go?"

"Yeah."

"Good," he said once again.

Next I called Father Kelly and told him the news. He reacted with joy. "We did it, Mark," he said. "We did it!"

"Yeah," I said, letting it all sink in. "We did, didn't we?"

27

That evening after dinner I stayed in my bedroom reading *Tis'* by Frank McCourt. I had meant to read it when it first came out but had never gotten around to it. He was one of my favorite authors, mostly because of his engaging voice and sharp sense of humor. Now that I didn't have to commute daily to and from Boston, I had more free time on my hands than I used to. Most days when I returned home from work, I spent my time upstairs in my room, either reading or on my laptop. If I closed the door and tried hard enough, I could almost fool myself into thinking I was living on my own.

My body felt pleasantly relaxed from my three-mile jog after work. It had been a warmer day than usual, and I much preferred running outside to being indoors on the treadmill. Running on pavement gave me a better workout, and it was more interesting to cover a distance on foot with the scenery passing by. I missed my old routes in Boston, running down Commonwealth Avenue or along the Charles River. I was trying to save money for a new place of my own, understanding that I wouldn't be able to afford to live in Boston without a roommate. I was torn about whether to do that or get my own place in Worcester. I absolutely hated the idea of having a roommate, but I considered that it might be preferable to the undesirability of living in Worcester. At the same time, I was in a kind of holding pattern, hoping that Sara might reconsider and take me back, though I was slowly realizing that was becoming less and less of a possibility.

I rested my book on my chest and glanced over at my cell phone on the night table next to my bed, wondering if I should call her. I had tried a number of times already, and each time she hadn't answered. After leaving her voicemails the first two times I called, I subsequently just hung up when she didn't answer. I knew she was avoiding me. Lately I had been thinking that we needed to be in contact so that we could figure out what we were going to do about our apartment. It seemed we would have to break the lease, and I wanted to retrieve my belongings, such as furniture, clothing, and CD's. That aside, more than anything else I called her because I longed to hear her voice.

Thinking about our break up saddened me, and I was no longer in the mood to read. My mind wandered lugubriously to the apartment we shared. It wasn't the biggest or fanciest place, by any means, but it had been ours and we had made it into our home: dinners together seated on the living room couch while watching TV; lying in bed at night, one of us draping an arm around the other; leaving the apartment together on weekend mornings to get breakfast. The rhythms of our life together originated there. Going back to it to collect my things would be tough.

I reached over for my cell phone, cradled it in my palm for a few moments, and then dialed Sara's number. I was nervous while it rang, and when her voice mail picked up, the sound of her voice on the recording pierced through me. When the beep sounded for me to leave a message, I decided to leave one this time, speaking in a soft, slow and halting manner. "Hi, Sara, it's me. I hope you're doing okay. I know you're avoiding my calls, but I'm just calling about the apartment. I don't know if you're still staying there, but I assume you are. I'm just calling to figure out what's happening, if you're moving out and if we're breaking the lease, if you're staying, or ... I also have to pick up some stuff, so I'm going to need to go there." I paused. "I'm sorry. I do love you."

I stood in front of my mailbox at the office, holding the envelope in front of me. Looking at the logo of the Commonwealth of Massachusetts in the return address location, I knew that the decision in Anna's case was inside of it. I tore open the envelope and began reading. On the first page Judge McCarthy concluded that Miguel was not a credible witness and that he was a participant in the drug deal. Right then I resigned myself to the fact that we had lost. But when I reached the end I was thrown for a loop. "Wow," I said out loud.

At that moment Alec happened to be getting his mail, too, and he asked, "What's going on?"

"Judge McCarthy issued a decision in my drug case. Here, check it out."

He began reading it while I just stood there. I wondered what his reaction would be. Judge McCarthy had done a very curious thing. He had, in effect, split the baby. He decided against Anna and granted possession of the apartment to the housing authority, but he also stayed the execution of the judgment until August 31 under the condition that Miguel not be allowed to visit the premises. As a result, Anna and David would get to stay in the apartment through the end of the school year and until the time he was set to go off to college. He would be able to keep the scholarship.

"He can't do that," Alec remarked after he finished reading. "The law doesn't allow a stay in this situation. He can't rule for the housing authority and at the same time give your client more time in the apartment. He should've just given your client possession."

Alec was right. Under the law the judge either had to allow an eviction or deny it. He had no discretion to give a tenant who lost a drug eviction case extra time in her apartment.

"I know. Obviously he was trying to strike a middle ground. What he did was unorthodox—"

"Unorthodox?" Alec said. "It's more than unorthodox."

"It's bad for Anna because she's going to lose the apartment, which isn't good, but I always thought we'd lose. This is good, though, because David gets to keep the scholarship. That's more than I expected. I don't care if the judge violated the law. That's not my problem."

"Merola will probably appeal."

"Let him. It'll take two years."

"True. But he could bring a motion for reconsideration right now. Judge McCarthy may realize he did something completely wrong and change his decision. He might be afraid of getting reversed on appeal."

"Yeah, maybe," I acknowledged. "But I'm not sure he'd reverse himself. He hates those motions. I've seen him really lay into lawyers who bring motions for reconsideration. He takes it personally."

"It's business, Mark. It's not personal," Alec said, riffing off *The Godfather.*

I joined him by saying, "Alec, you're my co-worker and I love you, but don't ever take sides with anyone against legal services again. Ever."

I went back to my office and called Anna to tell her the news. She reacted with a joyous yelp.

"It does mean you'll have to move at the end of the summer," I confirmed in order to make sure that she didn't lose sight of that fact.

"With him gone at school, I won't have nothing left for me here, anyway. I'll move to Puerto Rico to my family. I've been here so long, anyway, it's time for a change."

"Are you going to be all right?"

"I'll be okay. I have family. It'll be the right thing for me."

I cautioned her that we were not entirely out of the woods yet, that the housing authority might file a motion for reconsideration.

A CDBG meeting took place at the church the following day to decide on projects for the settlement money. Sitting around the table waiting for the meeting to begin, I noticed that we talked more easily with one another than we had at our initial meetings. Through the shared experience of fighting against the city we had grown closer with one another. Father Kelly began the meeting by thanking me for my work in obtaining the settlement, and everyone else joined in which felt very nice to hear. He then presented the idea that he had previously mentioned to me—rehabilitating a building on South Main Street to become transitional housing for single mothers who had been the victims of domestic violence. After sitting through so many meetings in the church basement that seemed never to end, in which divergent views were discussed at length, in which even simple decisions were difficult for us to make, it was quite surprising to see everyone readily agree on Father Kelly's proposal. Yet when I thought about it, it made perfect sense that they would, since the idea appealed in some way to everyone present. It would be located in Lawrence Geuss's territory, Nancy would like it because it would provide assistance to victims of domestic violence, and some of the women it would serve from the community would be Hispanic which was Gloria's constituency. Father Kelly had cleverly chosen a project that held an almost equal appeal for everyone. I wondered if he had done that intentionally or if it had come about by chance.

Any leftover funds, it was decided, would be applied to a rental assistance fund for tenants. Of course, there would have to be court approval of our plan, but we didn't foresee a problem with that. The uses we had in mind for the money fit squarely within the CDBG regulations.

28

A couple of days later Merola filed a motion for reconsideration, citing substantial legal authority that Judge McCarthy had committed legal error. After having been through so much in the case, and now with this additional hurdle to overcome, I felt a wave of exhaustion pass over me. I just wanted the matter to be over. It was frustrating that Anna and David were now on the chopping block again, their housing and his scholarship once more at risk. In my view, the housing authority was acting in a ridiculously bloodthirsty manner, like a legal version of *The Terminator*, not stopping until it evicted Anna and David.

Despite what I had said to Alec, I was a little nervous that the housing authority might get the decision overturned. It was true that Judge McCarthy very much disliked motions for reconsideration and often came down hard on lawyers who filed them. But his decision was so clearly erroneous that I feared he might change it.

When I called Anna to inform her of the motion, David answered the phone, and I explained to him what was happening in the case. Anna wasn't in and I asked him to have her give me a call. Before getting off the phone, I felt I should say something to try to forge a connection with him. After all, I had been to his apartment twice, we had taken a drive together to the Rite-Mart, and he had even seen me dance the salsa. And now his life had literally been changed by the outcome of the case, and I was a part of that. Yet there seemed to be a distance between us that was difficult to bridge. Nothing came to mind to say except to ask how school was going.

He responded that it was good, and then silence fell between us and we got off the phone.

By the time Saturday rolled around, Sara still hadn't returned my phone call, and I was sure she wasn't going to. I felt it was becoming urgent that I collect my things from the apartment; I had no idea how long she intended to stay there or, for that matter, if she was even still living there. I worried that she might have vacated and the landlord might have removed my stuff. I decided to drive into Boston, but beforehand, I placed another call to her. She still didn't answer, and I decided not to leave a message. If I left one she'd know I was coming and might make sure not to be there. And I wanted to see her again.

It felt strange and unfamiliar to walk through the front double doors of the apartment building and into the lobby. I felt nervous as I climbed the stairs and wondered if I might be walking into a bad situation. I slowly turned the key in the door and stepped inside. I heard footsteps from the direction of the kitchen and then Sara appeared from around the corner. Upon seeing me, she put her hand to her chest. "You scared me."

She looked prettier to me than before, somehow.

"Sorry to startle you. I just came to get my stuff. You didn't answer my calls, so I just came. I didn't know if you'd still be here."

"I'm moving," she said coldly.

"When?"

"In the next couple of days. I've already moved some of my clothes out."

I felt my stomach drop, knowing this meant that our relationship was surely over. She went into the living room, and I waited for a moment before I followed her. We stood facing one another.

"I'm sorry about things," I said, feeling my voice choke up.

She looked down at the floor. "I am too."

"All of a sudden we just ended, and it's hard for me to understand. We haven't even talked since that day."

"But it's not sudden, Mark, and you know that," she responded. "We fight a lot, we're not intimate. I mean, you haven't been emotionally available to me."

"What do you mean?"

"It's like there's no empathy or understanding in you for me. I've felt very alone for a long, long time."

"There is empathy and understanding," I protested. "You don't express your emotions. You leave me to guess them and when I don't do that successfully this is the result. You run away from me."

She shook her head. "See, I tell you how I feel and your first response is to reject my feelings, not to listen to them and actually feel what I'm feeling. It's the same old thing. You can't tell me we've been working for the past few years."

"But this is how it ends? Like this?"

"I don't know how else to do it." Her eyes welled up with tears and she wiped them away. "I'm going to come back later and get the rest of my stuff."

"This is how it ends?" I asked again.

"This is the only way I can do it. I don't know how else."

I noticed that a box filled with her belongings was positioned up against the wall in the hallway just outside of the bedroom, and it appeared that she had already moved some stuff out. She picked up her coat from the couch and put it on. I stood there hardly believing that she was leaving, that I might never see her again. She walked past me on her way to the door. I reached towards her hand to stop her.

"Don't," she said, jerking it away.

"I feel like I'm never going to see you again," I said, my voice breaking. "It feels like you're dying or something."

"I'm leaving," she said in a determined way, her upper lip quivering.

Tears began to stream down my cheeks.

All of a sudden Sara put her arms around me and held me tight. I embraced her, feeling her warmth against me, and then she pulled away and, without looking at me, left the apartment. I just stood there for a few minutes, staring ahead vacantly, the tears still coming as I softly cried.

29

I had time to kill before the motion was to be heard, so I went into the clerk's office to check a couple of files for cases that I had. Penny was stationed at the counter, and after we greeted one another she remarked, "So I see you and Kevin Merola are here again for that case."

"Unfortunately."

"It's been quite a saga, huh?"

"To say the least."

I wasn't particularly nervous this morning since not many cases were on the calendar, which meant a crowd wouldn't be watching me, and I was also in a much more advantageous position than Merola. I figured he'd be the one doing most of the arguing and that Judge McCarthy might even do my job for me by defending his decision. Our case was the first one called, and Judge McCarthy didn't even give Merola a chance to present his argument. "I made my decision clear, Mr. Merola," he barked.

Veteran that he was, Merola maintained his composure. "Your Honor, with all due respect, the decision contains legal error. In a fault eviction case, if the landlord wins, a stay of execution cannot be given to a tenant. Either the tenant wins and gets to stay or the tenant loses and has to move."

"How about if I change my decision so that the tenant wins?" Judge McCarthy taunted. "I could do that, couldn't I, Mr. Merola?" He leaned back in a self-satisfied way, like someone who has just finished a big meal. Now feeling certain that I was going to prevail, a surge of excitement ran through my body.

"Your Honor, I only bring this up because you already ruled in favor of the housing authority—"

"Yes, Mr. Merola, but a motion for reconsideration, which is what you have filed, asks the judge to change his decision. So how about I change my decision that way? I'm sure Mr. Langley would like that. It'd mean he'd win for a change."

Merola barreled straight ahead like a soldier who has just received an order to take a hill. "Your Honor could certainly do that. I'm duty bound to try to obtain a correct legal decision for my client. My argument is simply that a stay cannot be granted for this tenant, and I believe the evidence was pretty clear, as Your Honor wrote in the decision, that the son was involved in the drug deal. The law is also clear, most respectfully, that a stay cannot be given in these circumstances."

Judge McCarthy rose from his seat. "Counsel, chambers," he commanded.

I had never before visited his chambers, nor, for that matter, had I seen him order lawyers to join him there. Merola and I both paused and looked at each other as if to acknowledge the strangeness of the situation, as well as the fact that he was the one on the hot seat. We gathered up our things and followed Judge McCarthy into his chambers. While removing his robe, he told us to take seats across from his desk. The chambers were of a generous size, approximately twenty by twenty feet. The judge had an impressive mahogany desk that was very clean and organized. To the right of the desk, if facing it, there was a small brown leather couch and a coffee table with a newspaper and a hardcover book on it. To the left there was a bookcase filled with legal volumes. There were lots of framed photographs in the office, as well as degrees and certificates on the wall.

Judge McCarthy was dressed in black pants and a white shirt with a maroon tie. He had one of those rotund old-guy physiques with a balloon-like waist and short, skinny legs. He sat down and directed us to do the same.

"Mr. Merola, I am not going to change my decision." His tone was firm, but less angry than in the courtroom. "I am an old judge and my days are numbered on this bench. Not many positive things come out of this court. It's mostly just an assembly line of poor folks getting evicted. We have so many families lined up in the courtroom that sometimes there aren't enough seats for all of them. You two know that. I'm not telling you anything you don't know." The judge locked his fingers together. "Now, of course there is the law, which you are arguing, Mr. Merola, but sometimes the law isn't just and fair when applied to certain situations here in the Worcester Housing Court." Judge McCarthy leveled his gaze directly at Merola. "I'm not going to retire just yet, and so you have me for the next couple of years, unless I keel over from a heart attack or go insane or something. Why fight this particular battle when you are going to win in the end and the tenant will be out?"

Though phrased as a question, it was more than evident that Judge McCarthy was not inviting a response from Merola. We all knew what he was implying—mess with me on this case and things will be painful for you for the next couple years until I retire.

"I am denying your motion, Mr. Merola. Gentlemen, you're excused."

Merola and I exited the chambers. I had an urge to make a sarcastic comment to him, and it took great restraint for me to hold my tongue.

Instead of waiting until I returned to the office to call Anna and tell her what had happened, I gave her a ring on my cell phone while standing outside of the courthouse. A half hour later the two of us were sitting together in a booth at a Dunkin' Donuts about a half mile from George Washington. I sat drinking a cup of coffee, my tie loosened and legs crossed.

"I got nervous, you know, at court," Anna told me. "I should've told you before what that was all about. I don't know, I just didn't. I got this anxiety, like I get nervous about things."

"I understand," I said, thinking, I'm quite familiar with anxiety. "You did well, Anna."

"My plan is to go to Puerto Rico at the end of the summer and then David will go to school. I can live with my mother. There's room for me there. You know, the weather's better and it'll be a better life for me, too. It's hard here."

"He deserves a lot of credit for what he's accomplished. He's a good kid."

Anna took a sip of her coffee. "I was hard on him a lot of the time, and I felt bad about that, but I always saw the path ahead, you know? And I figured, if I don't push him, he'll go off the track, because other forces will be pulling on him. You know what I'm saying?"

I nodded. But I couldn't help wondering why Miguel had ended up on such a different path from David's. I wondered how much she had pushed or encouraged Miguel. It wasn't my place to ask, and right now, well, it was beside the point. I supposed that having one kid end up like David was more than enough to expect from a single mother residing in Washington.

I drove Anna back to Washington and we were quiet together during the ride. I think we both realized that this would probably be the last time we saw each other. I looked out the window and noticed that the passing landscape was becoming more second-nature to me. For the umpteenth time I thought about how unlikely it was that I would get an apartment in Boston, given that the rents were high and I really didn't want to have a roommate. It looked as if I would be living in Worcester, at least for the immediate future. But that fact didn't seem as gloom-inspiring as it had before. I was okay with it.

I pulled into a parking spot in front of Anna's apartment and shifted my car into park.

"Well, here we are." I turned to Anna. "I know I'm repeating myself, but I'm glad that this case worked out for David. I'm sorry that you'll have to move, though."

"I won't ever forget you." She hesitated for a moment, then reached over and hugged me tightly. Slowly I put my arms around her and pressed my fingers against the puffiness of her winter coat. We stayed like that for a few moments until we each gently let go. As I backed out of the parking space, Anna stood on the curb watching me, and when I put my car into drive, she waved.

30

When the summer arrived, I was still living with my parents, and I tried to make an effort to build a life for myself in Worcester. I got involved with the church by serving as an adult mentor to its youth group, and in August, I led a group of teenagers on a hiking trip at Mount Monadnock in New Hampshire. It wasn't exactly the best outing in youth group history. I read the trail map incorrectly and our group ended up lost for three hours until we were finally located by the park rangers. But hey, I figured, at least no one got hurt or injured. Margaret, a woman of about fifty who was very active with the youth group, set me up on a blind date with her friend's daughter who she described to me in glowing terms: "She's interesting, she's cute, she's really nice," adding that she used to live in Washington D.C., got transferred to Worcester for her job, and was looking to meet people. That was a good sign in my book. It meant she likely shared my urban orientation and probably wouldn't be terribly picky about guys, given that she was living in Worcester. She'd recognize there wasn't a good crop to pick from, thus upping my chances. We had a pleasant evening together, but I didn't find her attractive and we didn't quite click, so we never saw one another again.

Afterwards, I thought to myself, maybe we could just be friends? That way I'd have someone local who I could hang out with. But it seemed a difficult feat to pull off after a date that didn't quite work out. I probably shouldn't have even gone on the date in the first place. The truth was that I didn't quite feel ready to date again. I still missed Sara and couldn't manage to get her out of my heart and make room for someone else. I needed more time.

I jogged more than ever, about four miles nearly every day, and was in the best shape of my life. It was something that served as an anchor in my life, something that could fill part of an afternoon or evening if I had nothing else to do, and made me feel better mentally as well as physically.

It was in the late spring that I had my first visit with a therapist named Steve, who I had randomly selected out of my health plan catalog. He had a small office located on Park Avenue. It was configured so that he sat on a black leather chair, and I sat on a small black leather couch directly across from him, so close that our legs almost touched. The initial impression he made on me was of a rather scientific practitioner. He wore wire-rimmed glasses, had slightly longish brown hair, and at times leaned back in his chair and appraised me in a very exacting manner. I went to him partly to have someone to talk to about my breakup with Sara, and partly to finally address my performance anxiety issues. He ended up focusing much more on the latter. The goal Steve set for me was to learn to be more accepting of myself. For those days when I had to speak in court, he instructed me to review in my mind beforehand all of the instances when I had done it in the past. That would reassure me that I'd do just fine, since I had never really screwed things up in the past. He told me that we all make mistakes, and we all have uneven performances, and then offered the example of presidential debates where even seasoned candidates who undergo extensive preparation with a team of advisors sometimes do a poor job. If, with all of their training and preparation and prominence on the national stage, those candidates made mistakes, wasn't it unreasonable for me to expect perfection from myself?

That example really hit home with me. I had never quite thought of judging or gauging my own performance in those terms. I had accepted shortcomings and imperfection in others, but not in myself. Although I continued to feel a little nervous in performance situations, it was less than before. I was thirty-two and seeing a therapist for the first time in my life, and I often wondered, why didn't I see one years ago?

31

On a sunny, slightly windy Saturday afternoon in October, the groundbreaking ceremony was held for the transitional housing facility for women. I sat in the backseat of my parents' car as the three of us drove to the South Main section of the city to attend it together. The leaves had turned color and were at their peak, a magnificent mixture of red and gold, and I gazed out the window at them as we rode along. Near Main Street my father all of a sudden stopped short behind another car.

"Geez," my mother said, "you're going to kill us getting there."

As was typical of him, he didn't respond.

We parked a few blocks away from the facility and walked there together on the sidewalk.

I had survived the summer living with my parents, although, to be sure, I hadn't lived a lifestyle for anyone my age to be envious of. My social life was non-existent, and many a Friday and Saturday night was spent at home. When I went out to dinner at a restaurant, it was usually with my parents. I seldom went out to the movies and instead rented DVD's. In September I had enough money saved up to pay the security deposit and first month's rent on my own apartment, a one-bedroom unit on the top floor of a triple-decker near Elm Park. Luckily, the landlord didn't know that I represented tenants at housing court and accepted my application. My new place cost half as much as my Boston apartment and was slightly larger in size. I was thrilled to return to a life where I had personal freedom. A couple of times I went for drives at night, simply to bask in the joy of being able to come and go as I pleased without being subjected to questioning by my parents.

As my parents and I approached the transitional housing facility, I saw a banner posted above the front entrance and groups of people mingling outside it. There looked to be about fifty people in total. As we got closer, I looked up and down the exterior with its refurbished brick and new windows, and it pleased me to see how good it looked compared to just a few months earlier. I looked forward to checking out the inside. Having seen the floor plan drafted by the architect, I knew that located on the first floor would be a small office area, a child care center, and an all-purpose common area. Nine single mothers with children were to reside on the second, third, and fourth floors.

It was still hard to believe that this facility had actually come into being and was ready to house nine families. In fact, what had happened in the CDBG case still floored me—discovering the property transfer to Flanagan and then using it to get the upper hand over Arnold Landers and Chris Bloom at our meeting. I had recently read in the *Telegram* that both Flanagan and Miller had been indicted. It was a front page story written by the same reporter who had interviewed me and the others for the CDBG story. It was predicted that Flanagan would resign his seat, but he hadn't yet done so.

I introduced my parents to Lawrence Geuss who, to my surprise, actually seemed enthusiastic about meeting them. He told them that I had been a quiet presence at our meetings but had come through in a big way at the end. It was gratifying to hear him say that. I saw that Nancy Brightman was present with her husband, a lean guy with curly hair who appeared to be in his early-forties and had the look of a liberal college professor. It was the first time I had seen him and I thought he looked like a nice guy. They were there with their pretty, blonde-haired daughter who looked to be in the second or third grade. A few of the women who would be living in the building were present too. I had met them during the application process.

After a short while it was time for the ribbon-cutting ceremony, and it was then that I saw Father Kelly. He went up to the podium to address the assembled crowd, and everyone quieted down so that the only noise was from the cars passing by on the street.

"This is a special day," he announced. "Today we are going to officially open this transitional living center for women with children. This center will house nine families in need of emergency housing and will facilitate programs to help the residents with issues such as housing, domestic violence, benefits and employment. I should note that it was not easy to get where we are today. I want to thank the members of the social services community in Worcester who helped get us here." He pointed into the crowd. "Lawrence Geuss, Nancy Brightman, Gloria Ortiz." Between each name people politely applauded. "Thank you to each of you."

I saw Nancy Brightman's husband give her a kiss on the cheek after her name was called and felt a pang of emptiness inside because I didn't have someone special to share the moment with.

"I also want to especially thank Mark Langley, a legal services attorney, who I see is here today. He volunteered hours of his time to this cause, and his dedication and legal skills were instrumental in making this day happen. To my mind, he is the embodiment of what a lawyer and citizen should be. Aside from that, he is someone I value very much as a friend."

He paused so that the crowd could applaud for me. I looked straight ahead, a surge of warmth flooding through my body, feeling proud of what I had done and touched by Father Kelly's words.

Father Kelly spoke for a few minutes more, and after he finished, we all filed into the building for a tour. Following the crowd, I reflected on the past six months of my life and how so much had happened: CDBG, Anna's case, my breakup with Sara. I felt that I was at a point in my life where I was coasting along before figuring out what direction I'd ultimately head in. I was like a jogger who had just climbed a big hill and was going easy on the down slope, a good part of the race still ahead. Maybe I would stay at legal services, maybe I wouldn't. Maybe I'd get into a new relationship in the next few months or maybe it'd take a while. Maybe I'd continue to live in Worcester or instead return to Boston. I didn't know and didn't want to think about those things too much, at least not right then.

I also thought about the people who had been a part of my life only a few months earlier, but no longer were. They stayed with me in my heart and mind. Whenever I got a new intake involving a tenant who lived in Washington, Anna and David would enter my thoughts. I never saw either of them again after my visit to Dunkin' Donuts with Anna, and that saddened me a little. But I recognized that was just a part of life, and I hoped they were both doing well.

It was Sara who occupied my thoughts most of all. I hadn't talked to her since the day I moved my belongings out of the apartment. The pain from our breakup was still present, but it felt like it was finally lessening its hold on me, so that it was softer and less mournful. Sometimes I'd think of her in Boston walking along the street or sitting in a café and wish that I could be with her, talking and sharing with one another. But more and more, when I thought of her, I'd simply hope that she was doing well. I took it as a sign that I was repairing myself and moving forward.

I followed a small group upstairs to see the apartments there. I imagined women and their children moving into them, filled with joy at having their own place to live, finally safe from their violent pasts. It's something that most of us never take the time to think about, but man, it's so fundamentally important to have a roof over one's head. It's so important to have a home.